DISCARD

CAJUN NIGHTS

CAJUN NIGHTS

D.J. DONALDSON

St. Martin's Press
New York

Design by Claudia Carlson

Library of Congress Cataloging-in-Publication Data

Donaldson, D. J.
    Cajun nights / D.J. Donaldson.
        p.   cm.
    ISBN 0–312–02175–5
    I. Title
PS3554.04679C3   1988
813'.54—dc19   88–12012

First Edition
10 9 8 7 6 5 4 3 2 1

This book is dedicated with love to my wife June, who wasn't expecting it and who contributed numerous helpful ideas and suggestions during the writing. It is also dedicated to the memory of James Spencer Bell, who generously provided me with many insights into the life of a medical examiner.

afraid the w

Chapter 1

New Orleans—1738

Albair Fauquel's hands and feet were numb, their circulation cut off by the leather thongs that bound them. His ears still smarted from their encounter with the rough rope that now chaffed the tender skin of his neck. Below the gallows, a jeering crowd shook a sea of raised fists in his direction. Someone in the back began to chant, "By the neck until dead, by the neck until dead." The chant spread through the mob until the sound was deafening. Beside Fauquel, also wearing a rope was Malaqua, Fauquel's Haitian slave. Malaqua's eyes were tightly shut and his lips moved in silent communion with a god unknown to most of his tormentors. When the hooded hangman had slipped the rope over his head, Malaqua had fouled his clothing, and the smell now filled his master's nostrils. Unlike Malaqua, Fauquel was not afraid. He was angry.

A man in a powdered wig and dressed in a black cloak and black stockings and shoes mounted the gallows and unrolled the parchment he carried. The chanting stopped. In a sonorous voice that carried with ease to those farthest from the gallows, the charges were read.

"Inasmuch as you, Malaqua the slave, and you, Albair Fauquel, have conspired with the powers of darkness to cause a productive member of this community to commit the most heinous acts against his family and humanity and then, contrary to God's holy ordinances, take his own life, and whereas the evidence against you has been considered sufficient by a panel of your peers, you will this day be hanged by the neck until dead. Do either of you wish to speak?"

Malaqua seemed to be in a trance and gave no sign that he wished to respond. But Fauquel did. In a voice as strong as that of the parchment reader, Fauquel said, "When my land was taken, it was wrong. And today you wrong me again. But I tell you this, one day I will return and right this wrong as I did the other. And the streets of this city will run with blood as friend slays friend, fathers slay their children, and rampant suicide sends the souls of men by the hundreds to everlasting hell."

With this threat, the crowd went mad. A month of heavy rains had turned the ground around the cobblestoned square into a quagmire of foul-smelling muck. A man on the edge of the crowd scooped up a handful of the stuff and molded it into a wet ball with some Spanish moss from a nearby cart. Pushing his way through the throng, he let fly toward the gallows. It missed its mark, but was an inspiration to others.

Soon the air was thick with flying mud, and the ladies in the crowd screamed and fled to protect their dresses. A well-aimed handful struck Fauquel in the face, and the crowd cheered. Through a mouth full of grit, Fauquel spoke again as the cheer subsided. "Beware the songs you loved in youth," he shouted, his eyes burning with hatred.

Mud spattered the parchment reader's shoes and he gave the sign. The hangman pulled the wooden lever connected to the holding pins of both trapdoors, and the floor fell away from the condemned men. As they fell, the din that a moment before had battered the parchment reader's ears ceased as though cut with the blade of a guillotine.

The sound of Fauquel's neck snapping carried across the square like the crack of a whip. His eyes bulged grotesquely, and his face turned purple. The front of his trousers darkened with urine. Malaqua was a heavy man, and when he reached the end of his rope, his head was partially torn from his body.

The sound of retching could be heard from several quarters as ladies in attendance found the sight more than they had bargained for. Quietly, the mob turned and went back to their homes and shops.

New Orleans—The Present

"Daddy, Daddy." With her arms spread wide and her chubby legs tapping out a rhythmless beat on the blacktop, Lila Hollins, age two, gradually picked up speed. Oblivious to what it might do to his trousers, Barry Hollins, her father, dropped on one knee to catch her. Lila was a miracle, courtesy of the doctors at the Tulane fertility clinic. Before Lila, Barry and Pamela Hollins had felt incomplete. Now they were whole.

"Hello, baby. How's my sweetie?" Barry plucked Lila up in his arms and smothered her with exaggerated kisses. Eyes sparkling, she giggled and squeezed her daddy's nose.

"I swear. You act like you hadn't seen her for weeks the way you carry on," Mother Keltner said, wiping her hands on her apron. Pamela's mother had been living with them for about a month, and it was not at all like his buddies at work had said it was going to be. She more than earned her keep by doing all the cooking and taking care of Lila while he and Pamela were at work. She knew when to express an opinion and when to keep one to herself. More important, she was likable, all of which made it hard to understand why Pamela's sister was so set against taking her in.

A second car pulled into the drive and Pamela Hollins waved at them through the windshield. With Barry's help, Lila waved back. As his wife walked toward them, Barry took in every movement. His friend Aubrey's wife and Sammy's too still looked as good as ever . . . up close. But at a distance, it was obvious *they* were losing it. Calves and ankles beginning to thicken, once-firm buttocks now pushing acceptable limits, a subtle change in posture as though the years were pushing down on them like a winepress slowly being closed. But not Pamela. At forty-two, she still had the figure and carriage of a girl, and even now, standing here in the yard with the sun still up, he wanted her.

"Hi, babe," she said, kissing him lightly on the lips, and Lila on the forehead. "Have a good day?"

"You make them all good," he said, patting her on the fanny.

Mother Keltner clucked her tongue and shook her finger at him in mock scorn. "You two! Next thing, the neighbors will be calling the police on us for public lewdness, and I'm too old to go to jail."

"Yeah, you'd look awful in stripes," Barry teased. Turning to Pamela, he saw that she was troubled. "What's wrong?" he asked. "Boss still riding you about that contract mix-up?"

She shook her head. "No. It's not that. Somebody went through the parking lot today and cut the antennas off all the cars. Ours, too."

Barry adjusted Lila in his arms, took a few steps to the side, and looked again at Pamela's car. All that remained of the antenna was a six-inch stub. "Don't worry about it," he said, walking back to her. "I'll fix it on Saturday. No real harm done."

Pamela's face remained clouded. "But it was such a *mean* thing to do. I don't understand people like that."

He reached up and put a stray curl of his wife's hair back in place. "Forget it. They messed up your antenna, don't let them ruin your dinner, too." He looked at Pamela's mother. "So what are we having? Venison? Squab under glass?"

"Hamburgers and beans," Mother Keltner replied.

"Even better."

"It'll be ready by the time you get back from the store."

"Meaning we're out of . . . ?"

"Milk."

"No problem," he said, handing Lila to her grandmother. Pamela reached into her purse and took out her car keys. "Here hon, take mine. It'll be easier."

The car was not actually Pamela's but, rather, belonged to her mother, who had insisted that it become family property when she went to live with them. Inspection of the vandalized antenna revealed that it had been lopped off at an angle with a pair of bolt cutters that left the tip clean and sharp. This evidence of planned destruction of property was more irritating to Barry then if the antenna had been broken off in an impulsive act.

It was the first time he had driven the car and he did not expect that the seat would be so close to the dash. His knee collided with the steering column, and the pain made him curse. Guiltily, he looked toward the house and was relieved to find Lila inside, out of earshot.

His groping hand found nothing that felt like a seat-adjusting lever, and he had to practically stand on his head to find it. By the time he got underway, the pain in his knee had lessened to the point where he could appreciate how well the car handled. Much better than his, in fact. According to Pamela, though, it got lousy mileage. He nudged the blower on the air conditioner up to high and turned all the vents in his direction.

A kid on a motorbike suddenly appeared beside him and then sped away. Surprised, Barry looked in the rearview mirror and tried to figure out why he hadn't seen him coming. When he saw how little of the road was actually visible through the central oval and two portholes that served as a rear window, he understood. Better remind Pamela to be extra careful when changing lanes.

Figuring it wasn't worth driving all the way to Schwegmann's just to save twenty cents, he headed in the direction of the 7-Eleven six blocks away. At first he drove without thinking of anything in particular, but soon his mind was on Lila, and then on his own childhood and his favorite toy. His jack-in-the-box. Jack had red cheeks and freckles and was dressed in yellow-and-black stripes. When you turned the handle, the box played *"Pop goes the weasel. All around the cobbler's bench, the monkey chased the weasel . . ."* A trickle of saliva dribbled down his chin, and he wiped it away with the back of his hand. Puzzled, he studied his hand as though he'd never seen it before. There were no tissues in the car, and he was wondering what he could wipe it on when he thought of Jack. He could wipe it on Jack. . . .

"All around the cobbler's bench . . ." The tune ran lazily through his brain, and he began to bob his head in time to the music. Two blocks from the 7-Eleven, he began to whistle the tune softly, and his head stopped moving. His eyes became fixed on the road ahead. Saliva filled his mouth, and soon he could only whistle a few bars before having to swallow. He was still whistling and swallowing when he went in one side of the store's drive and out the other. At the Hebert Street intersection, he ran a stop sign. Over and over, between swallows, he whistled the tune . . .*"Pop goes the weasel."*

Art Meloy was taking the few minutes before dinner to spray some Ansar on a patch of weeds where his lawn ran beside the Hollins's driveway. When Barry got out of the car, Meloy suggested they play some golf on Saturday. But Barry paid no attention. He walked toward the house, still whistling the same song, a few bars at a time, followed by a short interval while his Adam's apple bobbed up and down. Meloy shrugged and went back to his weeds.

Barry went in the front door and through the den to the kitchen, where he heard Mother Keltner and Lila in the pantry. He walked over, shut the pantry door, and turned the key in the lock. *"Pop goes the weasel."* He hadn't blinked since the music began, and there were now tiny hemorrhages in the whites of his eyes. Hearing the shower running in the upstairs bathroom, he picked up a chair from the breakfast table, went up the stairs, and wedged it under the bathroom doorknob. *"Pop goes the weasel."* Then he went into the garage, got the gasoline for the lawnmower, and took it back into the kitchen, where he drenched the walls and floor. He proceeded from room to room, methodically wetting all the rugs and draperies. In the den, he poured the pungent fluid over his football-watching chair with the diligence and care of a fine craftsman whose reputation rides on the thoroughness of his work. *"Pop goes the weasel."*

He rattled the gasoline can against his ear. Satisfied that there was enough left, he took the gun-shaped cigarette lighter from the drawer next to his chair and placed it on the table. Deliberately, he upended the gas can and played the spout over his clothes. The tune in his head blocked all other sensation, and he neither felt the cold liquid that plastered his clothes against his skin nor smelled the heavy fumes that filled his nostrils. He sat down, picked the lighter off the table, and pushed back so that the hidden footstool under the chair slid out. With his feet up, he waited for the tune loop in his head to roll around again to the chorus. When it got to the next *"Pop,"* he pulled the lighter's trigger!

He continued to whistle until the flames burned away the flesh on his lips. For a few seconds more, there was just the sound of rushing air. The superheated smoke in his next breath cooked the delicate lining of his lungs and then he heard the tune no more.

Chapter 2

"Ummmm." Eyes closed in pleasure, Kit Franklyn pressed the back of her head deeper into the down pillow as David Andropoulas, assistant DA for the city of New Orleans, ran his tongue slowly up her thigh. She buried the fingers of both hands in his thick black hair and pulled him upward. Then the phone rang.

"Aggggh. Don't answer it," David pleaded, his lips moving against her hot skin.

"Have to." She pulled herself into a sitting position and plucked the receiver from its cradle. "Hello."

"This is Andy Broussard," a resonant voice said. "If you're free, I'll take you on a call."

"I'm free."

"I'll be there in fifteen minutes."

Her "thanks" was cut short by a click as her new boss, the chief medical examiner for Orleans Parish, hung up.

"You're leaving, aren't you," David whined.

"That was Broussard. We're going on a case."

As she slipped from under the sheet, David grabbed for her and missed, his fingers grazing the firm flesh of her flank. "Five more minutes," he pleaded.

"Can't." She turned on the light and picked up her panties from the chair where he had thrown them.

Lying on his belly, David watched her silken triangle

disappear behind the pink nylon. It was so like her, he thought, not to turn her back or insist on dressing in the dark. With her auburn hair free from the tortoiseshell combs she always used to hold it primly back from her face, she looked positively smoldering.

He very much approved of the way she downplayed her looks in public, wearing lipgloss instead of lipstick and doing little to call attention to her large brown eyes or hide the sprinkle of freckles on the bridge of her nose. He had liked her natural look from the moment he saw her, but more than anything, it was her self-assurance that had first attracted him eighteen months ago when they both were campaign workers for an ultimately unsuccessful candidate for Congress. The sweet body he had discovered later was pure lagniappe.

"How can you just shut your feelings off like that?" he asked, throwing his legs over the edge of the bed.

She shrugged into her bra, pulled her dress on, and padded into the bathroom to fix her face and put the combs back in her hair. "It's called discipline. You ought to try it." In the mirror, she could see David leaning against the doorframe, his arms folded across the fur on his chest.

"I just did. Can't say I care for it."

"Don't be so immature."

"Why is it immature to want to keep doing something you enjoy?"

"If you had your way, we'd spend most of each day in bed."

"Shows I'm healthy."

"Oversexed more likely."

"I will always consider it one of Nature's greatest perversities," he said, "that women were made so undersexed that when one with a reasonable appetite comes along, we say she's a nymphomaniac and we send her to a shrink . . . to a psychologist or psychiatrist for help."

David's use of the word *shrink* did not escape her notice. He had never said so directly, but she was sure that he thought very little of her profession. His ill-chosen word smothered any regrets she had for running off. She touched a finger to a tin of lipgloss and ran the finger around her mouth. "Stick to legal opinions, counselor," she said, cleaning her finger with a tissue. "At least there you know what you're talking about." She threw the tissue into a hammered brass wastebasket and brushed past him. ". . . And put your clothes on."

He followed her into the bedroom. "Did I miss something here? Why are you so sore all of a sudden?"

"I don't have time to talk now. Broussard will be here any minute."

"Later then . . . over dinner."

She looked at the ceiling. "I have no idea how long this will take."

"Look, it's . . ." David picked up his watch from the nightstand. "It's three-thirty. Say we make it for eight. That'll give you over four hours. If you see you can't make it or you finish earlier, call me at the office. I need to make up for taking the afternoon off, so I'll just work until I hear from you."

"Fine."

Outside, the humidity hung so heavily in the June air, it was like breathing molasses. Her town house, one of fifteen comprising the small rental community called Givenchy Village, was the first one on the right. The rest curved around the parking lot in a gentle half-circle. They were all structurally the same; two-story stucco with a red tile roof, but each one was painted a different pastel color. The young willows that lined the sidewalk shaded the doorways but little else.

In addition to David's Plymouth and her Nissan, there were only three other cars in the parking lot, all belonging to residents. So far, no Broussard. She put a hand to her hair and found it already warm to the touch. Even in the dappled shadows of her willow, it was extremely uncomfortable and she hoped for a short wait.

A few minutes after David's departure, a red '57 Thunderbird came down the drive and pulled up in front of her. Despite her belief that Broussard could never fit in such a small car, there he was, beckoning to her from behind the wheel.

The old medical examiner was not so much driving the car as he was wearing it, his great bulk appearing to have been poured into the seat as a liquid that had then set up, encasing the steering wheel in flesh. He showed her the fat fingers on one hand and flexed his bushy eyebrows in greeting. With her legs barely inside, he threw the car in reverse, made a tight turn, and shot up the drive. She had known him for less than six hours, the time that had elapsed since he had hired her as the country's first suicide-research investigator attached to a medical examiner's office.

It was her job to compile a psychological profile of the decedent in all cases where the physical evidence did not allow the examiner to determine whether death was accidental or suicide. The position had been created as a one-year experiment. If it proved useful, there was a good chance the administrators of Orleans Parish would make it permanent. Even with the drawback of an uncertain future for the job, she had found it hard to believe that Broussard had been willing to hire someone whose doctoral degree was so fresh that it had not yet come back from the place that laminates them onto wooden plaques. From her view, it was a great opportunity to study the suicide mentality firsthand. Maybe even write a book about it.

As they drove, she pretended to watch the road but was actually studying her new employer, who wore a short beard and mustache the same color as the unruly thatch of grizzled hair on his head. Through the beard and under layers of padded flesh, his features were delicate and his skin boyishly smooth. A clump of gray hairs guarded the entrance to the pink ear facing her.

Had she not seen the glass canister of lemon balls on his desk, and had there not been a marble-size bulge in his rosy cheek at this very moment, she might have been willing to concede that his weight problem was "glandular." But with the evidence, she concluded that, like David, he was undisciplined. *Broussard's* weakness, however, was food. And on that count, she was close to the mark, for Broussard really enjoyed only three things in life—his job, good food, and old T-birds.

However, when she concluded that his bow tie, mesh shoes, and the little black cord that ran from around his neck to the temples of his glasses were affectations, she was wrong. His choices in dress were strictly pragmatic. The cord allowed him to slip his glasses off when looking through a microscope and find them again when he was finished. Traditional ties would occasionally dangle in his work, much of which was conducted bending over. Mesh shoes were the only kind that kept his feet from sweating. On another point, though, she was absolutely correct. He *did* spend far too much time rubbing his fingers over the bristly hairs on the tip of his nose.

"How'm I doin'?" Broussard spoke in an effortless rumble with no corners and no edges, as though his words had been cooking all day over a low flame.

"Beg your pardon?"

He shifted the lemon drop into his left cheek. "You haven't taken your eyes off me since you got in the car and I was wonderin' what conclusions you'd reached."

"You sure you want to ask that of a relative stranger?" Kit replied. "Could be risky."

He glanced at her briefly, a smile tugging at the corners of his mouth. "You'd tell me the truth even though I sign your paycheck?"

"Isn't that one of my duties?"

His whole body chuckled in an appreciative basso profundo that rattled the dash. "I withdraw the question," he said.

Now that he had broken the silence, she felt obliged to say something in return. "Do we know any details of this case we're going to look at?"

He turned left and . . . Oh God! He was going over Huey P. Long. She *never*, absolutely *never*, used this dreadful bridge. It was just too high and too narrow. And in places, for a roadbed, it had only a see-through meshwork of metal through which the Mississippi and the tiny barges way below looked soooo scary.

"Cases," Broussard said. "There's two of 'em now. Got the second call just before leavin' the office. Seems like the population of this city's sole purpose for existin' is to make my days last well into the night. Inconsiderate buggers. What was it you asked. Oh yeah, details. Just addresses, that's all I want at first. Too much observer interpretation involved when someone tells you what happened. I want to be totally unbiased when I get my first look." He unbuttoned the pocket on his white shirt, plunged two fingers and a thumb into it, and brought out three lemon balls and some lint. He held them out in the palm of his small hand, a hand that she knew regularly handled human remains. "Care for one?" he asked.

The answer came easily. "No thanks."

A few minutes later, they pulled into a dirt driveway in Westwego that led to a little gray clapboard house set up on cement blocks. In front of them was a police cruiser, and in front of that, a brown Toyota. Two other cars, whose make Kit didn't recognize, were in the yard. Broussard eased onto the scraggly lawn, wrestled himself out of the car, and went inside, seeming to forget Kit completely. Figuring she was here to see what was happening, she followed him.

The house was a typical shotgun: a long hall leading from the front to the back, doorways on either side. She found Broussard in the first room on the left, a large sitting area. He was peering closely at the right temple of a man with blank staring eyes who lay slumped in a straight-backed chair, his head cocked crazily to one side. Had it not been protected by a piece of clear plastic, the Oriental rug under the chair would have been ruined by all the blood.

With her hand over her mouth, Kit remained in the doorway, her stomach doing greasy cartwheels. Maybe her suggestion that she accompany Broussard on a few cases to get the feel of things wasn't such a great idea after all. It certainly wasn't a necessary part of her job. As Broussard had pointed out in her interview, she would be working mostly from reports. Still, it *was* fascinating . . . in a morbid sort of way.

In addition to Broussard, the room held two uniformed policemen, a sallow-complexioned fellow with a Polaroid camera, and a middle-aged hulk of a man with tired eyes who was running a yellow tape measure from the back wall to the corpse. The man with the tape had a face as heavily lined as a dried apple and looked as though he'd dressed in the dark from a hamper full of dirty clothes. The photographer appeared to have been doing this sort of thing for a long time because he moved quickly around the room taking pictures with no instructions from anyone. Finally he told the man with the tired eyes what had been photographed and asked whether any other shots were needed. Receiving a shake of the head for an answer, he gave Broussard a thumbs-up sign and left, brushing Kit with his camera as he passed.

Broussard got down on one knee and, without touching it, flirted with the gun that lay next to the chair. With a stubby pencil, he made some notes in a small black book. The man with the tape then moved in and worked the area around the gun. It wouldn't have seemed at all out of place for the corpse to have been in his underwear. But to the contrary, he was nicely dressed: short-sleeve tan shirt, brown pants, and a pair of brown loafers that were either freshly polished or new. All that could be seen of his tie was the knot because the rest was obscured by a wad of papers clutched to his chest.

Broussard pulled gently on the arm that held the papers, inspected its underside, pressed on it with his fingers, and made more notes in his little book. He gingerly pulled one of the gore-soaked papers loose, looked at it, and gave it to Kit before beginning a stroll around the room. She took the paper reluctantly between her index finger and thumb. At the top, through the blood, she saw the words, "American History—

Mr. Rentdorff." The rest of the page alternated between lines of type and sentences written in an almost illegible scrawl with a soft pencil. The dead man was embracing a stack of exam papers.

Broussard was acting like a nosy relative. He read from a newspaper lying on a trestle table badly in need of refinishing, looked at the thermostat on the wall, and wrote again in his little book. He motioned to the man with the tape. "I've seen enough. When his ride gets here, have 'em tell Charlie I want a rectal readin' as soon as he can get it." He propelled himself in Kit's direction, sweeping his upturned palms through the air as though chasing a dog out of a flowerbed. "Time to go. We got another stop to make."

Kit reached the car first, dying to talk. She waited expectantly while her expansive colleague wedged himself behind the wheel, collected the sweat from his brow on the back of his hand, and wiped it across his trousers. She waited while he started the car and fiddled with the air conditioner. Finally, when she could wait no longer, she said, "What do you make of it?"

He looked out the rear window and backed up. "Self-inflicted. I saw that right away. Blew his brains out around nine-thirty, shortly after breakfast. Gonna be a lot of people unhappy over this one."

"Who?"

The steering wheel rubbed the buttons on his shirt. "All the little yahoos that'll have to write their American History exam over agin because teacher got the first set too soiled to grade. Gotta hand it to him. He found a pretty creative way to thumb his nose at 'em. Wonder if he used that kind of imagination in his teachin'?"

"That's what makes it a suicide?"

"Sometimes people who shoot themselves stand in the tub so's not to make a mess on the rug. This one used plastic."

"What do you need me for? Sounds like you're able to handle it all, including the psychology."

"I'm ninety-nine percent sure it was a suicide. But I don't like even a one percent possibility that I'm wrong. I'd still like for you to talk to his principal, the other teachers, the kids, and so on, and see if his behavior over the last few months fits a suicide. Don't feel useless. They're not all this clear. You'll have to tell *me* whether it is or isn't on some."

"How did you pinpoint the exact time he did it?"

He looked at her and his eyes glittered. "Elementary, my dear Franklyn. . . . You know, he never actually said that."

"Who never said what?"

"Sherlock Holmes never said, 'Elementary, my dear Watson.' He said, 'Elementary,' and he said, 'my dear Watson,' but he never said 'em together. Anyway, the deceased was in full rigor. With a room temperature of seventy-three degrees, rigor takes about twelve hours to develop. That alone would make it around five o'clock this mornin' when he did it. But there was a half-eaten sausage and biscuit from Burger Delight sittin' on the TV. While I'd never eat one myself, I know they serve 'em only for breakfast and they don't open 'til seven. The biscuit was fresh, so he must have been alive when they opened. The mornin' paper was turned to the TV schedule, where he'd circled the Larry Lambert program. You ever watch that thing? Seems like it's always about sex. I'll admit it's an assumption that he waited 'til after that show to do it, but when they take his body temperature back at the morgue, it can be plugged into a formula that'll help us determine the time of death."

"Is it really all that important to know exactly when he died?"

"In a murder, always. In a suicide, about one in fifty. But you never know which one until it's too late. Say we let this one slip by without gettin' too particular. A month from now, there'll be some snotty-nosed kid lawyer handin' me a summons in which a relative of our victim died the same day and left him a trunkful of money . . . providin', of course, he's still alive. If not, it goes to somebody else. Now, who gets the money? Our suicide's beneficiaries or the somebody else? Time of death of that schoolteacher then becomes real important. And I don't like bein' on a witness stand with lawyers pokin' holes in my work."

"Who was that with the tape measure?"

He probed his shirt pocket and slipped a lemon drop into his mouth. "Phillip Gatlin. He and the photographer are part of our VC squad."

"VC?"

"Violent Crimes. Phillip's one crackerjack of a detective . . . least he used to be."

"What happened?"

"A few months ago, his daughter disappeared. A lot of her clothes were missin' too, so it wasn't a kidnappin'. She'll show up in a few weeks tired and happy to be back. But it's killin' Phillip. I guess you noticed how he was dressed. He never used to look like that, but he's just been goin' through the motions ever since she left. Used to be, he had the highest solve rate in the department. Word is, it's now dead last. Our next case is in here."

He turned the car into a subdivision of neat middle-class homes and drove the winding streets until he came to a house with a fire truck and a chief's car out in front. Across the street, a flock of talked-out neighbors watched the firemen roll up their hoses. The door to the two-story house was standing open, and the siding around the windows was black with soot.

"Nuts," Broussard said, staring at the gutted house. "Tryin' to do my job after these folks have mucked around is like tryin' to put together a jigsaw puzzle after somebody's whittled on the pieces with a pocketknife."

They were met by a man in a tan canvas parka trimmed in flourescent yellow stripes. In the fading light, Kit could see pain in his eyes and the word *chief*, on his helmet.

"This is a bad one, Andy," he said. "Come on, I'll show you what we found when we got here."

Broussard had a sour look on his face as he followed the man inside. Kit could see that once again there would be no introductions or invitations to tag along, but under the circumstances, couldn't blame Broussard for forgetting her. Inside, the house smelled like a chicken that had been cooked without getting all the feathers off. She followed the chief to a room that showed considerably more damage than the small foyer through which they had come.

"It started here," the chief said. He pointed to the burned skeleton of a chair liberally covered in foam. "Poor devil was nothing but charcoal when we arrived."

Kit was thinking it odd that he would call the chair a "poor devil," then she saw the charred shoes protruding from the foam and realized there was a corpse attached to them. The foam danced with collapsing bubbles and the grinning remains of a face emerged. She shuddered and looked away.

"Found this next to the chair," the chief said. He turned and picked up a blackened can with flecks of red paint and the letters *G   S   INE* showing through a sooty haze. "I'm sure we'll find traces of gasoline in the hot spots. Now back here . . ."

He led the way into the kitchen where the wainscoting and the floor cabinets were blistered and black. Untouched by the flames, the drenched wallpaper above the chair rail had come loose at the ceiling and hung in flaps that were slowly creeping toward the floor. The linoleum was barely visible through a film of grimy sludge crisscrossed with bootprints.

"This door was locked. And we found these two inside. The woman was holding the little girl in her arms. They had to be separated to get oxygen to them, but as you can see . . ."

Broussard squeezed through the narrow pantry door and knelt to examine the two bodies. "Corneas are clear," he said. He stood up and put his penlight back in his shirt pocket. "Been dead less than two hours." He went back into the kitchen, pulled on the pantry door, and looked at the lock on the outside. "You said this door was locked. How did your men get it open without the key?"

"Isn't it there?"

"Afraid not." Broussard and Kit exchanged glances.

The chief shook his head and shrugged. "Why would you put a lock on a pantry?"

"Maybe to keep the little girl out of the cleaning supplies," Broussard suggested. "What else you got?"

"This way." They went back through the room where the fire started, up a flight of stairs, and down a narrow hall. "That chair was propped against the bathroom door," the chief said. "And we found this one inside."

On the floor, with her back against the wall, was the body of a woman wrapped in a towel. Broussard looked at her eyes, then stepped over her, and pulled the shower curtain back. "No window," he said as though he knew there wouldn't be one. "If there'd been a window, she might have escaped. Was this on when you found her?" For the first time, Kit realized the exhaust fan was running.

"I don't know," the chief replied.

Broussard switched it off and the quiet pall of death settled over the tiny space. "One of those things that seems like a good idea at the time," he mused. "All it did was draw smoke under the door. I've seen enough."

Kit and the chief started back down the hall and suddenly they heard the sound of splintering wood behind them. Broussard had put his fist through the hollow bathroom door. "It was hung wrong," he said quietly. "They're supposed to open in. Then that chair would have been useless. And there should have been a window," he added under his breath.

They all went downstairs, Broussard regretting his unprofessional display of emotion, Kit respecting him for it.

Outside, the chief looked up and down the street. "Wonder where the VC squad is?" he said.

"Phillip Gatlin is finishin' up a case a couple of miles from here," Broussard replied. "Jamison left even before we did. Shoulda been here by now. Maybe he stopped for a bite to eat."

From all she had seen, Kit was filled with disgust, shock, and pity. Hearing that Jamison might have an appetite after seeing the dead schoolteacher surprised her. For a moment, she disliked the photographer for being insensitive, but then she realized that he had responded to his job the only way he could . . . by adapting. It seemed to be happening to her already. This case, actually worse than the first, didn't make her feel quite as nauseated. Was it because there was no blood in this one?

They went back to the car and Broussard confidently retraced their path through the subdivision's winding streets. At the main drag, he turned right. Inwardly, Kit sighed with relief, for the Huey P. Long bridge was the other way. Though they were now on the opposite side of the Mississippi, they were still only a few miles from the heart of New Orleans. But the fast-food strip on either side of the highway might have led to any city in the country.

"When we get those folks from the fire downtown, we'll do a blood study on the child and the women and probably find lethal concentrations of carbon monoxide," Broussard said. "We'll do the same on the corpse in the chair and also look for burns in *his* trachea, providin' we can find some blood, and *if* there's a trachea left. Low monoxide and no tracheal burns would indicate he was dead before the fire started. It's more likely, though, we'll find that the fire killed him. Which will suggest a murder-suicide. But there's no way I can prove that from the autopsy. Phillip is goin' to be pretty interested in your report on this one. Once we identify the burned corpse, you should concentrate your efforts there."

"I will." Remembering the featureless face, Kit said, "How do you know the body in the chair was a male?"

"The shoes."

"You're awfully good at all this."

"Been doin' it a long time, and experience never made anybody worse at anything. It's not hard. You just have to pay attention to detail, and most folks don't." Squinting at her, he said, "Describe the wallpaper in the kitchen back there."

She thought about it and said, "I can't."

"Stripes or flowers?"

"Stripes."

"Wrong. Flowers. Big ones, yellow on blue, with a twelve-inch repeat."

"I'm impressed."

He waved away the compliment. "I do it now out of habit. Once you learn to pay attention to your surroundin's, it's simply a matter of playin' the odds to find the most likely explanation for what you see."

"For example?"

They were near a crowded shopping center and Broussard turned in and drove slowly past a sidewalk full of shoppers.

"See those two?" he said, pointing to a pair of overweight women. "Watch 'em 'til we go on by, but don't look back."

She had only a few seconds before the car was past them.

"What were they wearin'?"

"Jogging suits," she replied triumphantly.

"What color?"

"Gray and green."

"Both of 'em?"

"Yes."

Her smug smile lasted only until he said, "Which one recently felt the touch of a man other than her husband, on her bare skin?"

"Which one?" she asked, as though he couldn't possibly produce an acceptable answer.

"The one on the inside."

"Explain."

"Guess you didn't notice that her right shoe had been cut away for the cast on her foot."

Kit flushed at having missed something so grossly obvious. "And the man who touched her was . . ."

Together, they both said, "Her doctor."

"How do you know her doctor wasn't a woman?"

"Like I said, play the odds. There're not nearly as many women in medicine as men."

"But you're not absolutely sure it was a man."

"It doesn't accomplish a thing to withhold judgment just because unlikely explanations exist along with the likely. Unless, of course, you're a medical examiner lookin' for a permanent vacation."

He pulled back onto the highway.

"You've heard the sayin', 'Things are not always what they seem'?"

"Yes."

"Usually they are."

Chapter 3

Instead of heading for the heart of the city, Broussard turned onto a side road that quickly left all signs of human habitation behind.

"Where are we going now?" Kit asked.

"To pick up somethin' I should have taken with me when I left for work this mornin'. It won't take long."

On each side of the road, redwing blackbirds perched on nearly every structure that would hold their weight. Occasionally, the car passed a turtle that had gone up to the roadside to attempt a crossing. Once, she saw the snout and glistening eyes of a nutria push through the grass, then disappear back into it.

The abundant wildlife was one of the things Kit liked best about this part of the country. But she wished it didn't come with quite so much marshland. Sometimes when a rainstorm would hit where the drops were so big they sounded like baseballs hitting the roof, and geysers of water from the overloaded sewer system would blow the manhole covers off, she felt that New Orleans existed only at the pleasure of the natural forces around her, and one day they might just decide to call in the mortgage. Usually after such a storm, a trip across the Pontchartrain bridge to Covington was in order, where after a few hours on high ground, she would be ready for another few months in the crazy old city where the natives sound like they came from either New York or France, where politicians have nicknames like "Moon," and the water tastes like gasoline.

An armadillo blundered out of the grass and waddled across the blacktop a few yards ahead. Broussard jerked the wheel sharply and sent the right tires onto the shoulder. The left ones went over the tip of the armadillo's tail. Under the floorboard, there was a scraping noise as the car passed over a dead branch. In the mirror, Kit saw the armadillo pause, cock his head slightly, then go snuffling across the road.

"An armadillo pancake lookin' for a place to happen," Broussard said, guiding the car back onto the road.

Now they seemed to be dragging something. Broussard pulled over and got out.

"Nothin' serious," he reported a few seconds later. "Tail pipe came loose. We can change cars at my place."

After another mile or so, the car slowed and pulled off the road onto a drive that ran under a canopy of ghostly old live oaks draped with Spanish moss. It was the kind of drive that should have led to a brooding old mansion. Instead, they came to a stop in front of a sprawling structure so heavily hidden by flowering vines and other vegetation, it was almost invisible. Here and there through the foliage, Kit caught a brief glimpse of mottled white brick and an occasional tall window.

Leading to the house was a short flight of steps made from thick slabs of black stone. There was moss growing in the joints, and dozens of varieties of flowering plants and at least as many nonflowering species lay along and over the steps so naturally that it could only have been planned by someone very talented.

"This is lovely," Kit said.

"Come on in. I'll find the things I need and we'll get another car."

As they went up the steps, Kit said, "I get the feeling there used to be a different house on this site."

Broussard turned to look at her. "There *was* . . . an aristocrat of the old South, and I used to live in it."

"What happened?"

He squeezed his lips together and wiped the back of his neck. "Been almost seven years now and I still remember it like it was yesterday. I had inherited the place from my grandmother." He closed his eyes and lifted his face to a memory. "Columns so big two men couldn't reach around 'em, and a spiral staircase that rose through the house like a hawk ridin' a hot wind." His small eyes popped open. "Then one mornin' just after dawn, one of the upstairs ceilin's fell in. I ran into the room where the noise came from, and there they were, all wiggly and white on the fallen joists like maggots in a festerin' wound."

"What were they?"

"Termites!" He spit the word out like a bad taste. "I still see 'em about once a month in my dreams. The entire house was full of 'em, and the damage was so extensive, there was no way to save it. Even found 'em in the stairway. So I had the old house torn down and this one put up. It was too expensive to reproduce the old place, and since I don't like any other style of architecture, I decided to just have no style at all and make the exterior look like part of the landscape. Come on, I'll show you around."

At the top of the stairs, they passed through a cleft in the foliage and entered a recess lined by the same brick she had seen earlier. Using the light that filtered into the chamber through a skylight in the high ceiling, Broussard found the lock with his key, and they entered through tall French doors intricately inset with beveled and frosted glass. He thumbed a light switch and a great chandelier heavy with crystal garlands lit up a huge room with polished wide-planked floors that gleamed between the soft colors of Oriental rugs. Somehow, the ponderous bulbous-legged refectory table, the upholstered French chairs, the delicate tables, and the two overstuffed sofas all worked. It was a room fully capable of holding the grand piano to the right of the entrance without appearing crowded. Throughout, bouquets of real flowers or excellent fakes picked up the reds from the carpets and sofas.

"There'll be no termites in this house," Broussard pronounced. "There's not a piece of wood in any structural element. The walls are Sheetrock glued onto reinforced cement block. The ceiling is screwed to structural steel beams, and to keep the little beggars out of the floorin', the house was built on two eighteen-inch concrete slabs with a copper plate between 'em. Come on, my study is back here. I'll get my things and we'll go out through the garage."

Kit followed him into a wide hallway and watched him disappear through a door on the right. He was out quickly with a fat yellow file folder, and she got only a brief glimpse of his desk—huge and dark with the heads of mustachioed men as drawer pulls. She also had the impression that the room's freestanding bookcases with glass doors bore heavy carving that matched the desk. They passed the dining room so rapidly that only the gilded dining room chairs, whose armrests ended in small rams' heads, registered. Despite a loathing for all activities related to food preparation, she found the broad expanses of mauve Formica and the spotless copper utensils hanging from the kitchen ceiling inviting.

"You pick our transportation," Broussard said, holding the kitchen door for her.

The garage was as big as a gymnasium, and it had to be. Parked in a row, all looking as though they had just come off the assembly line, were five additional '57 T-birds.

"You need one more," Kit said. "Then the entire week would be taken care of."

Broussard shook his head. "Six is abundance. Seven would be eccentricity. Which shall we take?"

"How about the yellow one?"

"Always been *my* favorite."

Kit felt something heavy and soft against her ankles. She looked down and saw two big green eyes looking back at her.

"That's Chuck," Broussard said.

Chuck was a fat black tomcat with pink lips and a white bib. The upper half of one ear hung in a rakish droop. The other had a notch in it. When Kit bent to pet him, he began to honk like a goose, and she pulled her hand back in alarm.

"Worse cat I ever saw for hairballs," Broussard said, reaching for a bag of Cat Chow beside the door. "Been nearly twelve years since I found him half-dead, on my front porch, with an arrow in him. Guess he was shot by some kids, or a grown-up with a mean streak. Even now, you can't get near him if you're carryin' anything long and sharp." He filled a green plastic bowl with food and looked around the garage. "Princess should be around here somewhere. Guess she's afraid of you." Chuck, now recovered from his hairball, fell to his meal, keeping one eye on the stranger with the funny smell.

"I'm kind of surprised you'd be willing to take these cars out on the road," Kit said.

"Because they might get damaged?"

She nodded.

"If you're so afraid of damagin' what you own that you won't use it, you ought not to have it. Besides, anything one man can break, another can fix, and I've got a genius of a mechanic and body man I can call when I need help. And that area down there," he pointed to a portion of the garage partitioned off by a concrete-block wall with a picture window in it, "is fully equipped for any kind of eventuality, includin' enough parts for another complete car." He looked at his watch. "I'd better get you home before I take up your whole evenin'."

Broussard dropped her off a little after six. She considered calling David to cancel their date but then began to think of the bodies she had seen that evening and suddenly didn't want to be alone. David was still working as he said he would be, and they agreed to meet at the Rialto, a small restaurant on Dauphine Street, a few blocks from David's office.

In the shower, she soaped herself to a lather, rinsed, and was about to step from the tub when she changed her mind and did it all again. This time it was bloody exam papers, a kitchen floor with bootprints on it, and the memory of a fleshless face that she was trying to wash clean.

She walked the few blocks over to St. Charles and caught the trolley to Canal. It was getting late and there were only a few other riders, an old man reading a newspaper folded into a tiny square, a glassy-eyed maid in white holding a grocery bag on her lap, and in the back, a woman trying to get her little boy to stop climbing over the seats.

As often as she had made the trip, Kit never tired of it. With limbs of ancient oaks stretching over the sidewalks like the nave in a vast church and huge azaleas providing a rich green contrast to the sparkling white columns and porch balustrades of the great wedding-cake houses lining the avenue, it was a magical place. She could not understand how the old man could read his newspaper and how the maid could prefer staring into space when there was all this to see.

The trolley clattered its way past the immense houses, curled around Lee Circle, and entered the commercial canyons of downtown. At Canal Street, where the tracks made a return loop, she got off and walked the short distance to the Rialto.

Pausing at the top of the short flight of carpeted stairs, her hand on one of the brass rails that flanked the steps, Kit saw in the dim light of the restaurant that their favorite table, the one in the corner near the Australian fern, was occupied by four men in business suits. Most of the other tables were also occupied, none of them by David. She looked along the wall with the booths and saw him halfway back. He waved, the happy look on his face making her glad she had come.

As she walked toward him, she saw a man sitting alone two

booths to the rear. He was dark like David, but with a stronger jaw. Unlike David, whose hair was always combed meticulously straight back, his was casually arranged, but also with no part in it. His sensual lips made David's seem even thinner than they actually were. Shockingly, he raised his wineglass to her. Embarrassed and afraid that David might also have noticed where her attention lay, she lowered her eyes.

"How'd it go?" David asked as she slid into the seat opposite him.

With her palms on the checkered tablecloth, she poured out all she had seen. "Great, terrible, I'm not sure. Since I left you this afternoon, I've seen five bodies, one with his face burned off and another who'd shot himself in the head. Am I going to ruin your dinner with all this?"

David shook his head and Kit continued.

Talking about it here in clean, comfortable surroundings with the gentle murmur of other conversations in the background almost made it seem like it hadn't been real, that it hadn't really happened.

Her story was interrupted by a male waiter in black pants, a black sleeveless vest, and a white blouse. As he took their order to the kitchen, David said, "What kind of guy is Broussard? I've used him a couple of times as a witness, but have never talked with him outside the courtroom."

"You should. He's fantastic. If you were ever thinking of committing a murder, you wouldn't want him on the case."

"That's always been my impression. But he's a little on the large side, isn't he?"

"Just like you're going to be if you don't lay off the French bread."

He took her hand and kissed the skin between her finger and thumb. "When it comes to Greeks, more is better. Ummmm, you taste good."

Embarrassed, Kit looked around them. "Shhhh, people will hear you."

She tried to pull her hand back, but he held on and began to kiss each finger.

Kit dipped the fingers of her free hand in her water and flicked them in David's face. Surprised, he let go of her.

"Your table manners are atrocious," he said with mock seriousness, patting at his face with his checkered napkin.

"You got just what you deserved, you pervert."

He leaned forward and reached for her leg under the table.

"Daaaavid!" she hissed, sliding into the corner of the booth. "Behave."

She was saved by the waiter's arrival with two steaming plates of spaghetti, two baskets of French bread, and a bottle of wine. When they were finished eating, David said, "Got a dime?"

She knew him well enough to realize what was coming. "You've been to the magic shop again, haven't you?" she said.

"Never mind. Just give me a dime."

"I heard that it was illegal for anybody over twelve to go into those shops," she said, digging in her purse. "Here."

"You keep it and mark it with this so you'll be able to recognize it." She took the felt-tip pen he held out to her and made two dots on the head and one on the tail. "Now give it to me," he instructed.

He took the coin, dropped both hands below the table, then brought them up again almost immediately and offered her a small white matchbox tightly wrapped with rubber bands. His black eyes danced with that mischievous light that sometimes made him look like a little boy. It was at these times that she almost believed she loved him.

She removed the rubber bands and took off the lid. Inside was a smaller matchbox, wrapped like the first. "If my dime is in here, you're good," she said, tugging at the second set of rubber bands. Inside was a little red pouch with a rubber band around the neck. "I have to hand it to you, David, this is one of your better tricks." She opened the pouch, shook the contents into her hand, and inhaled sharply. Instead of the coin she expected to find, the pouch held a ring whose diamond setting burned with cold fire from the reflection of the table's flickering candle. "Oh, David." She sighed.

"'Oh, David, how wonderful'? Or, 'Oh, David, I wish you hadn't'?" he said.

She looked at him affectionately, yet with a certain sadness. "David, I . . ." She hoped he might anticipate the gist of what she was about to say and help her out. But he just sat there waiting, a well-trained lawyer allowing the witness to put her foot in her own mouth. ". . . It's too soon," she said.

He looked hurt. "What do you mean too soon? We've known each other for nearly two years. I thought that once you finished your degree you'd be ready to start a family."

Kit stiffened. "Why did you assume that? Were *you* satisfied after finishing law school? Of course not. That was just a beginning for you, a first step. Why did you believe my degree had any different meaning to me? David, I'm just starting my career, something I've been working toward for four hard years. I'm not going to jeopardize my professional future by getting tied down with children right now."

"I don't know what kind of people you come from," David said. "But to Greeks, family is everything; a blood tie to the past, a link to the future. A man without children has nothing."

"I wonder how eager you Greek men would be for kids if *you* had to drag the big belly around and wipe the strained pears off the wall. Being a mother is not my idea of a life's work."

"What is?" David asked. ". . . Hiding in toilet stalls and studying the effects of multiple patrons on bladder-emptying time?"

Kit glared at him without speaking, her face set in ice.

"I'm sorry," David said, running his fingers through his hair. "That was uncalled for."

"But very telling. I've felt for a long time that you think my work is frivolous and now I know you do."

"Come on, relax. Don't make more out of that remark than was there."

Kit thrust out her chin and said coldly, "I'm sorry, David. It's an occupational hazard. All us 'shrinks' do it." She reached over and dropped the ring in his half-filled wineglass. "If you'll excuse me, I'm going to take my headache home and go to bed." She worked herself free of the booth and stood up. In an elaborate gesture, she let her checkered napkin fall to the table.

David fished the ring from his glass. "I'll drive you," he said, pulling the napkin from his lap.

"Don't bother. I'll take the trolley."

"It's late. They aren't running now."

"A cab then. Good-bye, David."

She turned to go, but David grabbed her arm. "Do me a favor will you?" he said. "When you calm down, ask yourself if this career thing is something you *really* want, or is it something you *think* you should want? Does it come from your guts, or from the pages of *Cosmopolitan*? Think about it."

Allowing him the last word, she went into the night without looking back.

Later, as she lay in bed, she *did* think about it. What did it matter where her motivation came from? Some feminist's typewriter, an admired acquaintance, or a forgotten book read when she was a child. It's all the same. Desires that "come from your guts," as David put it, are simply feelings that can't be readily traced to their source. Poor David. There was so much about life that he didn't understand.

Unable to sleep, she turned her thoughts to a more troublesome point, his proposal. Perhaps she had been too hasty. She and David had enjoyed many good times together. He was witty, charming, and attentive, and she very much enjoyed the physical side of their relationship. But she didn't hear bells, and she didn't think of him every minute when they were apart. Wasn't *that* a big part of what had kept her from accepting his ring, the feeling that somewhere there was someone who could make her feel like Jell-O inside?

But maybe what she had with David was what love *is* when you grow up. Maybe the capacity for head-over-heels, sick-to-your-stomach love is something you leave behind like old high school yearbooks and your training bra. She halfheartedly considered reopening the matter to see whether they might reach some agreement about children and her career, but the thought of bargaining over terms for their marriage like a peasant haggling with a shopkeeper over a fish so repelled her that she put the thought out of her mind and finally went to sleep.

The next day, she was scheduled for her regular visit to the Happy Years nursing home where, for over a year, she had been doing volunteer work twice a month as a psychological counselor. The arrangement had begun when the administrators of the home had asked the Tulane psychology department whether they might have someone in their program who would be interested in helping old folks at the home cope with living in an institutional environment. They were particularly concerned about the periods of depression some of the residents were experiencing. Since suicide was Kit's special interest and depression was one of the chief causes of suicide, she had jumped at the opportunity. Broussard had not merely *allowed* her to continue her association with the home but had enthusiastically encouraged it. Investigation of the deaths from the previous day would have to wait awhile.

As she drove, she found herself inspecting the other cars on the highway for clues about their owners. The car ahead had a decal in the back window from Florida State University, and on the bumper, there was a current parking lot sticker from the same school. The owner was obviously a college student home for the summer. Big deal. Compared to the things Broussard could do with a simple observation, this was kid stuff. She concentrated on the facts, trying to extract something worthwhile from them, something not right on the surface, something worthy of Broussard. But before she could do it, the trip was over.

As always, a faint hint of urine met her at the door. From down the hall and around the corner, she heard the hysterical voice of the chief administrator, a woman named Ida Swenson. There was also another sound, one she couldn't identify.

"What on earth is the matter with you?" Swenson screamed. Then there was that other sound again. Rounding the corner, Kit saw Swenson with a frail old man in a blue bathrobe and street shoes. Swenson was hitting the old man on the head with a rolled-up newspaper.

At Kit's approach, Swenson turned, her newspaper poised for another blow. The woman had a grandmotherly face that usually radiated warmth, a face that could remind you of fresh-baked pies and warm bread. But today it was full of scorn.

"He's done it again," Swenson whined. "I don't know what you've been telling him, but it isn't working. You're going to have to try a new approach. We just can't have this sort of thing. And when you're through with him, I want you to talk to Minnie. She's still not eating."

Shindleman had been through it all before, and he shuffled toward the room they had given Kit for an office. Slipping behind her battered desk, Kit said, "Have a seat, Mr. Shindleman, and I'll be with you in a minute." She got out the old man's file and reviewed it briefly. Six times in the last three months, Shindleman had taken a folding chair out onto the lawn early in the morning to watch the rush-hour traffic. And each time, except for his shoes and socks, he had left his clothing inside.

She studied the old man over the top of the file folder, perplexed as to the proper course to take. As sickly old men go, he was a pretty average specimen. His thin hair barely concealed a pate generously speckled with liver spots, and there was a shiny lump the size of a gumdrop just above his right eye. On his left cheek, a tuft of hair grew out of a mole that resembled a tiny cauliflower. His neck was all cords and strings and his head never stopped shaking. He picked at some lint on his bathrobe.

"Mr. Shindleman." He jumped when she addressed him. "Do you remember promising me two weeks ago that you would stop exhibiting yourself on the lawn?"

His wiry brows met over his nose. "Why's that get everybody so goddam excited? I don't see it. Everybody knows pretty much what everybody else has got, so what difference does it make? What's everybody afraid of? Lightning gonna strike us dead if we see a bare butt?"

"You didn't answer my question."

"What question?"

"About your promise to stop going outside without your clothes."

"You sure it was me that made that promise?" He shook his head. "Don't sound like me." He rolled down one sock and scratched a white leg. "Mighta been me, though, bad as my memory is."

This was getting her nowhere. He was hopeless . . . or was he? A crazy idea popped into her head and she opened his file and checked the dates he had gone naked into the world. Ha! There it was.

In every instance, he had misbehaved on the morning of one of her days at the home. It was her fault as much as it was Shindleman's. The old man was just making sure he would get to talk with her each time she had office hours. "Tell you what, Mr. Shindleman. Why don't you and I have a little chat whenever I'm here. Would you like that?"

His eyes didn't exactly gleam at her suggestion but they did the best they could, and he broke into a lopsided grin. "Could we? I mean, we could talk even though I hadn't been bad?"

"Even though you hadn't been bad. Now I need to see someone else. Would you tell Mrs. Swenson that I'm ready for Minnie now?" Shindleman got up and backed his way to the door in a half-bow, and Kit thought she would have no more trouble with him. But Minnie Mrocheck was a different situation.

She picked up Minnie's file and refreshed her memory. Minnie Mrocheck, sixty-year-old widow, had come to Happy Years four months ago with severe arthritis and had gone steadily downhill, dropping from 130 pounds to a pole-thin current weight of 80 pounds. She ate practically nothing, professing to have no appetite. A thorough medical examination had revealed no organic cause for this situation.

The door opened, and a cadaverous face peeked into the room. "Come in, Minnie," Kit said brightly. The old lady hobbled inside and took a seat without being told. She barely indented the chair's cushion. But then all the residents of Happy Years were small. Come to think of it, Kit could not remember ever having seen a tall old person. Where do the tall people go when they get old, she wondered. Is there a special home for them somewhere?

Many of the residents who ended up in Kit's office would stare at the floor or into their lap. Some let their eyes drift over the room, as though finding it interesting, an unlikely possibility in view of its drab gray walls and the sparse dilapidated furnishings. Minnie, however, had her eyes firmly fixed on Kit. Her stare was so unwavering that it made the younger woman uncomfortable.

"Minnie, why are you not eating?" There, a good direct question with an implied accusation in it would show the old girl who was in charge.

"I'm not hungry. Do *you* eat when you're not hungry?"

Don't answer, Kit counseled herself. Answer and you become equals. "Is the food not to your liking?"

"I've had better . . . and worse."

"You know you've lost a great deal of weight since you came to us."

"Thank you."

"It wasn't a compliment. I was calling your attention to the fact that if this continues, it can lead to only one thing."

"And what is that?"

"Death. You will die."

"How extraordinary. I'll die. Surely the media will find that such a remarkable event, they'll converge in droves to this establishment and interview you extensively for your views on the matter."

"Is that your purpose then, to starve yourself to death?"

"Let's assume for the sake of argument that it is? What would you propose to do about it?"

"Why, try to talk you out of it, of course."

"You say that like it's the only rational thing to do. Tell me dear, why do you feel so driven to meddle in the one thing above all else that should be left to individual discretion?"

"Because such a decision is contrary to the human spirit."

"Wouldn't the mere fact that someone chooses such a course negate your argument?"

"Not when the decision, as it always is, is made by a mind temporarily disturbed by stress, grief, or depression."

"Let me see if I have it straight. Whenever the decision to end one's life is dictated by temporary brain malfunction, you have the right, in fact the moral duty, to intervene. Is that correct?" Kit nodded reluctantly, knowing she was being led down the garden path. "And how can we tell when a brain is malfunctioning? Why, whenever suicide is seriously contemplated. I'm afraid, my dear, that you have never come to grips with why you feel compelled to involve yourself in the most private of acts. You simply are unable to accept a decision that repudiates your own values."

"Surely life is *always* preferable to death."

"It all depends on the life you're talking about."

Early in the conversation, Kit had considered showing the old lady some inkblots to get her talking, thinking that a clue as to why she was starving herself might emerge. Now, that didn't seem like such a good idea. It would be like showing a physicist how a yo-yo works. Kit was not accustomed to being debated so capably by anyone at the home. Most of the clientele had long ago given their brain over to keeping track of their bowel movements and committing to memory every pain and twinge so that they would have something to talk about. It was hard to imagine Minnie doing that. But right now, Kit would have traded Minnie for the worst of them. They were dull but easy to control. Kit was clearly not in control of this interview. Maybe a tough approach would shift things her way.

"Minnie, earlier I said you would die if you persisted in starving yourself. That wasn't entirely correct. Because before that happens, I'll see that Dr. Peeples straps you to your bed and feeds you through a tube in your arm."

"That would be illegal," Minnie said haughtily.

"It most certainly would not," Kit replied, trying to sound as though she knew what she was talking about. "Who told you it was illegal?"

"Mr. Graybar. He was a lawyer before he retired, you know."

"Real estate law, I believe."

Minnie's proud demeanor collapsed. "Then he may be misinformed? Oh dear." The old woman dropped her eyes and the debate was over. "I'd like to go now and think this over."

"You do that Minnie. And we'll talk again next week."

After Minnie left, Kit did nothing for a full minute but enjoy the way she had turned the tables on the old girl. Maybe now Minnie would start eating. She wrote optimistic paragraphs in both files and was putting them away when a different interpretation of her discussion with Minnie suggested itself, one that could have disastrous consequences. She added three sentences to what she had already written in Minnie's folder and underlined them.

Before leaving, she stopped at Swenson's office to report the results of her two interviews but found no one in. Eager to get on with her investigation for Broussard, she decided not to seek the woman but instead tore a page from the pink memo pad next to the telephone and jotted down the words, "Extremely important that you read latest entry in Minnie's file. File is in my desk, K. F." She put the message on top of a neat stack of papers and placed a stapler on one edge to hold it in place. Then she called Broussard on Swenson's phone to see what they had learned about the previous day's victims.

So far, all they knew for sure was that the name of the dead schoolteacher was Thad Rentdorff, that he was single, and that he taught at Craigmont High. That was the school she passed every time she went to the home, and it was only fifteen minutes away.

Chapter 4

Craigmont lay atop the crest of a small hill that paralleled the street. With its Palladian windows and ornamental pink stonework, it was too pretty to be a school. It looked more like a French palace. Inside, classes were changing and the lockered hallway was choked with noisy teenagers. There wasn't room between them for another notebook, let alone another body, so Kit decided to wait for it all to clear. In two minutes, it was a different place; quiet and empty, like a palace ought to be. She found the administrative office a few doors from the entrance.

Behind a long wooden counter she saw three desks to the left of a door with the faded word "PRINCIPA" on it, the L having worn off for some reason before the other letters. The two most distant desks were facing the far wall, implying that visitors were of no concern to the occupants. The other desk faced forward and it was from here that a woman in a baggy flowered dress and brown Hush Puppies came to inquire as to her business.

"Mr. Callicot, please," Kit said, reading the principal's name off his door.

"Is he expecting you?"

"No. It's about Mr. Rentdorff."

The woman's mouth pursed. "Ohhh, Mr. Callicot is not very happy with Mr. Rentdorff. He didn't call in sick and his first class was half over before anybody realized he was absent. And no one answered at his home. Is he ill?"

Kit hadn't anticipated that she would be the bearer of the bad news, and she had no intention of telling more people than necessary. "Would you just tell Mr. Callicot I'm here please?"

The principal's office was pretty much standard issue, right down to the American flag on a pole in the corner and the unfinished picture of Washington that schools always have on the wall. Behind the desk, a black-and-white picture of a football team in a thin gold frame hung above a lacquered wooden paddle with "The Voice of Reason" stenciled on it. She had time to see all this because Callicot had yet to look up from his work.

She cleared her throat, and he said, "Just one minute. Please find a seat." And he still hadn't looked at her.

Find a seat. It was so typically a teacher's phrase that she had to smile. As the seconds ticked by, she began to get the feeling he had hastily pulled out a stack of papers and had begun writing on them just so she would have to wait. A way of setting the pecking order straight. A heartbeat before she expressed a sharp sentiment about his rudeness, he looked up, put his pen in the polished wood holder in front of him, and said, "You have a message from Mr. Rentdorff?"

It was the first crew cut she had seen in years. With his rough-hewn features and a nose that looked as though it had healed poorly after being broken, he might have stepped right off a marine recruiting poster. *We need a few good men with no neck.* Probably a former coach, come up through the ranks. "I'm Dr. Franklyn, from the medical examiner's office." Ordinarily, she wouldn't have used the "Dr.," but felt he needed to hear it. "Mr. Rentdorff's body was found late yesterday at his home."

"Guess I can't fault his excuse for not calling in then, can I?" the man said as calmly as if she had said Rentdorff had come down with athlete's foot. "What happened?"

"We're not sure, but we think it was suicide."

"How did he do it?"

"There was a gun next to the body."

"I wouldn't have thought he'd use a gun. Seemed more the poison type to me."

"What do you mean?"

"A gun is a man's weapon. Rentdorff was a wimp." Seeing the expression on Kit's face, he said, "Well, he *was*. Always whining about how unmotivated his students were and how poorly he was paid. He took every act of nature that interfered in any way with his plans as a personal attack, as though when it rained, it only rained on him. Sometimes it was all I could do to keep from kicking his butt. His students were the rowdiest in school. Kids who were no problem in other classes went wild in his. He had this talent for generating contempt in everyone around him. *We're* better off and so's he for what he did."

Look who's calling someone else contemptuous, Kit thought angrily. He had told her exactly what she wanted to know, but in such an unfeeling way she felt an irrational desire to strike back on Rentdorff's behalf. Suppressing the desire to taunt Callicot with what she knew about the exam papers, she said, "Did you notice anything different in his behavior recently?"

"Now that you mention it, he seemed almost normal the last few weeks. I mean I actually saw him smile a couple of times. The change was so obvious that one of the other teachers asked me if I'd given him a big raise. A raise! That's a laugh. My foot in his behind is the only raise he deserved."

This last comment gave her all she needed. It was a classic suicide. A morose, depressed personality suddenly seems to have solved his problems, then a few weeks later, kills himself, his apparent cheerfulness arising from the fact that he had not only made the irrevocable decision to take his own life but had the plan completely worked out down to the exact day he would do it. She thanked Callicot for his time and left, pleased that her first report to Broussard would be so clearly correct.

* * *

John Griffin wiped his forehead with the back of a greasy hand and looked at the clock. The woman whose car he was working on would be back any minute, and he still had to put in the new plugs and figure out what was wrong with the brake lights.

He looked for his boss, Freddie Watts, and saw him out by the pumps, closing the trunk on a Volkswagen bug. The scene brought back memories of a day six years ago, and he smiled.

He had known nothing about cars then but had lied and told Freddie he'd worked for two years in a station in Florida. Then the first day on the job, he'd spent ten minutes looking for the radiator on a VW minibus. Boy did he feel stupid when the owner came out of the john and told him it didn't have a radiator. That and the amount of time he'd spent wandering around cars searching for the gas cap made it pretty clear that he didn't know anything about being a station attendant. But Freddie had kept him on and gradually taught him to be a passable mechanic. Hell of a guy, that Freddie.

At the pumps, Freddie carefully ran his squeegee as close to the edge of the windshield as he could. With his fingernail and a paper towel, he worked at a stubborn bit of dried insect until the driver told him to forget it. When he went inside to put the credit slip in the cash register, Griffin leaned into the office. "Hey boss. Can you give me a hand for a few minutes? The owner of this buggy will be here any minute, and I haven't had a chance to work on her brake lights yet."

Freddie pushed the register closed and went into the work bay where he opened the car's front door and lay across the seat with his head under the dash. When he found the fuse box, he snapped off the plastic cover and rose up for a look. Before he could accomplish anything, his stomach muscles cried out in agony and he dropped back to a more relaxed position.

As he lay there, he began to think that maybe his body was trying to tell him to give it up. Sell the damn station and retire. Put an end to the dirty fingernails he could never get clean, the scraped knuckles, and the dirt in his hair. The thought of putting all these things behind him was satisfying and he began to sing softly. ". . . *She cut off their tails with the carving knife, three blind mice.*" Saliva ran into his throat, and he began to cough. Sitting up, he coughed some more and put his hand to his neck. His mouth was filling again. He was about to say something to Griffin, who was in the office reading about sparkplug settings, when suddenly it didn't seem important anymore. *"Three blind mice."* That was more important.

He slid out of the car and slammed the hood. Griffin came out of the office just as he backed the car out of the garage and caught the edge of the tire display, sending its contents bouncing and rolling over the pavement.

With Griffin calling out to him, Freddie headed east, eyes fixed on the road, body rigid. Saliva began to run from one corner of his mouth and he swallowed hard. ". . . *Three blind mice. See how they run.*" The song had become everything to him. He needed nothing else. Not that new oscilloscope, not another work bay, not anything. The song was enough.

At the first intersection, where there was a small knot of people queuing up for the silver-and-blue bus that could be seen above the cars three blocks away, he turned the wheel sharply to the right. Most of the crowd didn't see him, and the few who did, stood rooted in disbelief as the car jumped the curb. Watts never even felt the impact. ". . . *Did you ever see such a sight in your life?*" He swallowed hard, and more saliva came.

He guided the vehicle back onto the street and proceeded east. A cabbie, unhappy with the way he ignored the stop sign at the Huey P. Long interchange, flashed him "the bird." By the time he was well onto the bridge, the scleras of both eyes had become pale pink as a curtain of blood spread over them.

". . . *Three blind mice.*" Cars going in the opposite direction passed without incident, but when a school bus appeared in the oncoming lane, Watts aimed his car directly at it. The driver saw what was happening and swerved to the left. Freddie tore out the guardrail on one side a fraction of a second before the school bus went through on the other. The bus hit the water upside down. Freddie's car fell without flipping, and when it hit, his head snapped forward, displacing his first two cervical vertebrae just far enough to sever his spinal cord.

"Cause of death was a through-and-through gunshot wound that entered on the right side, penetrated both ventricles, and exited on the left," Broussard said into the telephone.

While he talked, Kit sat clutching her reports on the two cases she had been assigned, grateful for the delay, however brief, of the moment she would have to let go of them. Trying to relax, she studied the picture on the wall behind Broussard's desk. The sepia photograph of a negligee-clad young woman seated at a vanity was not particularly attractive, and she wondered why he had chosen it. Then she saw for herself. Hidden in the figure, so that it was not apparent at first, was a leering human skull.

"By itself the second bullet would not have caused death. . . . That's right. . . . Exactly. . . . Anytime." Broussard hung up and scrabbled for a lemon ball in the glass fishbowl near his desk calendar. With the candy tucked safely into his cheek, he said, "Let's see what you've got for me."

She handed the two files across the desk and waited nervously while he read them. He rolled the lemon ball from side to side in his mouth and nodded while reading her report on the schoolteacher. He winked at her when he put that file down and picked up the other. He rolled the lemon candy but did *not* nod at the contents of the second file. And why should he? She had followed every lead the police had given her and some they hadn't. She had talked to relatives, employers, neighbors, and friends, and still could not find even a hint of a suicidal personality in Barry Hollins. She knew that Broussard was convinced it was a case of murder-suicide, and she was more than a little upset that she had not been able to verify that. Thus, as he read the second report with no expression on his face, she felt he was trying hard not to show his disappointment.

Finally, he put the report down and said, "Babe Ruth struck out over thirteen hundred times. But nobody remembers that. They only remember that he was the greatest home run hitter in the history of baseball. Bein' one for two at this stage of your career is not bad."

Kit gave him a wan smile and nodded weakly. Having always found sports analogies juvenile, she found no solace in this one. "If no one knows how many times Babe Ruth struck out, how do you know it?" she said.

"I read it in a book. Now stop feelin' sorry for yourself. You made a thorough investigation and that's all anyone could ask. Go on home and forget it."

But she couldn't forget it, and it was still on her mind when she put the key in the door of her town house. If he really thought she hadn't screwed up, he wouldn't have gone to so much trouble to make her feel better.

As the door opened, a small dog she had never seen before dashed past her legs and was inside before she was. He sat up and examined her with his head tilted to one side. Kit's heart melted at the sight of him and she forgave him instantly for barging in uninvited. He barked sharply three times in greeting, and she bent to scratch his head.

Before she could touch the gray curls that hung into his brown eyes, he darted away and began to race around the room. Each time he encountered it, he went onto the sofa instead of around it. Sitting up was cute, scrambling over the furniture was not. With a piece of ham from the refrigerator held close to the floor, she coaxed him from his game and sent him charging through the open door by flinging the meat into the parking lot.

Sighing in relief, she shut the door, put her back against it, and closed her eyes. A sharp kick of each foot sent her shoes flying. The first message on her answering machine was from

David: "I'm sorry for what I said the other night at dinner. I really *do* have an explanation. Give me a call, will you? And we'll talk it over."

The next voice was Broussard's. "If you're still interested in what it's like in the field, meet me at the foot of the Huey P. Long bridge as soon as you can."

When leaving, she opened the front door just a crack and peeked through it. There was no sign of the little dog. Fearing that he might be hiding close by, she slipped out quickly through the smallest possible opening.

It was four-fifteen and South Claiborne was beginning to fill with rush-hour traffic. Thirty minutes later and she would have been hopelessly mired in it. A half mile from the bridge, traffic came almost to a standstill as drivers and passengers twisted in their seats to see why there were three ambulances at the Carrolton intersection. Kit had no better luck than anyone else at seeing through the large crowd that had gathered.

Ten minutes later, at the bridge, she saw a small cluster of people, a tow truck, and an assortment of cars, including Broussard's yellow T-bird, on a grassy spot at the end of a dirt road leading to the river's edge. On the highway, two policemen were making life difficult for the curious.

"Keep it moving. . . . You! Yes, you! Get that thing out of here. Come on, come on. Let's go."

As she drew near the cop on her side, she rolled her window down and leaned out.

"You can read about it in the papers, lady," the cop said sharply.

"I'm with the medical examiner's office." She pointed to the dirt road. "Can you get me down there?"

"Got any ID?"

"None that will satisfy you."

He looked hard at her for what seemed like an awfully long time, then yelled at the other cop and together they opened a path in the traffic. Her little Nissan took the rutted road badly, and by the time it had jiggled and bounced her to the water's edge, she didn't like the car quite as much as she had.

Phil Gatlin was there and, along with Broussard, was watching a police boat work its way across the river. In the boat's stern she could just make out two men hanging on to a line playing out from a winch.

Hearing her swish through the dry grass behind them, Gatlin and Broussard turned around. From the look on Gatlin's face, Broussard hadn't yet told him who she was.

"Phillip, this is Kit Franklyn, my new assistant. Kit's specialty is suicide."

Gatlin put out a huge hand at the end of a wide forearm. "Never knew a lady before whose specialty was suicide," he said, shaking her hand as gently as King Kong ever held Fay Wray. With all the lines in his face, he reminded her of a worried Robert Mitchum.

"Somewhere out there in all the mud, catfish, and garbage, there's a school bus and a car," Broussard said. "The car ran down some pedestrians back up the road. You probably saw that on your way here. Then it tried to ram a school bus on the bridge. Both of 'em went over the edge."

It was a long long way to the bridge from where they were standing, but when Kit looked up, she thought she saw a gap in the steel meshwork of the rail. She pictured herself plunging off the bridge and somewhere in her pelvis, she felt a muscle contract. Gatlin moved off downriver.

"Somebody saw the car plow into that crowd and then leave the scene. They followed the car to the bridge and saw what looked like a deliberate attempt to ram the bus head-on," Broussard said.

"Could it have been some kind of dizzy spell that waxed and waned?" Kit suggested.

"If you had a dizzy spell and ran over some people, I think you'd stop the car when your head cleared and help the injured. Whoever was behind the wheel of this car had a clear enough head to drive a half mile in a normal manner after he hit those folks."

"Drugs?"

"Maybe. But I don't think so. More likely a suicide involvin' a man angry over somethin' and not satisfied to die alone. One determined to take as many people as possible with him. That's why he waited for the school bus."

"God, I forgot about that. How many kids were in the bus?"

"We think it was empty."

"That's a break."

"Doesn't do much for the dead at the bus stop."

"Looks like they got something," Phillip shouted, his hand shading his eyes.

The police boat had hoisted a red flag. The vessel made a wide turn and headed for shore, stopping about fifteen feet out. An unshaven man in jeans and a gray T-shirt got out of the tow truck and waded to his knees to catch the steel cable that was tossed to him. He fastened it to the winch on the truck and cranked up the engine. As the winch groaned and the cable strained, Kit thought of what Broussard had said about the case likely being a suicide. Would he be willing to change his mind if she found no evidence of a suicidal personality? She doubted it. She found herself hoping that the autopsy would disclose a heart attack or a brain tumor, anything to shift the responsibility for this one away from her.

The winch continued its tortured labor and almost imperceptibly it began to gain ground. The object on the end of the cable was moving. Unexpectedly, with the sound of a rifle shot, the cable parted and the end attached to the winch sliced through the air in a curving arc. To Kit, it all seemed to be happening in slow motion. She could see the ruptured end glinting in the sun as it traveled a course that would intersect the spot where she stood. It was going to hit her.

She was jolted backward and the world turned upside down. Seconds later, she felt as though a great weight lay upon her, and the right side of her face felt as though it had been filleted. She couldn't move and, for a terrible moment, she was sure she was paralyzed. She let out a small cry. Her ear! She could see one of her ears! Then she realized it was not *her* ear, it was the ear of someone on top of her, someone whose sharp whiskers were still pressed against her cheek.

Breathing heavily, Broussard struggled to his feet and offered her his hand. "I didn't think you were goin' to duck in time," he said apologetically.

"Neither did I," she replied, looking at a small sapling that had been sheared off its trunk by the cable.

Broussard brushed himself off and picked a piece of chaff from his hair. "Guess you weren't lookin' at the wallpaper," he said.

It was a nice way of saying she had picked herself a pretty stupid spot in which to stand. From now on, she was definitely going to be looking at the wallpaper.

The tow truck driver spliced the broken cable with four U bolts, and in less than ten minutes, the car that had gone off the bridge was leaking water onto the bank. Jamison, the police photographer, appeared from somewhere and circled the car, clicking pictures as he went. While he was taking one from the rear, the tow truck operator climbed up on the hood, wiped the windshield on the driver's side with a rag, and looked in.

"Christ! Take a look at this," he exclaimed.

Everyone crowded around, and soon they were all trying to talk at the same time. Kit had overdone her new respect for winch cables and was nearly forty feet away. Curious as to what could produce this kind of excitement in such veterans of mayhem, she walked to the car, squeezed between two uniformed policemen, and saw what had caused the stir. The corpse was smiling!

Chapter 5

Kit walked slowly along the cement steps that lined Lake Pontchartrain's New Orleans shore. Overhead, the cloudless sky made the calm water of the shallow lake deceptively blue. In the water above the first submerged step, she could see small fish that darted into deeper water at her approach. It was early and the benches that dotted the wide grassy strip that ran beside the steps were empty. Except for two figures on the steps ahead and some robins scratching under the big fir trees along the lake, the place was all hers.

She could not remember a worse time in her life. The autopsy had produced no explanation for the vicious behavior of the man who had gone off the bridge, and four days ago, she had set about her investigation of the case. It had ended just like the one involving the fire. A series of events had occurred for which there was no discernible cause. Fred Watts was not suicidal, or if he was, had done a helluva good job of keeping it to himself.

She drew near the two figures on the steps, a little boy about seven and a man in his early forties, just as the boy jerked on his cane pole and hauled a flopping silver fish onto the steps. The boy and the fish scuffled briefly. The fish lost.

"Look what I caught," he said, pointing his prize in her direction. The fish made soft croaking noises, and the boy put its mouth to his ear and giggled. "It talks," he said happily.

Kit walked on, the child's joy making her own problems seem even worse. What had caused Barry Hollins to kill himself and his family? Why had Fred Watts driven into a crowd of innocent people and then tried to kill himself in a head-on collision with a school bus? The great psychologist who was going to write a book on suicide couldn't do a thing with two of her first three cases. And then yesterday, she'd learned that Minnie Mrocheck was in the hospital in a coma . . . from an overdose of sleeping pills. Kit angrily kicked a pinecone into the lake. She had anticipated that Minnie might try something like that, had even put it in her report the previous week. But Swenson claimed she'd never gotten the note telling her to check the file. Damn it! Something that important shouldn't have been left to chance. She should have spoken to Swenson personally instead of leaving a note.

The turn of events at the home along with the results of her investigations for Broussard made her feel utterly worthless, and she had gone to the lake to consider her options . . . one of which was to resign from the medical examiner's office and give up her efforts at the home. For all she knew, Shindleman might this very minute be standing naked on the *roof* at Happy Years.

In one sense, her difficulty in dealing with what she perceived as failures came from her profession. All the ego-defense mechanisms people unconsciously use to survive bad times were well known to her and were, therefore, unavailable for her use. She was forced to view all her actions in the glaring light of objectivity.

Then too, there were her years of growing up. Years when everything she wanted seemed to come without effort. Good grades, lots of friends, college scholarships, all were a normal part of life for her, and they went unquestioned and unexamined, like the money her father had sent her each month when she was still in school. It was just the natural order of things. Working mothers, lawyers with divorce papers, fractured bones, and tight budgets were concerns other people had to contend with. In her view of the world, trapeze artists were born to do triple somersaults, and concert pianists inherited the genes for long fingers and musical ability. The role of pain and frustration in human achievement had escaped her notice, and she, therefore, felt that her failure to prevent Minnie's suicide attempt and her inability to explain Broussard's cases simply meant she was unfit for the work.

Even if she and David hadn't argued at the Rialto, her deep-seated desire to avoid any hint of a clinging-vine personality in her own makeup would have prevented her from looking to him for solace. Thus, her desolation was all the worse because she had to bear it alone.

Around nine o'clock, with the decision to resign still on her mind, she went to her office in Charity Hospital to put the final touches on her report for Broussard. There she ran into Charlie Franks, the deputy medical examiner.

"Want to see something interesting?" he asked, obviously pleased with himself over something. The gaps between Franks's teeth made him resemble a carved Halloween pumpkin.

"Sure. What have you got?" she said, more brightly than she felt.

"Come on, I'll show you."

Franks was lanky and built like a hammer, wide at the shoulders and narrow at the waist. He walked with a peculiar rocking gait that made Kit feel like she was on a ship listing from side to side. To all outward appearances, he was an extremely dedicated employee who worked seven days a week. But Kit had learned that he simply took three times longer than it should to do anything. Mostly because he was one of those people who just couldn't sort out the priorities in life. He spent so much time cataloging, cross-indexing, and rearranging his reprint collection that he didn't have time to read any of the papers in it. The joke around the office was that he proofread even the things that came off the Xerox machine.

He was a hit with Broussard, though, no small part of that being his willingness to do all the floater autopsies. It wasn't that Franks enjoyed working on partially decomposed corpses pulled from the local bayous. It was just that because of some childhood accident, the details of which no one seemed to know, he had lost his sense of smell.

They went into his office, where he sat down at a computer terminal. "Ask me anything about homicides in New Orleans," he said.

"What do you mean?"

"Make up a question that you'd like answered about murder in this city."

There was nothing particular that Kit was curious about, but she liked Franks and didn't want to appear uninterested so she managed a question. "What percentage of murders are committed by women?"

"Over what time span?" Franks asked, his fingers poised over the keyboard.

She decided to make it challenging. "Broken down by years for the last five."

Franks's eyes glistened, and the keyboard made busy clicking noises as his fingers flew over it. A few seconds after he finished, a bar graph flashed onto the screen with the data she had requested. He pushed a button and the printer on the adjacent table began to clatter. From the paper bail, a sheet appeared containing the diagram on the screen. Franks pulled it free and presented it to her.

"No money necessary," he said.

She took the paper from him and examined it with a forced look of admiration.

"Took me six months, but every case that's come through here in the last ten years is in this baby's memory. Come on, ask me something else."

She wanted to be alone with her own thoughts right now, but because Franks was so excited and proud of his accomplishment, she decided to humor him a while longer.

"Make it a hard one this time," he said.

She thought a minute and said, "Show me a yearly breakdown of all cases classed as murder-suicide over the last ten years."

"Too easy," Franks said as he worried the keyboard. When the data appeared on the screen, Kit saw something so surprising and unexpected that it completely changed her expression.

"Look at that," she said, pointing to the monitor where the data was displayed as before, in a bar graph.

For the first seven years of the period, the bars were all about the same size, very short. In two of those years, there had been no incidents that fit the criteria. The last three bars on the page, though, dwarfed all the others.

"I'll be damned," Franks muttered. "I never realized how the number of those kinds of cases was increasing."

"Can you do statistics on this thing?"

"Sure. The numbers are pretty small, so let's run the last three years against the previous seven."

A minute later, the results flashed on the screen, and they both searched eagerly for the p value among the other numbers.

"Less than point oh-one!" Kit said enthusiastically, leaving a greasy fingerprint on the screen.

"That's better than I expected with n so small."

Kit was no longer a reluctant participant. Playing a hunch, she asked Franks whether he could break the data down into *known* and *probable* suicides, and silently blessed him for his methodical ways when he said he could.

They discovered that during the first seven years of the period surveyed, almost all of those suicides were classed as *known*. To the contrary, much of the increase in the last three years could be accounted for by an escalation in the number of *probables*. She could not have been happier. The two cases that had so stumped her were part of a pattern. It wasn't a question of her being unfit for the job, she had simply stumbled onto an unexplained behavioral phenomenon. For the next hour, they had the computer examine the data from every possible angle. She left Franks's office with a thick bundle of fanfold paper, eager to get off by herself and assimilate the results.

Thirty minutes later, she burst into Broussard's office and showed him her findings. His response was disappointing.

"I'm sorry to have to say this, because enthusiasm over your work is a commendable virtue, but I think in this case, it's premature."

"But the statistics show . . ."

He lifted a cherubic hand to ward off her rebuttal. "A good statistician can stand in the middle of a thunderstorm and prove it can't possibly be rainin'."

"Didn't you tell me, a few days ago, to always play the odds?"

"I did. Now I'm suggestin' you do it with a little healthy skepticism. You may be on to somethin', then again, it could be nothin'. But for the moment, let's assume the increases are real. What else do we know?"

"Two things. For one, the increases appear to be caused by people with blood type O." She looked expectantly at Broussard, hoping his eyes would light up and he would say something brilliant. But he just sat there, his fingers laced over his belly.

"And?"

"And we found a correlation between the probable suicides for the last three years and scleral hemorrhaging. Does *that* tell you anything?"

"Not really. It's a findin' that can occur anytime there's hypoxia. Certain poisons, inhalation of toxic fumes, a violent coughin' spell, even a gunshot wound if it's in the trachea. It's fairly common. A correlation doesn't mean much. Where would you go from here?"

"I'm not sure. I haven't had time to think about it. After all, it's only been about an hour since we generated the data."

"And you believe that the Hollins case and the Watts case are part of this pattern?"

"The records show that the blood type of both men was O."

"So's mine," Broussard said. ". . . along with about a hundred and twenty million other folks in this country."

"Just out of curiosity, did either of those two have scleral hemorrhages?"

Broussard looked at her sternly and she was afraid she'd gone too far, asking about something he had already dismissed.

"No way to tell. The first body was burned too badly. But I would have expected it anyway. Toxic fumes, remember? With the one in the river, the water would have washed it away."

His face softened and he said, "I can see you're very much taken with this theory of yours and I respect that. Nothin' of value ever gets done without a champion behind it. So if you'd like to get into this, go on, and if I can help in any way, let me know."

"Fair enough." She left Broussard's office and found Franks waiting for her in the hall.

"How'd he like our discovery?" Franks asked.

"Not much. Seems that our esteemed colleague isn't swayed by statistics."

"There's a little more to it than that. He's a fine fellow in many respects and I'd stack him up against the best medical examiners in the country . . . when *he's* the one with the hypothesis. But he's got a blind spot for other people's ideas. If you're the one to suggest a possibility, it takes twice the evidence to convince him than it would if *he* had the idea. It's a problem he's well aware of. That's why he won't talk to anyone about a scene until he's examined it himself. He doesn't do it willfully, it's just something he can't help. Let him chew on it awhile. That's what I do."

"Would it be possible to check with some other cities to see if they're having similar experiences? If they are, that would be more proof that there's a real phenomenon taking place."

"I know the homicide files are computerized in L.A., New York, and Boston, so it should be an easy matter to get their data. I'll send the letters off this afternoon. Ought to have an answer in a week, two at the most."

"Have you got a hematology book I could borrow?"

"Sure."

Alone in her office, Kit looked up "Blood Groups" in the index of Franks's book and turned to the appropriate page. A small table there showed the percent distribution of each of the major blood groups in different races. While there were minor racial differences in the distribution of the four primary blood types, the bottom line was that A and O, the two types found in eighty-five percent of the population, occurred in nearly equal numbers.

She closed the book, convinced that the absence of blood type A in the recent rash of murder-suicides could not be a random event. She got Franks to pull the files on all cases the computer had categorized as probable suicides for the last three years and began reviewing them. Since they included copies of the police reports, there was a fair amount in each file to read. If these cases were related in some way, as she felt sure they were, there must be a clue somewhere in the files.

Three hours later, with all the cases reviewed, she still had not found the thread she was searching for, and she had begun to think that maybe none existed. There was a knock on the door and Broussard leaned in. "The police forensic lab is havin' an open house to show off their new mass spec. Let's walk over and see if they've got anything good to eat."

Weary of the files and pleased that he had thought of her, Kit pushed her chair back and stood up. "What's a mass spec?"

He was still trying to describe it as they left the hospital's cool interior and set off down the hot sidewalk toward the Criminal Justice Center two blocks over on LaSalle. She had just about decided that he wasn't too clear himself on the nature of the thing when an apparition stumbled out of an alley and turned to face them. He was without shoes or socks, and a wide expanse of shirtless skin showed from between the lapels of his gaping sport coat. One hand held a whiskey bottle loosely by its neck, the other was all that was holding his pants up. He glared at her and Kit's steps slowed.

"'Tell me I'm imagining this and he isn't really there," she breathed.

Broussard put his hand in the small of her back and urged her on. "Just act like you don't see him."

She pretended to look at the cars in the street, the Coppertone billboard on the roof of the Mutual building two blocks ahead, and the litter in the gutter. But she was actually watching *him*. As they neared, he tensed and she was sure he was about to spring, instead, he abruptly turned and shuffled back into the alley.

She sighed with relief.

"Local color," Broussard said.

The Justice Center extended over a square city block. It housed the city and parish courts and attorneys, the holding cells for prisoners facing arraignment, and the central offices of the city police, including the forensic division. Completed a year earlier, it still looked fresh and new from the sidewalk. Inside, it was aging rapidly. The tall weeping figs in their washed-gravel containers showed the yellowing evidence of continuing neglect, and cups and papers littered the soil around their roots. To the left of the elevator, there was a long meandering slash in the wall covering, and on the right, an obscenity, originally written in lipstick now cleaned away, was still legible.

Forensics was on the sixth floor where, under a picture of a microscope tipping the scales of justice in the favor of law and order, they had set up a long table covered with a white cloth.

From the color of the contents of the crystal bowl on each end, there were two kinds of punch, red and yellow. A long plate of finger sandwiches flanked by silver bowls of nuts rounded out the consumable part of the festivities. The punch was being dispensed by a young woman with cover-girl eyes and a wide red mouth.

Suddenly everything disappeared in a blinding light. When it cleared, there was a grinning mug in its place.

"Lord-a-mighty, Raymond," Broussard said. "Give somebody a warnin' why don't you."

"Candid shots are always the best," the grinning face said. "When people know they're gonna have their picture made, they get tense and they don't look natural."

The man with the camera looked to be in his early fifties. He had a bland flat face with the eyes right on the surface. Kit recognized him as the photographer at the Hollins and Watts cases. He turned to her and said, "I'm Ray Jamison. Haven't I seen you a couple of times in the field?"

Kit introduced herself and said, "I was at the fire in Gretna and I was there when they pulled that car out of the river a few days ago."

"So what are you; medical student, writer, M.E. in training, lady with an odd hobby?"

"Would-be suicide investigator."

"Why do you say, 'would-be'?"

"There's Phillip," Broussard said, touching Kit's arm. "I'll be over there with him." He patted the photographer on the shoulder. "Good seein' you, Ray."

"So why did you say, 'would-be'?" Jamison asked again.

Kit wished she had been less candid. She had no intention of discussing her career problems with someone she had just met.

"I'm new at it. That's all I meant."

"No, I think there's more to it," Jamison said slyly.

She suppressed the impulse to tell him to mind his own business and instead took advantage of his inability to see Broussard from where he stood.

"Oh, sorry, Dr. Broussard wants me. Nice to meet you." At her approach, Phil Gatlin paused in mid-sentence.

"Go on with what you were saying," Kit said.

"I was just asking Andy why forensics sends out Christmas cards. I can understand why businesses do it, but why does forensics do it? They afraid I'll take my ballistics work to another firm?"

Before either of them could reply, they were joined by an angular woman in a tailored gray suit that she wore over a white shirt and tie. Her short hair was nearly the same color as her horn-rimmed glasses. She had probably never been pretty.

"So glad you all could come," she said.

According to Broussard, she was Beverly Delong, director of the whole forensic division.

"Where's the new machine?" Gatlin said.

A crimson blotch appeared on the woman's neck and spread upward to her face. Her eyes blazed with indignation. "Fields are plowed by machines," she said. "A mass spectrometer is a scientific *instrument!*"

Gatlin drained his glass and set it on the table. "If I wasn't afraid you'd quit sending me a Christmas card, I'd tell you what you could do with your *instrument*," he said, and headed for the stairs.

"Peasant," Delong said under her breath.

"Don't be too hard on him," Broussard said, "He's havin' personal problems."

Delong made some noises that presumably meant she was offended, then said, "Actually his question about the new instrument was a good one. We should see it now." She tapped on a punch bowl with a knife from the table. "May I have your attention everyone."

The murmur of conversation stopped.

"If you'll all follow me, I'll show you the reason for this celebration."

Kit stopped to snatch a sandwich and brought up the rear of the small group following Delong down the hall. They convened in a simple room that contained a long gray rectangular object slightly taller than anyone present. It had an instrument panel with a few dials and switches and a TV screen above a writing surface. It looked far less complex than Kit had expected.

Jamison took a few pictures of it, then turned his camera on the people jammed in the doorway. Delong told what the instrument could do, how fast it could do it, and how much it had cost. When she asked for questions, a hand went up in the front.

"How do you justify spending that kind of money on new equipment when our salaries are so far below the national average?"

Delong looked surprised and started to sputter. Finally, when she was able to put a complete sentence together, she said, "Al, this is neither the time nor the place to discuss that."

"Why not?" the voice said.

An embarrassed silence filled the room as the crowd waited for the little drama to play out. Kit went up on her toes to get a look at the person who had asked the question, but was thwarted by Broussard's back.

"I'd be happy to discuss the matter with you later *in my office*," Delong said through a clenched jaw. Shifting to a happy tone, she said, "Thank you all for coming. Do stay and help us finish the refreshments."

The crowd filtered back to the food and Kit drew Broussard aside. "Who asked the pointed question?"

"Al Vogel. He's the forensic fabric expert."

"For how much longer, I wonder?"

"Oh, he's too good to fire. That's him over there." He nodded toward a dark-complexioned man in a white lab coat filling his plate from the refreshment table. Kit was surprised to see that she recognized the face. It was the fellow who had been sitting behind David at the Rialto. And she felt now the same interest she had then.

"Well that was certainly an inexcusable performance," a breathless voice said from over Kit's shoulder.

Broussard introduced her to Gil Bertram, forensic expert on glass fragments and cigarette butts.

He was a slight man whose face was mostly cheekbones. From beneath a mustache that looked as though he had glued a caterpillar on his lip, a thin cigar protruded from a wide fishlike mouth. He removed the cigar from between his lips and held it in one hand while supporting his elbow with the other. "It's not that I don't agree with the point he made," Bertram said. "It's just the way he went about it. Beverly was exactly right. Dirty linen should be washed in private, not flapped in a guest's face. Please don't think too badly of us, will you?"

Bertram seemed so concerned that Kit assured him she would put the matter out of her mind. Broussard said something similar and Bertram floated off, presumably to extract the same pledge from others.

"And they really solve crimes here?" Kit said.

"Remember the promise you just made," Broussard cautioned.

"Sorry."

From out of the corner of her eye, Kit saw Vogel coming their way.

"Let me guess," he said. "Bertram thought I was out of line in there."

"Hello Al," Broussard said. "Actually, he thought you had a good point."

Vogel looked at Kit and jerked his head in Broussard's direction. "Ever the diplomat. That's why everyone loves the man. Hi, Al Vogel, dissident," he said, offering Kit his hand.

Vogel's grip was firm and warm. He held her hand a trifle longer than was necessary and their eyes locked. His were a compelling pale blue that made her feel that she was on a high mountain looking into a clear limitless sky.

"We've met somewhere," he said, releasing her hand.

"We didn't actually meet. I saw you in the Rialto about a week ago."

"Of course. You were wearing a black dress with white pinstripes."

Flattered that he remembered her so well, she looked at Broussard. "Here's someone else with an eye for detail."

After learning her name and where she fit in, Vogel said, "Well, I guess I'll have to be real careful what I say, you being a psychologist and all. Wouldn't want you to learn all my secrets."

"People always seem to feel that way when they find out what I do," Kit said. "I think I'll start saying I'm a dog groomer."

"You strike me as someone who couldn't shade the truth even a little."

"You're probably right."

Behind him, Beverly Delong was staring coldly at Vogel's back. Decision made, she strode over and touched him lightly on the shoulder. "May I speak with you privately," she said.

Recognizing the voice, Vogel made an "oh-oh" expression for Kit's benefit and said, "I'd like that, Beverly."

He excused himself and followed Delong to an unoccupied corner of the room where, from the look of it, he was getting a good dressing down.

"Well," Broussard said, "we've eaten their food. . . . You tried it, didn't you?" Kit nodded. "We've seen them fight and we've looked at their *instrument*. So I'd say we've gotten our money's worth."

The open house had briefly taken Kit's mind off the pile of cases on her desk. Alone at home that night, she thought about them some more but could come up with nothing new. And that's where the matter stayed for several days, a time during which Broussard assigned her an additional case that turned out to be a classic textbook suicide much like the schoolteacher, and during which David called every night to apologize, calls that she let her answering machine handle even though she was home.

* * *

On the morning of the fourth day, in a section of the city that never appeared on tourist brochures and never heard the clatter of horse-drawn sight-seeing carriages, Leon Washington and his friend "Burnt Larry" Brown were going fishing. Leon, a former LSU tackle, pulled up in front of Burnt Larry's weathered gray shack and honked three times. The screen door opened and a slightly built man, many years Leon's junior, and hugging a bamboo thicket of cane poles, fought his way free of the house.

"Damn, you sure you got enough poles there," Leon called out.

"Fishin' license don't say nothin' 'bout how many poles you can put in the water," Burnt Larry said with a lopsided grin. The other side of his face was marred by burn scars that looked like pink corrugated tin.

"Say what? If right now I gave you *my* license, you'd still only have *one*."

Larry put his poles and cricket box in the back and slid onto the dirty blue vinyl front seat. "You don't have to *gimme* your license," he said. "Just *show* it to me." They both laughed as Leon pulled away from the curb.

"Say man, where'd you get the wheels?" Burnt Larry asked.

"Police auction. It was in some kinda accident, but it runs pretty good."

The engine backfired as Burnt Larry fiddled with the radio dials.

"It don't work," Leon said.

"How about the AC?" Larry asked, flipping switches and pulling levers.

"I dunno, never tried it."

"Damn! I bet you never even looked to see if it had a motor before you bought it." Leon said nothing. Larry chuckled and poked him in the ribs. "You didn't. You didn't. I knew it." While Larry slapped his hands together in glee and chuckled some more, Leon slid his free hand along the back of the seat and cuffed his friend playfully on the head. Larry slumped in the seat as though knocked unconscious, then sat up and put his hand over the air-conditioning duct. "Roll up your window. I think the AC is workin'." Larry cranked up the window on his side and the plastic knob came off in his hand. "How much you pay for this thing?" he asked.

Leon rolled up his window and said, "You think anybody'd pick up a smartass hitchhiker carryin' a bunch of cane poles?"

"I don't know," Larry said. "Why don't I drop you off at the next corner and we'll find out." He poked Leon in the ribs again and chuckled.

Leon put his hand out and tested the air-conditioner vent on his side. "Say, this is all right. It's really puttin' out."

He pulled up at the stop sign at the corner of Chelsea and Highway 39, looked both ways, and eased out fifty yards in front of a Colonial bread truck. When he accelerated, a great billow of gray smoke rolled out of the exhaust and drifted over the truck.

With lips compressed into a thin line, the driver of the truck, a man who'd once given ten dollars to the Sierra Club, glanced at the car ahead, wishing he could wrap the offending tail pipe around the owner's neck.

Leon had never owned a car *without* a visible exhaust, so it didn't bother him.

The road ran parallel to the Louisiana-Southern railroad tracks and there was a very long train about a half-mile behind them. Up ahead, the road passed over the tracks. "Goose it, man," Larry said, jerking his thumb toward the train when Leon looked his way.

When they were thirty yards from the crossing, bells began to clang and a black- and white-striped wooden arm descended to block the road. "Shit," Larry said. "If that dude ahead of us wasn't such a candy ass, we both coulda made it. Must be somethin' wrong with that gate. Hell, it'll be five minutes before that train gets here."

"You want a . . ." Leon hesitated, losing for a moment what he was about to say. "You want some . . ."

"Say what?"

"You want a beer?"

"Sure, you got some?"

"In the trunk," Leon said, handing Larry the key.

Larry went around to the back of the car and promptly dropped the keys. Inside the bread truck, which was right behind Leon's car, the driver wondered what was going on.

Leon's thoughts had shifted from beer to his mother, dead now, five years. How he missed her! Why he could almost hear her voice . . . no, he *could* hear it, singing the tune that had always made him laugh when he was little. All about ducks and chickens and cows. And she used to tickle him under the chin when she made the animal sounds. He liked that part best. *"Here a chick, there a chick . . ."* He laughed, and as he did, a spray of saliva speckled the steering wheel.

A few seconds later, he got out of the car and went around back to where Larry was halfway into the trunk trying to reach the six-pack that had shifted to the front. Grabbing his friend by the legs, Leon threw him all the way in, then shut and locked the lid.

The driver of the bread truck squeezed the steering wheel in disbelief. Had he really seen the big guy lock the little one in the trunk? He slid the truck's door open far enough to hear Leon's gravelly voice murdering *"Old MacDonald Had a Farm."* He checked the impulse to intervene. It wasn't any of his business if someone wanted to play a joke on a friend. It didn't seem like much of a joke, though, considering how hot that trunk was going to get in the next few minutes with the sun beating on it. He was too far away to see the saliva on Leon's chin and the broken blood vessels in his eyes.

With his mother's sweet voice filling his senses, Leon put the car in gear and moved forward until he made contact with the bumper of the compact car in front. Then he began to push it toward the striped barricade. When the driver of the car ahead felt his car begin to move, he increased his pressure on the brakes. But Leon responded by pressing harder on the accelerator, blocking the truck driver's view with billows of gray fumes.

The trucker fled the smoke and, from a vantage point outside the cloud, was shocked at what was taking place. Even though Leon's car was far older than its years, it still had enough horsepower to inch the smaller car's locked wheels over the pavement.

The train was now only a hundred yards from the crossing, and its shrieking whistle seemed to be coming from the two adults and two children who were looking backward, their mouths gaping in horror at the car behind them. With saliva dripping onto his shirt, Leon kept working on the smaller car, pushing it until the barricade passed over its hood and came to rest against its windshield. He continued to push until the barricade splintered. The sound disappeared in the steady scream of the onrushing train, now only seconds away. When the front wheels of the car Leon was pushing came to rest between the tracks, the truck driver shut his eyes, unable to watch the imminent carnage. But as the train thundered through the crossing, he heard only the roar of its passing and the rhythmic pounding of its wheels against the rails. He opened his eyes and was able to relax, for he saw between the railroad cars racing by that the doomed family's vehicle had somehow made it safely to the other side of the tracks.

But Leon was not finished. He backed up until he touched the bread truck's bumper. Then he raced his engine, popped the clutch, and lurched toward the mountain of steel hurtling by. His momentum carried him deeply under an empty passenger coach whose wheels rolled the car over and over like a hog on a barbecue spit until the train derailed.

Chapter 6

"I was hoping you were here," Charlie Franks, the deputy medical examiner, said, stepping partway into Kit's office. "I'm taking all the fieldwork today and I've just been called to a scene that sounds like it might match the murder-suicide profiles the computer gave us the other day. Like to come along?"

"Would I ever!" she replied, leaping to her feet.

Franks grinned. "Kind of thought that'd be your answer."

Franks's car held no surprises. Fixed with rubber bands to the visor on the driver's side was a ball-point pen, a little green notebook, and a tire-pressure gauge. Riding the hump between the driver and passenger was an empty color-coordinated combination wastebasket and a full Kleenex dispenser. Near her feet on the right sidewall was a small fire extinguisher. The floor mats were clean and bright, and the dash wouldn't dirty a white glove. She was sure that he could produce emergency flares if asked.

About a hundred yards from their destination, they encountered a roadblock. After identifying themselves to the cop who was turning everyone else around, they were allowed through. Railroad cars lay scattered along the tracks like toys flung by an angry child. The remains of Leon's car lay upside down beneath the belly of a derailed flatcar carrying a massive piece of blue machinery partially covered by a green tarp. A half-dozen men were working a row of jacks that had been placed under the railway car. Near a tow truck that had been attached to the pinned auto by a huge chain, a man kneeling by a welder's helmet was fiddling with the hoses from a pair of metal tanks.

They pulled onto the sandy shoulder behind a string of other cars and got out, Kit having to fight through grass nearly up to her knees. As they approached the crossing, a pear shape in a blue-striped seersucker suit appeared from between two jackknifed railway cars up the line. With his tiny feet and close-cropped hair, the man inside the suit reminded Kit of a bowling pin. Seeing Franks, he waved them over.

"We figure you've got two customers in there," he said, pointing to the wrecked auto. "But it's gonna be awhile before we can get 'em out."

"Any in the train?" Franks asked.

"No, but we nearly had some more. I dunno if it's because we get our drinking water out of the Mississippi or what, but the people in this town are gettin' crazier every day. This was no accident. We got an eyewitness who said this car rammed the train deliberately. And before it did, the driver tried to push somebody else onto the tracks."

"So I heard. Dispatch also said something about him locking a guy in the trunk."

"Just another day in the big city."

"Where's the other car?"

"What other car?"

"The one that was pushed onto tl e tracks."

"Split. Guess they didn't want to get involved. Probably never will know who they were."

"You said there was an eyewitness," Kit interjected. "Where is he?"

"We taped his statement and let him go."

Responding to the puzzled look on the man's face, Franks introduced Kit to detective Gabe Santos.

"May I hear the tape?" Kit asked.

"Sure, it's over there on the floor of my car." He gestured toward the first car in the line on the shoulder. "Just don't erase anything by mistake. If you have any doubts about which button to push, come and ask me."

The sun had made the detective's car unbearable. Noticing that he had left the keys, she slid behind the wheel, started it, and flicked on the air conditioning. It was a cheeky thing to do, but the heat made it necessary. As the tape played, she found the witness so articulate, and Santos so thorough in his questioning, that she felt as though she had been there herself.

While listening, she watched the workmen's progress at the crossing, where they soon had the railroad car raised enough for the wrecker to pull the pinned auto free. When they got it flipped over, it was obvious that no one inside could still be alive. The front part of the roof and the trunk were crushed nearly flat. Only the rear window was recognizable. As Kit looked at its odd configuration, a central oval flanked by two circles, she felt she had seen the pattern before.

When Santos asked the witness whether there was any evidence that the driver of the death car might have been drinking or on drugs, the answer made her forget all about the car's rear window.

"He moved kind of stiff, like a windup toy, only not so obvious," the taped voice said. "It's kinda hard to explain, but it just wasn't right, and he was . . . not exactly humming, but was doing something like this." The witness reeled off a few bars of music using grunts instead of words. The tune was familiar and she said it to herself at the same time Santos said it on the tape.

" '*Old MacDonald Had a Farm*'?"

"Yeah, that's it," the witness said. "And his face had no expression on it."

She let the tape run to the end of the interview and turned it off. "*Old MacDonald Had a Farm*"! Her eyes glazed and she withdrew into the memory of a conversation she'd had with one of Barry Hollins's neighbors. He had said that a few minutes before the fire, Hollins had walked by whistling *"Pop goes the weasel,"* and had ignored an invitation to play golf. This was the second time she had thought about that interview, which initially seemed of no value. The first time was when she was going over the old files on her desk.

One of those files contained a case that had begun with two friends out for a day of duck hunting. Before reaching their destination, the fellow driving was suddenly hit in the face with the butt of his passenger's shotgun. When he came to, the car was against an overpass guardrail and his friend was blasting away at vehicles on the highway below. Fearing for his own life, the driver pretended to still be unconscious. A short time later, the other man jumped or fell from the overpass and was killed.

She had read the police transcript of the driver's testimony so often that she had no trouble recalling it now. The driver had said that the whole time his friend was behaving so strangely, he was singing about the woods and teddy bears and picnics. A song from an old kiddy radio show, he said. He couldn't remember the name of the program but could recall some of the song. *"If you go down in the woods today, you're sure to have a surprise"* . . . something . . . something . . . something. *"Today's the day the teddy bears have their picnic."*

That song was what had first reminded her of Barry Hollins whistling before the Gretna fire. It was such a weak coincidence that she had completely forgotten it. But here it was again. A few hours ago, a man singing "Old MacDonald" had locked his passenger in the trunk and driven into the side of a train. Three cases, all similar, all where the killer was either singing or whistling a children's song. She switched off the engine, knowing as surely as she ever knew anything that she was on to something. She also knew just as surely that she wasn't going to present such a wild idea to Broussard without a lot more evidence. But where to get it?

* * *

The next evening as the local news was starting, Kit heard a knock at the door. Through the peephole, she saw David clutching a huge bouquet of flowers. Not at all sure it was the right move, she shot the deadbolt and opened the door.

"You wouldn't answer your phone or return my calls, so I had to do something," he said, thrusting twenty or thirty dollars' worth of pink sweetheart roses, white shasta daisies, and baby's breath toward her.

How many times had she decided to break off with him only to be coaxed into giving it one more try? Five times? Six? Surely this was not the way two people who really loved each other behaved. She took the flowers and went inside, letting David decide for himself whether to follow. He did.

"When you hold a grudge, you sure do it right," he said, watching her go into the kitchen. Through the passthrough, he saw her lay the flowers next to the sink and begin to rummage around in the cupboards. He found encouragement in the fact that she had not thrown the flowers in his face at the door, nor had she put them down the disposal like she did the last time. Things were definitely looking good.

"I can understand your anger over that crack about . . ." He paused, realizing that it would be dangerous to repeat his reference to psychologists hiding in toilet stalls. ". . . that careless remark about your work, but there was a reason for it and you've never let me tell you what it was."

"I know the reason," she said, putting a white vase under the cold-water tap. *"That's* why I haven't been available."

Now she was talking to him, another good sign. The words didn't matter. He went into the kitchen and stood beside her while she arranged the flowers. "I was free for the afternoon on the day we argued because earlier we got a hung jury out of the Krupp case and I was in no mood to work. I didn't say anything at the time because it made me furious to think about it and I didn't want to ruin our time together."

Kit remembered reading about the case in the newspaper but said nothing.

"The sonofabitch strangled six women, had an apartment full of incriminating evidence, gave a full confession, and we couldn't get a conviction. And you know why? Because only ten jurors believed *our* psychologist, who said that the killings were premeditated and that Krupp knew what he was doing. Two believed the defense psychiatrist, who said Krupp was compelled to kill by a long-standing hatred for his mother . . . that every time he killed he believed he was killing her. Ten for our side, two for theirs . . . and a hung jury. Probably cost the state two hundred thousand for that trial and in a couple of months we can do it all over again. Maybe next time the defense will find a more persuasive psychiatrist. Maybe then the *whole* jury will believe that Krupp can't tell right from wrong and we'll have to settle for a short stint at Shreveport, where he'll eventually be declared 'cured' and allowed to walk away."

Kit carried the vase into the living room. "What's your point?"

"Simply that psychologists and psychiatrists have no place in the courtroom. They confuse the proceedings and obstruct justice."

She put the vase on a serpentine-front commode to the left of the door and stepped back to see how it looked. "You don't believe in mental illness then."

"Not as a defense. He took six human lives. There has to be a penalty for that. If this guy isn't executed, we *have* no judicial system. I don't care *why* he did it."

She turned and brushed past him. "Is it justice you want or revenge?"

"One life for six isn't justice, but I'd settle for that, preferably done in public where other sadists like him could see it."

Kit dropped into a wing chair, pulled the latest *Newsweek* from the magazine rack next to the chair, and began to leaf through it. "The threat of punishment does not deter others from committing the same offense," she said icily.

"It's a hell of a deterrent on the one executed, though," David said, the lawyer in him pleased at being able to get in such a good shot. He'd given himself over so fully to venting his feelings about psychiatrists in the courtroom that he'd momentarily forgotten the real purpose of the conversation. Realizing that things were going sour, he tried to get back on track. "It wasn't my intent to argue the merits of the insanity plea as a murder defense, but simply to show you why I said what I did that night. I said it out of frustration. That's all. In the eight years I've been with the DA's office, there hasn't been a single year that someone hasn't tried to cop an insanity plea for murder, often successfully. And I can't help but feel that when they get away with it, it's partly my fault for not working hard enough or being smart enough, or . . . whatever."

David's attempt to explain his actions made Kit wonder more than ever whether they had a future together. How could a man despise your profession without some of that hostility coloring the relationship? His views hadn't changed, most likely would never change. He'd just be careful not to make the same slip again. And the next time a psychiatrist contributed to a verdict that went against him, he'd say nothing but would always find a little of the reason for his defeat in her. She expressed none of this but kept flipping pages while he continued to plead his case.

"It's been years now, but I can still see the surprised look on George Delberg's face when he got Abe Shindleman off with his 'Rock-A-Bye-Baby' defense."

Kit slapped her magazine shut. "What was that you said about Shindleman and 'Rock-A-Bye-Baby'?"

"Three or four years ago a night watchman at . . . Crescent City Industries, I think it was, emptied a gun into his employer's head, reloaded, and tried to shoot himself. But the final bullet was defective and simply ricocheted off his skull and knocked him out for a few hours. His attorney pled temporary insanity based on a lot of crap about his client remembering nothing about the event except hearing voices singing 'Rock-A-Bye-Baby' over and over. He was sent to Shreveport, where they observed him for awhile, and goddam if six months later he wasn't back in court petitioning for release. The Shreveport shrin . . ." He caught himself about to say the magic word and quickly substituted another, hoping Kit hadn't noticed yet knowing she had. "The Shreveport staff testified they could find no trace of mental illness. His attorney argued that legally he had to be released because he hadn't been found *guilty* by reason of insanity, he had been found *not guilty*. Therefore, if he wasn't insane, he was entitled to go free. We argued that if he wasn't crazy in Shreveport, he wasn't ever crazy, and therefore should pay the penalty for murdering his boss. But with our screwed-up laws, once they convinced the judge he wasn't crazy *now*, he was free. And that's what I've been forced to put up with all these years."

"Could you get hold of the file on that case?" Kit asked excitedly.

"I suppose. Why?"

"Would there be a photograph of Shindleman in it?"

"Probably not."

She jumped to her feet. "You've got to leave now. I just remembered something important I need to do at the examiner's office." From behind, she pushed him gently toward the door.

He balked. "Wait a minute. We haven't settled anything."

"We'll talk later."

"When?"

David looked so hurt, she felt a pang of remorse. "I don't know . . . later . . . whenever you want."

"Dinner tomorrow night."

"Okay." She smiled.

"I'll be by around seven."

She pushed him through the door and looked at the clock on the TV as she headed for the phone. Six-thirty. Would Charlie still be at the office? He often worked until eight or nine, so there was a good chance.

"Rock-A-Bye-Baby" defense. That's what David had said. And if the man who had plowed into the train had lived, his attorney might have been able to get him off with an "Old MacDonald" defense. The similarities in David's case and her three were too obvious to ignore. All four men had childhood songs on their mind coincident with an act of violence against another person or persons followed by a self-destructive action. The Shindleman in David's story had been a night watchman. The Shindleman at Happy Years had once mentioned how boring night security work could be. But were they the same man? *Come on Charlie,* she urged as the phone rang a fourth time. Then there was a click and the sound of Franks on the other end.

"Charlie, this is Kit. Are you going to be there for awhile yet?"

"Actually, I had just locked the door and was on my way out when the phone rang. What's up?"

"I need to see a file and I was hoping I could come down and you'd find it for me. But if you're . . ."

"What's the case?"

"It's an old one. Three or four years ago, a fellow named Shindleman killed his boss and then tried to shoot himself in the head. I'm curious about the circumstances."

"The case is that old and it can't wait until tomorrow?" Franks said, good-naturedly.

"I suppose if you're leaving, it'll have to," Kit said, making no effort to hide her disappointment.

"Where do you live?" he asked. When he found out how close it was, he said, "Tell you what. Why don't I drop the file by on my way home?"

"Would you? You're a dear."

"Glad to help. See you in about twenty minutes."

Waiting was not something Kit did well. She paced the room for a few minutes, then looked out the window, knowing Franks couldn't possibly be out there after so short a time. She sat in her wing chair, picked up *Newsweek* again, and tried to follow the numbered pictures showing step by step how terrorists blew up the U.S. embassy in Uruguay. Finding it all unintelligible, she tossed the article aside and went into the kitchen.

She took a TV dinner out of the freezer and folded the foil in all the right places, wondering what kind of house Mr. Swanson lived in and whether the Morton place was bigger. She put the dinner in the oven and set the timer. Noticing a trail of ants attracted by a drop of syrup on the counter, she reached for the Mr. Clean and gave them a shot. As the little black specs were rolled and tumbled by the spray, she briefly imagined them screaming with voices so tiny they couldn't be heard. She wiped the counter with a paper towel, tossed the towel into the grocery bag she was using for a wastebasket, and went back to the living-room window. Still no Franks.

She switched on the TV and ran the channel selector to the right, giving each program a mere second or two. At channel thirty-six, she ran the selector all the way back to the left, shut the set off, and looked out the window. When Franks finally arrived, his third knock hit only air.

"Jesus," he said. "You *are* anxious to get hold of this file, aren't you?"

"I think there may be a lead in there on those statistics we generated."

"Sounds interesting. I'd like to stick around and talk but my daughter's having a piano recital at . . ." He looked at his watch. ". . . Oh God, in fifteen minutes—Enjoy!"

Without sitting, she ruffled through the file looking for photographs, soon finding a grisly series of pictures of a man with multiple gunshot wounds to the head. The oven timer went off and she put the file down, pulled her dinner out, and set it aside, seriously doubting that she would be able to eat it after seeing those pictures. David had said Shindleman was shot only once. Those first pictures then must be of his employer.

A few pages deeper into the file, she found another picture, a profile of a man with dried blood in his hair above his right ear. She was not accustomed to looking at *her* Shindleman in profile, and he was now a little older, so it was difficult to decide whether this was the man she knew. There were definite similarities, though. Then she noticed a tan swelling over the right eyebrow on the man in the picture. The swelling was slightly bigger now, but this was definitely a picture of the Shindleman at Happy Years.

Chapter 7

When Kit arrived at the home the following morning to question Shindleman, she found everyone gathered in the meeting room for the once-a-week "Armchair Traveler" series. The guest speaker, a man with a red face and huge ears, was just making his opening remarks.

". . . and so, because they sent our supplies to the *north* face of the mountain, and we were waiting at the *south* face, our expedition got off to a shaky start."

She scanned the room looking for Shindleman and saw him over the take-up reel on the movie projector set up between the rows of chairs. When he saw her, he waved and motioned toward the empty seat in front of him. Noticing that she would be sitting next to Mrs. Overholtzer, who had recently embarked on a bathing boycott, she shook off his invitation and sat instead between the two newest residents, the Duran sisters. They were a sight not often seen; identical twin old ladies dressed exactly alike. Today they were wearing light-gray pullovers with dark-gray horizontal stripes, and gray pants. Each had a golden butterfly pinned to her sweater in precisely the same place.

Kit soon discovered why they had left a seat between them. Mandy began to talk into one ear while Mindy did the same to the other. The speaker heard them too because he would get halfway through a sentence, then glance at the sisters and lose his thought. The sisters brought shiny droplets of perspiration to his forehead. But it was Lester Goldman, endlessly coughing into his hankie, who silenced him completely. While Mrs. Swenson helped Goldman from the room, Kit changed seats. When everyone had settled down, the speaker took a deep breath, looked quickly around the room like a cornered rodent, and tried again. "The wind . . ."

"I took a trip once," Mrs. Annafanna said, standing up and turning to face the others. "It was to someplace in Iowa." She paused and her mouth trembled. "Or was it Nebraska? Where do they grow all the corn? Gracious me, we saw a lot of cornfields on that trip. There were four of us in the car and I got so sick. . . ."

Mrs. Swenson swooped into the room, seized the rambling old lady's thin shoulders, and pushed her into her seat. "I'm sure we'd all like to hear about *your* trip, dear," she said sweetly. "But someone else has the floor now."

The speaker never finished his point about the wind but went directly to the film he'd brought. Things then went nicely until one of the mountain climbers swung out on his "peetons" to scale a nasty overhang. The "peeton" pulled out of the crevice into which it had been pounded and. . . . The picture suddenly darted from the screen and flashed across the wall as Mrs. Woolridge, who had fallen asleep, toppled off her chair and fell onto the table holding the projector. As the projector hit the floor, the lamp shattered and the take-up reel popped loose and rolled across the floor, leaving a trail of film as it went. In the ensuing scuffle, the film was damaged rather badly by chairs and feet. Mrs. Swenson apologized for the short program, and the gathering broke up amid much muttering.

Shindleman went over to Kit and said, "Good program. Best one this year in fact. How come *you're* here today? Isn't tomorrow your regular day?"

"I came early just to see you." No one had ever looked

happier than the old man did just then. "Let's go into my office where it's quiet."

As he followed her down the hall, Shindleman said, "Did you hear about Minnie? She's in the hospital. Tried to kill herself, they say. And for awhile, it looked like maybe she had. But I heard she was going to be all right. Have you seen her?"

Kit's face reddened. "No, I haven't." Ashamed once again of her sloppy handling of Minnie's case and embarrassed at not having visited her, she added, "My new job is keeping me terribly busy." That was certainly the truth, but the primary reason she hadn't gone to see the old woman was that she just didn't know what to say to her. She had no answer for Minnie's wish to die and had simply taken a coward's way out.

"I'm going to see her later today," Shindleman said. "You can get a bus out front that goes right by the hospital. Anything you want me to tell her?"

She had begun to wonder whether the old man was needling her, but his face was innocence itself and she decided he wasn't. "Just say, I hope she's better soon."

Instead of sitting behind her desk as usual, she sat next to him and said, "I realize what I'm about to ask you to discuss may be painful, but I want you to know that I wouldn't bring it up if it wasn't extremely important."

The happiness on his face was immediately replaced by suspicion. "What is it you want?"

"I want you to tell me what happened the night you . . . the night your employer was shot."

The old man clapped his hands over both ears as though trying to shut out a loud noise. "No," he said through clenched teeth. "That's over. I won't talk about it, I won't. It ain't right for you to remind me of this." The old man dropped his eyes to his lap and continued to hold his head in both hands.

She pulled her chair closer and put a hand on his knee. "I thought we were friends. And friends share their troubles with each other."

The old man slowly raised his head. "You'd still be my friend, knowing what I did?"

"That's another part of friendship, understanding when no one else does."

"They said I was insane, and maybe I was, 'cause I don't remember any of it. If someone does a terrible thing without knowing it, is he crazy?"

"Why don't you tell me exactly what you *do* remember about the day it happened."

"Why are you so interested?"

"The same kind of thing has been happening to others and I'd like to find out why."

"You mean there's a chance that I never *was* crazy?"

"I think that during those brief few minutes you were . . . being driven by some urge beyond your control, one whose origins could have been entirely external."

"I don't understand."

"Nor do I . . . yet. But after you tell me your story, I may."

The old man nodded in agreement. "It was December ninth. I remember that 'cause it was one of the coldest nights ever in New Orleans. When I started my rounds, I looked at the illuminated temperature sign over on the billboard across the street and saw the number twelve and wondered if the thing was broke. But as I worked my way around the plant . . . did I say I was a night watchman?"

"No, but I was aware of that."

"Well, after about ten minutes, my fingers and toes began to ache, so I figured the billboard was right. On the back of the building there was this big vent, and on that night, there was a nice warm breeze coming out of it, so I took off my gloves and warmed my hands awhile. Then I decided to have a smoke. Course I don't smoke anymore. Can't afford it. Do you smoke?"

"No, I don't. You took off your gloves and decided to have a smoke and then . . . ?"

"I lit up, leaned against the vent, and smoked about half a cigarette. That's the last thing I remember until I woke up in the hospital with a dull ache in my head and three men in suits sitting on chairs around the bed. Do you want to hear about the trial and the place they sent me?"

"At the trial, your attorney said that you heard voices that night . . . singing to you. Can you tell me about that?"

"Sorry about leaving that out; I ain't got the memory I used to have. Used to be, I could remember everything. Now though . . ."

She put her hand on his knee again. "You were hearing voices and . . ."

"That's what really convinced 'em I was crazy. Actually it wasn't all that big a deal. It was nice and warm next to the vent and I was feeling pretty good. I didn't hear them voices like I hear what you say, but more like they was inside my head. Pretty little-girl voices singing 'Rock-A-Bye-Baby.' I remember singing along with them for awhile and from then on, it's all a blank."

"Do you have any idea what part of the plant that vent served?"

"No."

There was no doubt in Kit's mind that she was going over to Crescent City Industries and check out that vent. It was equally clear that it would not be wise to take the old man along. It might be too much for him emotionally, or they might run into a relative or friend of the man he shot and there would be an unpleasantness. She went to her desk, withdrew a legal tablet and a pencil, and handed them to Shindleman. "Would you draw me a diagram of the plant and mark the location of the vent?"

He took the paper and his speckled hand set about the task. When he finished, she looked at the rough sketch and said, "Where's the street in relation to the drawing?" He reached over and drew two wobbly lines parallel to the long rectangle that represented the plant. "And where's north?" He took the drawing back, rotated it a few times, then drew an arrow and put an "N" at its sharp end. "This 'X' is the vent?" He nodded. "Were there vents in any other position around the plant?"

"One on the roof, I think."

"But no others opening through the walls?"

"No."

She tore the diagram out of the tablet, folded it, and put it in the pocket of her slacks. "Thank you for trusting me," she said.

"Will you be coming in at your regular time?" Shindleman asked. "I mean, does this count as our talk for this week?"

"No, this one doesn't count."

"You . . . won't tell the others about this, will you? No one here knows what happened and I don't want them to know."

"Of course I won't tell them. It will be our secret."

Chapter 8

The phone book listed Crescent City Industries at 6023 Waring. Around the three-thousand block, the character of the structures lining the street began to change from fast-food joints and gas stations to small manufacturing plants. Soon Kit was surrounded by industrial blight. On one side, the towers of a petroleum cracking plant spewed out clouds of gray smoke and streamers of flame. On the other, the view was dominated by the silos and treadmills of the place where they make Delta Cat Chow. The smell resulting from these two endeavors so close together was awful. It seemed like a good excuse for exceeding the speed limit.

Eventually, the bleak landscape on her left was replaced by a long meadow. Even here, industry superseded tranquility as a road-construction crew poured sweat and concrete into forms for an additional lane. At the end of the meadow, a wall of fieldstone with CRESECENT CITY INDUSTRIES spelled out in big white letters came into view. Behind the sign and cupping it on each side was a cool stand of pines. In front was a well-tended bed of red geraniums. The most eye-catching feature was the dense green lawn that surrounded the sign and stretched along the plant itself, a four-story, white-over-beige, corrugated-metal building set well back from the road. On the esthetic down side, the plant had an ugly smokestack big enough to do the air some real damage but presently sending out only a thin, nearly transparent discharge. On the opposite side of the street was a billboard that still told the temperature.

The parking lot had recently been relined, and the yellow paint marking off each space was crisp and bright. The lot was half-full, probably with employees' cars since they were all clustered in the back. Scattered through the lot, unpaved rectangular patches of ground had been planted with small fir trees and variegated monkey grass. At the rear, beyond a wide grassy expanse, was a drive that came from behind the plant and ran to a small one-story concrete-block structure painted to match the main building. Beyond this drive were two huge metal storage tanks with the words AMMONIUM NITRATE stenciled on them. Behind the tanks was another meadow. The plant site, being higher than the surrounding meadows, looked as though it had been built on a landfill.

The parking lot was separated from the plant by a ribbon of grass. Next to the wide steps leading to the plant's main entrance, the grass was marred by a small sign reserving the best parking space for someone named Weston. Pulling into the second-best space, Kit studied the corrugated-metal wall stretching away to her left. Except for a row of tiny windows under the eaves, it was smooth and unbroken. There were no vents to be seen. Getting out, she walked to the rear of the lot and, with a definite feeling of guilt, stepped onto the grass. She was so deep into the property, she failed to hear the red Porsche that pulled into the space she had avoided.

Rounding the corner, she found only more grass, more corrugated metal, and more of those small windows under the eaves. She took Shindleman's drawing from her pocket and turned it round and round, finally deciding that this was definitely the spot indicated on the diagram. The vent just wasn't there. But Shindleman was old and confused. He could easily have forgotten the exact layout of the place. He had admitted his memory was poor.

She continued on, her finger trailing lightly over the

building. Around the next corner, she came upon a loading dock beyond which the main road could be seen. The dock was the only difference between this side and the back. She had now been completely around the building and there simply was no vent.

A forklift carrying a black barrel came out of the plant and deposited its burden on the tailgate of a small pickup. After wrestling the barrel against a dozen others, the forklift operator secured the tailgate and gave it a loud slap. The truck went off toward the small building near the ammonium nitrate tanks. From somewhere deep inside the plant, there was a bellow of laughter.

"Shit," Kit muttered in disappointment.

"No, Turfglo," a voice said.

She drew a sharp breath and hiccoughed in surprise. When she looked behind her, she saw a gorgeous man. He was a head taller than she and the head had wavy brown hair on it that looked as though it might spring into tight little curls if you bumped him. His features were craggy and his teeth were straight and white. His mustache didn't droop or curl up at the ends, or continue into muttonchop whiskers, or look like it would get in his food, but was full and neatly trimmed. His eyes were soft and brown with deep creases in the corners. He was ruggedly handsome in a way that Kit could appreciate even though she was not personally drawn to such types.

"I'm sorry. What did you say?" She asked.

"I said, 'Turfglo'. . . . You said 'shit' and I said 'Turfglo.' It's not shit that makes our grass so green, it's Turfglo, although I expect your way would work just as well. I wouldn't be telling you this, but Turfglo is our best-selling product. I'm Bert Weston, company president."

Kit took his outstretched hand and felt calluses on his palm. A company president who apparently did more than push pencils. "Kit Franklyn," she said. "I'm with the Orleans Parish medical examiner's office."

"Kit," he said, trying her name himself. "Short for what?"

"Nothing, just Kit." She hadn't told even David what it stood for. It was too ridiculous. "Is there a place where we can talk?"

Just outside Weston's office, there was a small anteroom with rose-colored carpet so plush that Kit's shoes were nearly swallowed up by it. The walls were papered with a large beige-and-brown floral on a rose background. Hung in just the right places, there were a number of small Impressionist paintings of rainy street scenes in oversize gold frames. Kit couldn't talk for more than a few minutes about art, but she did notice that unlike the Impressionist painting she owned ($18.95, frame included, from Starving Artists, Inc.) the characters in Weston's paintings were not all dressed the same.

Behind a small desk was a young woman with iridescent black hair that made her skin look nearly as white as the face on a street mime. As they approached, she looked up from her word processor and gave them a plastic smile. Weston pushed his office door open and stepped aside for Kit to pass. To the young woman, he said, "Hold all calls until we're finished."

Kit glanced backward and saw the secretary put her tongue between her teeth and raise her middle finger to Weston's back in a Bronx salute. The two women's eyes met briefly and the girl put her index finger in front of her lips and shook her head gently in a plea for silence.

Despite its immense size and warm yellow paneling, which was either very old or very cleverly made to look that way, Kit found Weston's office unattractive, primarily because of all those *things* hanging on the wall. Behind his desk, a half-dozen wide-eyed antelope heads stared off into space. The far wall was reserved for heads from the bigger species: an elephant, a tiger, and a rhino. She found the elephant-foot ashtrays distributed about the room particularly offensive. To her right, on a long table, a stuffed alligator stared hungrily at two wood ducks floating on a placid pond in a watercolor hanging on the wall.

"Got him right through the eye from seventy yards," Weston said, coming up beside her. "My bearers carried on like they'd never seen such a shot. That's one of the reasons I like Africa so much. The natives don't seem to resent having hold of the shitty end of the stick, and if there's one trait I admire in a people, it's obsequiousness, even if it's faked." He shook his head. "It won't last, though. When that mess in the south spills over into the rest of the continent, they'll be too good to carry a pack."

"You're responsible for all this?" Kit said, looking about the room.

"Ah, you don't approve," Weston said, noticing the tight set to her lips.

"It's not for me to say."

"Would it make any difference if I told you that many of these animals were man killers? I've operated businesses in parts of the world that have never seen a sidewalk, and occasionally an animal like that elephant will decide he'd rather not live near a mine or plantation and he'll set out to improve the neighborhood. Or a big cat will realize that my workers are easier to catch than a gazelle. Then something has to be done. Absenteeism becomes a real problem when being eaten or smashed against a tree becomes a hazard of the workplace."

She gave him a wry smile. "Just making sure the old wheels keep turning, huh?"

"Isn't that the major responsibility of the chief executive officer in any business? Let productivity fall or the profit margin slip, and suddenly you're signing chapter eleven papers. No company has ever lost money while I've been in control and none ever will."

Kit glanced at the heads behind his desk and nearly asked how many workers the beautiful creature with the spiral horns and big brown eyes had killed. But she wasn't here to debate the pros and cons of killing animals for sport. She was here to find out why mass murder and suicide had become one of New Orleans's favorite sports.

"Can I get you something to drink?" Weston asked. "Coffee, iced tea, soft drink?"

"No thanks, I'm fine."

"Well, you didn't come here to discuss rogue animals. Have a seat over here and tell me what I can do for you."

She followed him to a matching pair of burgundy leather sofas facing each other under the great heads at the far end of the room. Motioning her into one, Weston took the other and, with one arm resting along the sofa back, waited for her to begin.

"A little over three years ago, a man employed here as a night watchman shot his boss to death and I'm trying to find out why. They said at the time he was crazy, but there have been a lot of cases lately similar to that one and I'm looking for an explanation."

"How is what happened here similar to the other cases?"

"The night watchman said that when he leaned against a vent on the back of this building, he began to hear voices singing a children's song. Then he said he blacked out and remembered nothing about the shooting. We have three other cases in our files where a man singing a childhood song took several lives and then killed himself."

"And you'd like to know what was coming out of that vent?"

"Exactly."

He shook his head. "Afraid I can't help you. Shortly after the shooting, the business closed. When I took over, the place had been vacant for a year and there wasn't much in the way of assets; some fairly modern machinery and an antiquated building. I had the place gutted and completely remodeled inside and out. I have no idea what purpose that vent served."

Until the last few sentences, Weston's face had been that of someone with nothing to hide. No involuntary shudders, or eyebrow twitches, or jerking jaw muscles. But when he said he had no idea what purpose the vent served, there had been the barest flinch around one eye, a cue that he had lied.

"What about old blueprints?"

"Never had any."

Unlikely, Kit thought. "Old employees then," she said. "They might know. Did you take on any of the people who worked for the previous owner?"

"I told you, the place had been shut down for a year. They all had other jobs by then. All my people are new."

"Surely you remember the kind of business they were in."

"It was primarily a fabric mill."

"What kind of fabrics?"

"Mostly upholstering, I think."

"How could I find some of the people who used to work here?"

Weston shrugged. "Detective work is kind of out of my line. Now if it was a grizzly bear you were afraid of, I could help you. But with this . . ."

His jaw muscles tensed and he averted his eyes.

Kit stood up and offered her hand. "Well, thanks for talking with me anyway."

"Maybe you should give me your address and phone number in case I think of anything."

She jotted the information down on the back of a business card for a beauty shop that had made a mess of her hair on the last visit, handed it to him, and left.

The girl at the desk outside was so involved in prelunch maneuvers, touching up her lipstick and pulling at her hair, that Kit didn't even get the plastic smile this time. Why had Weston lied? And she was virtually certain he *had* lied . . . a lot. What did he have to hide?

Outside the plant she had a thought. Instead of leaving, she moved her car to a spot opposite the entrance and waited. A few minutes later, Weston's secretary came out and started across the lot. Kit couldn't help but envy her just a little for the ease with which she navigated on stiletto heels. As the girl passed by, Kit rolled her window down and said, "Hi. Remember me? I was just talking with your boss."

"You didn't tell him what I did behind his back, did you?" the girl said behind hostile eyes.

"No, of course not."

She smiled and immediately grew more friendly. "Thanks. I know I shouldn't have done that, but he deserved it. Everytime I bend over in that office, it's like my ass is sending out a signal that says, 'Here Bert, give this a squeeze.' Yesterday I asked him if I could leave a half hour early and he said, sure . . . if I'd go for a ride with him . . . on one of those big sofas in his office. I don't have to put up with that stuff, at least I won't when I find a new job. And I'm looking every day. By the way, I'm Cheryl."

Kit introduced herself, went quickly through the reason for her visit, then said, "During my conversation with your boss, I had the feeling he lied in response to some of my questions, and I was hoping you might help me get at the truth."

Cheryl's eyes narrowed. "Is he likely to get in any trouble over this?"

"It's too early to say for sure, but I suppose it's possible."

"Good," Cheryl said, going around to the other side of the car and getting in. "Now what was it you think he lied about?"

"For one thing, he said he didn't have any blueprints of the way the plant was laid out before it was remodeled."

A disappointed look passed across the other woman's face and she shook her head. "Afraid I can't help you on that one. Why did you want old blueprints?"

"Before the remodeling, there was a vent on the side of the plant facing that meadow, and I have reason to believe that a few years ago the discharge from that vent might have played a part in causing the night watchman to become temporarily deranged and shoot his boss. I want to know what went on in the rooms connected to that vent."

"Why didn't you just ask Weston that instead of asking for blueprints?"

"He said he didn't know what the room was used for because the plant had been vacant for a year before he took over." Cheryl shrugged. "That's all before my time. I've only been here six months." A flicker of an idea passed across her face. "You need to talk to Ethyl."

"Who's Ethyl?"

"One of our maids. I heard her talking to another maid who was complaining about how hard it is to keep the plant clean and Ethyl told her she should have seen it before it was redone."

"Weston told me he brought in all new people."

"Well, you said he was a liar."

A maid! She couldn't have asked for a better contact. A maid would likely have been in every room in the plant at one time or other. "Could you give me this person's name and phone number?"

"If you like. But why don't I just go inside and ask her right now about that vent? After all, I should leave Weston something to remember me by." As she spoke, she made a claw with her right hand and twisted it in a disemboweling motion.

It was nearly ten minutes before she returned. From the look on her face, she had good news. "Ethyl knew all about that part of the building. There was only one room vented to the outside like that. It was where they tested each batch of dyed material for colorfastness. It was usually real hot because each piece of cloth would have a sunlamp shining on it. Does that help any?"

"Do you think she'd have any idea what products were made from those fabrics?"

"Hey, she was a maid, not head of product development." Seeing Kit's face fall, Cheryl opened the car door. "Wouldn't hurt to ask, though."

She returned this time in only five minutes.

"Ethyl couldn't answer your question," she said. "But she

sent me to someone *else* who worked here then. He thought some of the fabrics being made then might have been used in automobile interiors."

Automobiles! There were cars involved in each of the three cases connected by childhood songs. Hollins had just gotten out of a car before the fire started; the sniper incident had begun in a car; the events at the railroad crossing involved a car—and the Huey P. Long murders were committed by a man in a car. . . . *So What?* the voice of reason said. In an automobile-oriented society, almost *any* three events could be related to them somehow.

"Is any of this useful?" Cheryl asked.

"I don't see the whole picture yet, but I'm sure it's all important. You've been a great help."

"Like the duke says in the Schwepp's commercial, 'my pleasuah.'"

As their two cars moved up the drive, Bert Weston watched them from the plant entrance, a dark scowl distorting his handsome features.

Chapter 9

Upon reaching her office in Charity Hospital, Kit went back to the files, looking for another common denominator of the three cases related by children's songs. But there were none except . . . she was back to cars again. Damn it! What kept bringing her back there? Cheryl's comments for one thing. There was reason to believe that Shindleman had been driven over the edge by vapors from fabric samples being tested at CCI, fabrics that might have ended up in the hands of automobile manufacturers. Why not cars? It wasn't that unreasonable. Or was it?

For hours there had been an itch in her brain that she couldn't scratch. She sifted through the files and pulled out the Huey P. Long case, wanting to see again the photographs taken immediately after the death car was pulled from the river.

The first few shots were close-ups of the driver's face taken through the windshield. These were not what she wanted, and she began shifting them one by one to the bottom of the stack until she came to those showing more of the car. The first was a head-on view of the entire front end. She put this one on her desk, shifted a close-up of the corpse taken through the side window to the bottom of the pile, then saved a long shot of the driver's side. The itch was still there. But not for long. The last picture was taken from the rear, and it clearly showed the unusual rear window: a central oval and two portholes . . . *just like the car pinned under the train.* She grabbed up the other two photographs and headed for Broussard's office. Before reaching it, she hesitated and knocked instead on Charlie Franks's door. It was still too soon for Broussard. She found Franks rubbing his chin and staring into the monitor on his computer.

"Charlie, what kind of car is this?" She handed him the pictures.

He ran quickly through them and handed them back. "It's an Escadrille."

"Never heard of it. Who made it?"

"I don't remember the name of the company, but they only put out this one model, then folded. What's up?"

She explained where the pictures had come from, then told him of her suspicions that Crescent City Industries might have provided toxic fabrics for the car, recounting in detail her reasons for thinking so.

"Interesting idea," Franks said. "How are you going to pursue it?"

"I don't know." She looked at him for a second or two, then said, "Where would that car in the photographs be now?"

"Probably at the impoundment station on Poydras."

"Suppose I took some laboratory mice down there and put them inside the car to see their reaction?"

He shook his head. "I wouldn't use that car. You might come up empty simply because it had been totally immersed in water. Not only might that have washed away any toxic material but knowing the Mississippi, there's probably a crust of mud all over the inside. That could also work against you."

"I guess the flattened car is at the Poydras lot, too."

"Probably. But there's no way to test *it*. You need to find one that's not damaged. And I may know where . . . the automotive museum next to the amusement pier at the lake. Because of the short life of the company that made it, the car should already be of historical significance."

* * *

In the parking lot some jerk had parked his Land Rover a foot over the yellow line on Kit's side and she had to wiggle into her car through a mere crack. Once inside, her troubles continued, for the car would not start but produced only a metallic click every time she turned the key.

Exasperated by the heat and the inconvenience, she roundly cursed the driver of the other car as she squirmed out of her dead vehicle. While pausing to consider her options, a voice from behind her said, "Got you hemmed in, has he?"

It was Al Vogel, the handsome and outspoken forensic chemist she had met at the open house Broussard had taken her to. "Worse than that," Kit said. "It won't start. There's nothing I hate worse than car trouble."

"What's it sound like when you try to start it?"

"Hardly makes a sound at all, just a click."

"Hold on. My car's right over there. I'll get my tools."

He was gone before Kit could stop him. In a minute, he was back, a rolled-up fabric tool pouch in one hand.

"Look," Kit said. "It's awfully hot out here and you're not dressed to be doing this sort of thing. Let me call a garage."

"If it's what I think it might be, it won't take any time at all to fix."

He opened the hood, took a quick look around, then spread his tools out on the fender and went to work with a wrench. "Try it now."

This time the engine came to life with a touch of the key. He dropped the hood and made an A-Okay sign with his finger and thumb. She rolled down her window, pulled slowly from the cramped parking space, and stopped beside him.

"Loose battery cable," he said.

"I wish I knew of a way to thank you," she replied, looking into his bottomless blue eyes.

"There *is* a way," he said. "Have dinner with me tonight."

Tempted, Kit remembered her date with David. "Sorry, but I already have plans."

Vogel's face fell. "Of course. It was stupid of me to think you wouldn't. How about Saturday?"

Kit hesitated. David hadn't said anything about Saturday, but he might. About to make an excuse, she thought of all the arguments she and David had been having lately and how she had been wondering whether he was really the right man. Maybe it *was* time to test new waters. "I'd love to," she said.

A big grin spread over Vogel's face. "You're in the book?"

"Yes."

"See you at seven then."

She started to pull away and Vogel said, "I thought we'd go to K-Paul's, so you better wear comfortable shoes. You don't mind waiting in line, do you?"

"For food like that? No problem," Kit said.

As she watched Vogel grow smaller and smaller in her rear-view mirror, Kit felt a twinge of guilt mixed with anticipation.

On the roof of the automotive museum, there were six huge plywood pictures of odd-looking cars missing enough paint to give the impression that the business was doing poorly. Kit got the same feeling from the number of cars in the parking lot; one from Texas and one from Iowa.

Just inside the door was a room that smelled of old seatcovers. It was full of things only people on vacation would buy: miniature license plates with "Bob," "Nancy," or some other name where the number should be; postcards showing a picture of the roof display (minus the peeling paint); and bumper stickers saying "I've been to the Old Car Museum in New Orleans, La." The walls were covered with bright prints of old cars in stained wooden frames. She couldn't see the cars themselves because they were on the other side of a curtained doorway with a sign over it that said ADULTS 2.50, CHILDREN 1.00, S. GROSSMAN, PROP.

Beside the draped doorway was a glass case filled with yellow T-shirts. Behind the case, a thin black man with hair like cotton operated an ancient, silver cash register from a tall stool.

"Is Mr. Grossman in?" Kit asked.

Without replying, or changing his blank expression, the man on the stool pushed an ivory button on the wall behind him. Presently, a short man with a thatch of fading red hair and a face dotted with age spots came through the drapes.

"Mr. Grossman?"

"All day today and probably tomorrow too," he said, glancing at the black man as though checking to see if his employee still thought the line was as funny as ever. If he did, he didn't show it.

"Mr. Grossman, I . . ."

"Call me Shami," he said. "Ain't that some name for a guy who owns a car museum? Course it ain't c-h-a-m-o-i-s, like the rag you use to wipe a car off. It's S-h-a-m-i." Grossman's upper and lower teeth were blunt and broad, as though he had purposefully had the ends ground off.

"Shami, I'm Kit Franklyn, from the Orleans Parish medical examiner's office. Do you have one of these cars in your collection?" She handed him the pictures.

"You betcha!" he said. "It qualifies on two counts. Not only was it made by the company with the shortest life in automotive history but it got the worst mileage of any car ever made. Kinda makes you think the two facts were related, don't it?"

After she explained the reason for her visit, Grossman said, "Let's go have a look at her." But as she parted the drapes, he touched her arm. When she turned, he pointed at the admission prices and gave her a contented smile. She thought about getting a receipt, but figuring it was worth $2.50 of her own money, didn't bother.

The display area was partitioned off into a multitude of rooms by black drapes on cables suspended from the ceiling. A yellow arrow on the floor pointed the way through the maze. With Grossman in the lead, they passed a row of cars with thin little tires that looked as though they were mounted on wagon wheels, Grossman talking all the while.

"Used to be you could tell one car from another. Now, they all look alike. It's this preoccupation with efficiency. Why can't you have efficiency *and* style?" He shook his head and sighed. "Until a few years ago, you could make a statement about yourself by the car you drove. Your car could . . . whaddya call it . . . be an extension of your personality. People who couldn't afford anything else could have a car that made them feel special. How's anybody gonna feel special now?" Grossman suddenly veered from the direction indicated by the arrow. "We go this way. Pretty soon every car that's made will get a hundred miles to the gallon and they'll all be khaki-colored. Here she is."

He had stopped in front of a white car loaded with chrome. Through the windshield, she could see the familiar oval rear window with its two porthole companions. She walked around it, looked inside at the black vinyl seats and artificial burlwood inset on the dash, and imagined the driver of the car that went off the Huey P. Long bridge, staring at the road through bloodshot eyes, his will destroyed.

"All that chrome was a good idea," Grossman said. "You know, like a return to the fifties. Everybody's into nostalgia these days." A wistful look came into his eyes. "If only it woulda got better mileage."

"Have you ever been in this car with the windows closed?" Kit asked.

"Sure. From time to time, we move everything around. One month, we may feature hood ornaments and we'll put all the cars with fancy hood decorations in one place. Or we may line up the twenty worst gas guzzlers in history, or . . ."

"What's the longest time you ever spent in this car with the windows rolled up?"

"Twenty minutes maybe."

"Do you know your blood type?"

Grossman looked puzzled. "Type O."

His answer shattered Kit's hopes. According to Freddie Watts's employee, Watts had been working inside the car for only a few minutes before he drove off in it. As a type O, Grossman should have been affected by twenty minutes exposure . . . unless of course her whole theory was worthless. In a last attempt to salvage her foundering hopes, she said, "Is the interior of this car all original?"

"You betcha! I bought it from a friend of mine in Chicago who's a fanatic about keeping his cars clean."

With his answer, Kit's only lead now evaporated completely. Mustering a brave face, she thanked Grossman and left.

David arrived for their date that night with an armful of groceries. He whirled past her and set everything down in the kitchen.

"What's all this?" Kit asked.

"A domestic demonstration," David said, spreading things out on the counter. "*I'm* cooking dinner."

"Then *I'm* leaving," Kit teased.

David pulled out her gadget drawer and rummaged around till he found a corkscrew. "You'll be sorry if you do," he said, twisting the screw into the cork of a long-necked green bottle. "The menu tonight is flank steak medallions, asparagus with hollandaise, a tossed salad, bananas flambé, and to start . . ." The cork slipped from the wine bottle with only a tiny squeak. David looked crestfallen.

"Jake's Discount Liquors, right?" Kit said, forgetting for the moment how Grossman had blown her car theory.

David unrolled a package of white butcher paper with two flank steaks inside. "Why were you so interested in that 'Rock-A-Bye-Baby' case?" he said, reaching into the cupboard for a plate.

"I thought it would help me unravel some cases of my own."

David scored the steaks with a knife and began cutting them into strips. "And did it help?"

"Yes and no."

He stopped cutting and looked up.

"I thought it was leading somewhere, but this afternoon things just played out."

"I'm sorry it wasn't more useful," David said, rolling a strip of steak and a piece of bacon up together. "Tell me about it. Sometimes an outsider can bring a new perspective to a problem."

"I'd rather just let tonight be a little vacation from it."

All through dinner, David watched her intently to see what she thought of his effort. But Kit carefully kept any telltale sign from her face until he brought in the bananas flambé and lit them. Then her eyes gave her away.

"Pretty good, huh?" David said, giving her a generous portion.

Tasting them, Kit nodded. "Pretty good," she agreed.

Later, sitting together on the sofa, David proposed a toast. "To Greek men who can cook."

Kit touched her glass to his, beginning to feel the effects of the liquor she had already consumed.

"I sense that there was a hidden purpose in this display of culinary perspicacity," Kit said, hiccoughing.

Perspicacity? David thought. She had totally misused the word. He took her glass and put it on the end table. "I think you could use some coffee," he said.

"And he makes coffee too," Kit said with a slightly goofy look on her face.

The coffee brought her back from the brink on which she had been teetering.

Head cleared, she said, "I didn't know you could cook like this. How many other talents do you have that I don't know about?"

David's face glowed. "Hundreds," he said. "This is merely the tip of a great iceberg of untapped potential. In short, I'm a great catch. Look at the facts. I'm well-off financially, I'm reasonably good-looking . . ."

Kit put her hand out and tilted it back and forth. David grabbed it. "And I know what you like," he said, kissing his way from her fingers to her ear. "You smell good," he whispered, trailing kisses down her neck.

Kit rocked her head back, enjoying the smell of his aftershave and the touch of his skin against hers. Her hand went to the back of his neck. His lips grazed her cheek and came to a stop on her mouth. She let herself go, let the tide of desire blot out everything else. His hand cupped her breast and she sighed into his mouth. They pressed against each other, her hand exploring him. Tearing himself free, he pulled her to her feet and they went to the bedroom.

The next morning, with David gone, Kit reflected on the previous night over a fresh cup of coffee. It had been enjoyable, no question about that, but still no bells. She thought briefly of her upcoming date with Al Vogel. Thankfully, David had a big drug case pending and would be tied down all weekend. There had been no need to tell him about Al. Idly, she wondered what Vogel would be like in bed, then her mind brought her back to reality, to those perplexing suicides and her shattered theory. Feeling unable to get her mind on someone *else's* problems, she called Ida Swenson at Happy Years and coaxed her into saying that no harm would be done by canceling that day's counseling visit.

For more than a week now, there had been no sign of the dog that had run into her house and she no longer looked for him before opening the door. It was a habit she had discontinued too soon. Today, he was waiting. Experienced now, she got the ham out much faster than last time. But he was more experienced, too, and was not quite so eager to chase it. He stopped at the threshold and looked at it draped over the creeping evergreen on which it had fallen. She gently helped him toward it with the side of her shoe and followed him out.

Later, at the office, she recounted to Charlie Franks the results of her visit with Grossman.

". . . so when he said the interior was all original and he hadn't been affected by being in the car, there didn't seem to be any point in pursuing the matter."

"That's not all." Franks shuffled through his "to be filed" box and pulled out a piece of paper. "This came in yesterday afternoon's mail."

The letter he handed her bore the return address of the medical examiner's office in Boston. The message was short. They had experienced no increase in murder-suicides over the time span specified in Franks's letter of inquiry. She tossed the letter onto Franks's desk. "I'm sure glad that I didn't say anything to Broussard about those cars."

"What cars?" Broussard said from behind her.

Too surprised to think of an effective way to parry his question, Kit reluctantly related everything that had happened since he had first scoffed at her suggestion that the Hollins and Watts cases were part of a larger pattern. While she talked, he worked the lemon drop in his mouth from side to side and occasionally rubbed the short hairs on the tip of his nose.

". . . and then the final blow came when the Boston M.E. said they hadn't been having a similar increase in those kinds of cases."

With arms folded across his chest, Broussard leaned against the wall and caressed his nose for a very long time. Then he said, "How many cases was it where kiddy songs were involved?"

"Four, counting Shindleman."

He lapsed back into thought and mulled her story over awhile longer. ". . . And three Escadrilles," he said abruptly.

"No, just two."

He shook his head. "There was also one in the Hollins's driveway. Two could be a coincidence. Three may be somethin' more."

"But the car at the museum . . ." she began.

"Potentially explainable. How'd you like to take a look at the two Escadrilles in police custody?"

"I'd like it."

"Charlie, Phil Gatlin is waitin' for me near the Tulane campus. We'll be there for a few minutes, then we're goin' to the impoundment station."

Fifteen minutes later, Broussard's yellow T-bird came to a stop in the driveway of a dirty stucco story-and-a-half on Magnolia

Street. Phil Gatlin was swinging back and forth on the porch, smoking a cigarette, and blowing smoke rings toward the beaded ceiling.

"Sorry to have taken so long, Phillip. Where's the body?" Broussard asked.

"Rec room in the basement," Gatlin replied, throwing his cigarette to the cement and grinding it underfoot.

They all went inside where, at the bottom of a flight of stairs off the kitchen, they found the body of a man dressed out in a first-rate Dracula outfit. There was an ugly kitchen knife protruding from his chest. Next to the body was another knife, heavy-handled and masculine-looking. Near the victim's outstretched left hand was a claw hammer.

"What's with the costume?" Broussard said.

"Something going on at his fraternity," Gatlin replied. "When he didn't show up or answer the telephone, his roommate came looking for him. The kid was so shook up, I had the uniforms take him over to student health."

Exhaling loudly as if letting the air out of his legs, Broussard sank to one knee, raked the knife on the floor with his eyes, and said, "Looks like a bayonet." He waved his hand over the body. "Has all this been photographed?"

Gatlin nodded and Broussard's stubby fingers began to unbutton the dead man's shirt. Where the garment was not pinned to the body by the knife, he laid it back. There were two pieces of pine strapped to the man's chest with duct tape. The tape ran in an unbroken line across the two pieces of wood. The knife rested neatly in the seam between. Broussard studied the bottom of the seam, then struggled to his feet. "An accident," he said. "Stupid and avoidable. He was hammerin' the kitchen knife into that board strapped to his chest when the board split. He'd tried the bayonet first but didn't like it for some reason and switched knives. The bayonet had weakened the board and when he hit the kitchen knife a solid blow . . . Phillip, did you tell Jamison he could leave?"

Gatlin nodded.

"Would've been good to have some pictures with his shirt open before we move him."

"You're sure it was an accident?" Gatlin said.

"It's the only explanation that fits the facts. He was left-handed and the hammer is on the left side of the body. . . ."

"How do you know he's left-handed?" Gatlin interrupted.

"His watch. It's on his right wrist and has a band that buckles. Most people would have to use their dominant hand to fasten a buckle. That makes his the left."

Kit hadn't even realized that the man wore a watch.

"Oh yeah, I did notice that," Gatlin said unconvincingly.

The clump of heavy footsteps was heard overhead and two men in white came down the stairs.

"They told us it wasn't an emergency," a portly fellow with fine yellow hair said. "So we took another case first."

"You did right," Broussard said. "There he is."

While the two men loaded the body, the others filed upstairs.

When they reached the kitchen, Broussard touched Kit's arm and whispered, "Wait for me on the porch, will you? I'd like a few words with Phillip."

Gatlin came up a few steps behind the stretcher. As he followed it out, Broussard said, "All through?"

"Yeah."

"How long we been friends, Phillip?"

"Long time," Gatlin said, looking at Broussard from beneath eyebrows that had crept together at the question.

"I figure maybe that gives me the right to talk to you straight out."

"About what?"

"There was a time when you wouldn't have let Jamison leave until every last thing was covered. And now you just walked off and left the hammer and that bayonet on the basement floor."

Gatlin grimaced and turned back toward the basement but was stopped by Broussard's hand on his arm. "Phillip, I hate

tellin' you this, but instead of 'Slick,' they're beginnin' to call
you 'Slack' Gatlin."

Gatlin looked at the floor. "You saying I've lost it?"

"You're just not usin' it."

"I didn't know it showed so much."

"It shows."

Gatlin's shoulders slumped a little more. "It's my daughter. I
miss her so much I . . . I can't concentrate." He looked at his
old friend from under eyelids that drooped sadly. "I go to bed
early every night and sleep all weekend so I won't have to
think about it. Andy, she doesn't know how dangerous the
streets really are. I've tried to tell her. But you know kids,
they don't think parents know anything. And I'm afraid she
might be . . ." He was unable to put into words the nightmare he carried within him for fear that saying it aloud might
somehow make it true.

"Phillip, I'm not goin' to tell you I understand what you're
goin' through, but I do know that what you're doin' is not
helpin' her. And it's destroyin' you. You're no good to the
department this way, and you're no good to yourself. When
Shelby comes home, she's goin' to need a stable environment.
How can you provide that if you've lost your job?"

Gatlin's eyes widened in surprise.

"They'll carry you for as long as they can because of your
record. But eventually they'll have to let you go. Don't let that
happen, Phillip. Come to terms with it."

Gatlin looked at his friend and nodded. "I'll try, Andy. I'll
try."

Chapter 10

The tiny white cement-block building that housed the clerk at the vehicle impoundment station was empty. On the sliding glass window above a Formica counter worn through to where the black backing showed in spots was a sign that said, PRESS BUTTON FOR SERVICE. A large red arrow pointed to a shirt button that had been glued onto the side of the building.

A sound started in Broussard's throat as a rattle, then gained in volume like a siren. "aaaaaaaAAAATTENDANT!" he roared. "IS THERE AN ATTENDANT ON THESE PREMISES?"

"Why you wanna make all dat noise?" a man dressed in coveralls and a greasy T-shirt said, stepping out from behind the little building. He had long black hair that billowed from under a green baseball cap that bore a decal of an ocean wave showing its teeth and carrying a football. Only his eyes and two fat cheeks showed through a bushy beard the same color as his hair. And he was even shorter than Shami Grossman.

"WHAT'S THE MEANING OF THIS?" Broussard said sternly, pointing at the button.

"You tryin' to tell me dat someone as old as you don't know what da word *dis* means. Dat's criminal. It really is." The little fellow looked at Kit. "You work wit dis man?" She nodded. "Well, you got mah sympat'y. Ah can tell by his small eyes, he a slow learner."

Kit was shocked by the diminutive Cajun's sharp tongue. "What made them hire *you* for this job?" Broussard asked. "Did they want somebody who could disconnect tow bars without bending over?"

Now *Broussard* was doing it!

Both men started to laugh. "How you doin' dis mornin', Andy?" the attendant asked warmly.

"So far so good, Bubba. But then it's early. Plenty of time yet for things to go wrong. Kit, this is Bubba Oustellette, the best crawdad fisherman and mechanic in Loosiana. Bubba, meet Kit Franklyn, our new suicide investigator."

Bubba looked at his hand, wiped it on his coveralls, and offered it up. As she bent to shake it, he jerked his head toward Broussard and said, "You too pretty a lady to be seen wid dis fella." Turning to his friend, he said, "Whatsa mattah, Andy? One of da birds sick?"

"Now that you mention it, the red one could use a new strap on the tail pipe. Anytime you can get to it will be okay. But that's not why we're here. We'd like to see the Escadrille that came in a week or so ago, and also the latest one."

"Ohhh dat last one was some squashed. How many die in dere?"

"Two."

Bubba shook his head and made noises of sympathy. "Which one you wanna see first?"

"The one that wasn't wrecked."

Bubba led them through the main gate, past the front of a corrugated-metal barn with doorless openings at each end, and down a row of cars parked with their rear bumpers against the chain link that surrounded the place. The cars, the blacktop, and the sun conspired to push the temperature up near the hundred mark. When they reached the mud-encrusted Escadrille that had been pulled from the Mississippi, Broussard stepped up to it and ran his hand under the upper lip of the grill. There was a *clunk* and the hood popped up an inch. He felt around until he found the second release and raised the hood. To support himself as he looked into the engine, he put both hands on the hot fender but quickly pulled them back and shook them.

"Here, use dis," Bubba said, whipping an orange rag from the back pocket of his coveralls.

Broussard spread the small rag on the fender, put both hands on it to keep his clothes off the mud, and leaned into the car's engine. "Too dirty," he said, straightening up. "Bubba, could you clean off the ID plate on the fire wall for me?"

Bubba took the rag from the fender, worked it around in the engine's depths, and carefully put it back on the fender, dirty side down.

After a quick inspection of Bubba's work, Broussard grunted with satisfaction and stood up.

"What is it?" Kit asked.

With a raised finger, Broussard solicited patience. "Now, where's the other one?" he said.

The wreck from the railroad crossing was behind the metal barn. "Bubba, can you get me into the engine on this one?" Broussard said.

"Might take fifteen or twenty minutes. You got dat much time?"

Broussard said they did, and Bubba set off for the rear entrance to the barn, reappearing a few minutes later wheeling an ancient welder's torch and carrying a welder's helmet. "You two might oughtta stand over dere," he said, pointing to a narrow band of shade next to the barn.

As soon as they were a safe distance away, Bubba fired up the torch and, in a white-hot shower of sparks, began cutting away the Escadrille's hood, which had collapsed so tightly against the engine that the dim outline of the air cleaner could be seen among the sharp wrinkles that had been thrust up through the paint. The light from the torch was so intense that Kit glanced in that direction only enough to check his progress.

Finally, Bubba yanked off his helmet, pulled a large irregular piece of metal free, and threw it to the ground. He extinguished the torch and waved them over. His cheeks were the color of a clay pot and his hair lay in wet curls against his scalp.

With the sun providing all the light he needed, Broussard knelt onto the crushed fender and peered into the hole Bubba had cut in the hood. He made the same sound as when he had looked into the other engine, then stood up.

"*Now* will you tell me what you're looking for?" Kit asked.

"There's a rectangular silver tag on the fire wall down about eight inches. Take a look and read it to me."

She knelt as he had and found the tag. "NAM-NO-663– 02 . . ."

"That's enough." Broussard said. "The rest is just a serial number. The letters are the important part."

When she stood up, a drop of sweat ran down her nose and hung on the end till she wiped it away with the back of her hand.

"Let's get back in the shade," Broussard suggested.

When they were out of the sun's reach, he unbuttoned his shirt pocket, pulled out a lemon drop, and pushed it into his mouth. The heat and the waiting had worn Kit's patience away, and she was on the verge of demanding he get on with his explanation when he said, "Bubba, you probably know this story better than I do, so you speak up if I go astray.

"The NAM on the tag stands for 'North American Motors,' the company that made the car. They went bankrupt practically before the ink was dry on their union contracts. Primarily because they set up assembly plants near all the major cities and bought as many of their supplies as possible from regional businesses, believin' that by providin' jobs for the locals, they'd build enough goodwill to give them a competitive edge in the marketplace. But the overhead of operatin' all those plants proved to be prohibitive. They also found that even though gas prices had come down from what they were in the seventies, folks were still leery of cars that got poor mileage and Escadrilles were inefficient as all get out. The point in all this is that the 'NO' on the tag I showed you means that particular car was assembled in the New Orleans plant, and so was the first one we looked at."

"And it's possible that the one at the museum was *not* assembled in the New Orleans plant, and therefore would contain materials from different suppliers than New Orleans models would," Kit said excitedly. "It's all so right. That would also explain why the Boston ME hasn't seen the same increase in murder-suicides we have. It's only *our* Escadrilles that cause it." Then she remembered what Shami Grossman had said, and her eyes grew even brighter. "The one in the car museum was previously owned by someone from *Chicago!*" She nearly laughed aloud. "It's *not* a New Orleans model."

"Let's do this," Broussard said. "You go back to the car museum and check the tag on their car. If it's not an NO edition, see if you can get hold of the one that was in the Hollinses' driveway. If you can, call Bubba, and he'll tow it to my place." He turned to his friend. "Bubba, you can tow a car without havin' to get inside it, can't you?"

"If Ah use a dolly."

"Do that. We could be lookin' down an empty burrow on this, but I don't want you takin' any chances. There may be a toxin of some sort in that car, so you stay out of it. Put it in the work bay and don't hang around." He turned to Kit. "I'll be leavin' for Dallas shortly and won't be back till sometime Monday. If by the time I return you've got a car, we'll set up some tests and see if we can get our theory on a factual basis."

It did not escape Kit's notice that what had been *her* theory when they first arrived had now become *our* theory. It felt good.

An hour later, having just left the car museum, Kit was poorer by another $2.50. But Grossman's car *had* been assembled in another state. After driving by the Hollinses' house and seeing that their Escadrille was no longer in the driveway, she set about tracking it down.

That night, while packing for his consultation in Dallas, Broussard got a phone call from Bubba.

"Hey, Andy. You got time tonight to visit with Gramma O. I was tellin' her about dose cars an' she asked me to bring you by . . . tonight if possible."

Broussard hesitated. Bubba's grandmother was a real kick and he always enjoyed their talks, but he didn't particularly look forward to going out there at night.

"She tol' me to say dere'll be a big piece of warm zucchini cake waitin' for you."

That settled it. There was no way he could pass up Grandma O's zucchini cake.

Bubba lived alone, about twenty miles outside the city, in a log house he had built with his own hands on Goose Bayou. His grandmother lived two hundred wet yards away in a shanty perched on stilts. She was accessible only by boat, and it was this part of the trip that had made Broussard reluctant to pay a call at night.

On the outskirts of the city, he stopped at a liquor store and bought Grandma O a fifth of her favorite whiskey. By the time he turned into the two dirt tracks that led to Bubba's cabin, it was as dark as it was going to get.

Aided by a floodlight at the top of a long cypress two-by-four nailed to the side of the cabin, Broussard eased his car between the bathtub Bubba grew his red worms in and the picnic table where he cleaned fish, coming to a stop a few feet from a pile of cypress planks. With hordes of insects around the floodlight casting eerie shadows on the ground, and frogs croaking so loud the sound seemed to come from inside his head, Broussard found the bayou at night an unsettling place.

Bubba was waiting on the porch. In his outstretched hand was a can of Pearl River beer, its sides wet with condensation.

Pearl River and zucchini cake. It was a combination that could get him drummed out of his gourmet society.

Bubba watched approvingly as Broussard drained the can and tossed it into a wire wastebasket by the cabin door. "What's in da bag?" Bubba asked. "Somethin' for Gramma?"

"She still partial to Cutty Sark?"

"Won't drink nothin' else. C'mon, she's anxious to see you."

Bubba flipped a switch on one of the posts supporting the porch roof and a string of light bulbs illuminated the path to the boat dock.

"Been makin' some improvements, I see," Broussard said, following Bubba to the dock.

"Wait, you can't see it all yet."

Bubba's pirogue was tied to the very end of the dock and when they reached it, Broussard saw what Bubba meant. The string of bulbs stretched from tree to tree way down the bayou, lighting it all the way to Grandma O's.

"She don' wanna stay with me so Ah had to do somethin' to make it easier to get to her at night in case she needs me in a hurry."

"I like it," Broussard said, stepping carefully into the pirogue while Bubba held it steady. "Makes the swamp kind of festive."

Bubba stepped lightly into the bow and pushed off with his forked push pole. Glistening black water that came within two inches of sinking them slipped silently by. There was a loud splash a few yards ahead.

Looking over his shoulder, Bubba said, "Ah been tryin' to catch dat frog for two years. He got legs on him like a Tulane runnin' back."

Water hyacinths now crowded both sides of the bayou, and Bubba grunted as he poled the pirogue through them. "Ah'm gonna have to get out here soon and do somethin' about dis," Bubba complained.

"How's Gramma O doin' these days? She still runnin' her traps?"

"Oh, she sets 'em out, but most days she don' put 'em where she's likely to catch anything. That way she don't have to skin 'em."

"Why does she want to see me?"

"Dat's somethin' she'll have to tell you. It's kinda involved."

When they got to Grandma O's dock, she was waiting for them, a huge woman with long black hair that hung down her back, and hips that made her look like a tree surrounded by a park bench. She was wearing enough black taffeta to clothe several lesser women. Broussard took her hand and was hauled onto the dock.

"See you still got your grip," he said.

Her smile was enhanced by a gold star inlay on one front tooth. "Listen city boy, you skin as many nutria as Ah have, you boun' to have strong hands. You gonna make me wrestle you for dat bag?"

"No ma'am. I know when I'm overmatched."

She pulled the bottle out of the bag and looked at the label in the glare from one of Bubba's light bulbs. A hoarse cackle rolled through the swamp and she patted the bottle. "Le's go inside."

The dock jiggled ominously as the formidable woman tested its limits with her heavy step. Broussard let her get a few strides ahead so that his weight and hers would not stress the same timbers. In her wake, she left the sweet smell of gardenias, her favorite scent.

The shanty she lived in had only one room, divided functionally into a kitchen and a sitting room. On the kitchen side, every horizontal surface was covered in the same white linoleum, embossed to suggest brickwork. It covered the floor, the countertops, and the kitchen table. On the sitting room side, there was a long sofa, a rocking chair, and two armchairs, all covered in a white chameleon print on a green ground.

"You boys sit here at da table," Grandma O said.

From an old stove on legs, she brought out two foil

packages, put their contents on plates, and set a huge piece of heaven in front of each man.

"Aren't you havin' any?" Broussard asked.

"You're gonna eat, Ah'm gonna talk," she replied, pouring each of them a cup of coffee in cups honeycombed with hairline cracks.

If he had been allowed only that first forkful, the trip would have been worth it, Broussard thought as the moist cake melted in his mouth.

"Bubba tells me you been seein' an increase in murder-suicides in da city."

Caught with a mouthful, Broussard nodded and reached for his coffee. "Don't know what it means yet, but somethin' unusual seems to be happenin'."

"Ah'm gonna tell you a story that mah gramma tol' me, an' her gramma tol' her 'bout somethin' that happen a long time ago . . . when da city was jus' gettin' started with maybe two, three thousand folks in it. It's da reason why no Oustellette has ever lived in da city an' why Ah keep tryin' to get dis bonehead here," she nodded at Bubba, "to give up his job dere.

"Long time back, a fella named Albair Fauquel was hanged right out where everybody could see it. It all start one day when Fauquel drink too much and drive his carriage fast an' wild, down da main street. At a corner, he slide out of control and hit a man on a horse. Da horse go down with a broken leg, but da man all right. Da horse he have to be shot. An' it wasn't no ordinary horse, neither. Best racehorse for two, three hunnert miles around. A judge say Fauquel have to pay for da horse. But he won't do it. So da judge take a piece of Fauquel's land an' sell it, givin' some of da money to da man for his horse an' give da rest to Fauquel.

"Fauquel get mad an' say he gonna get even with da judge. One night somebody see Fauquel an' his slave creepin' aroun' da judge's house when ain't nobody home. 'Bout nine o'clock da judge come home, an' later dat same night, kill his wife an' little girl, den himself. Da police, or whatever dey was called in dose days foun' a slippery smooth black stone on da front porch of da judge's house. An' da stone had a cross inside a circle scratched on it. Well, somebody reconized that pattern as a voodoo symbol dat helps a spell take hold."

"Sort of a good luck charm in reverse," Broussard suggested.

Grandma O shook a finger across the table. "Tha's a good description of it. Anyway, da person who saw Fauquel hangin' around da judge's house happen to mention it. Big crowd goes over to Fauquel's place and runs all over it. In a little house where one of Fauquel's slaves lives, dey foun' a bag of smooth stones jus' like da one foun' on da judge's porch.

Nex' thing you know, Fauquel and da slave are bein' asked if dey have any las' words. Da slave, he don' say nothin', but Fauquel, he say plenty. And if anybody dere didn' think he was guilty, Fauquel set 'em straight when he say . . ."

Grandma O closed her eyes and she seemed to go into an almost trancelike state. Her voice changed to that of a man. Oddly, she lost her Cajun accent.

"When my land was taken, it was wrong. And today you wrong me again. But I tell you this, one day I will return and right this wrong as I did the other. And the streets of this city will run with blood as friend slays friend, fathers slay their children, and rampant suicide sends the souls of men by the hundreds to everlasting hell. . . . Beware the songs you loved in youth."

A shiver ran through Bubba's body and he sloshed some coffee onto the table. Self-consciously he looked into his cup. "Dis part always gets to me," he explained.

Even before she finished, Broussard had dismissed Grandma O's tale as a quaint bit of Cajun folklore.

"Dat's all da story dere is," she said.

"And you think our increase in murder-suicides is related to your story?" Broussard asked politely, his eyes glinting with amusement.

"Ah'm not sayin' it is, an' Ah'm not sayin' it ain't. Dat's for you to decide. But Ah didn' want you goin' around ignorant of da possibility. An' because you been such a good friend to Bubba an' me, Ah'm gonna give you somethin' to protec' you jus' in case. Stay right here."

She went to a drawer, took out some things, and came back to the kitchen table. "Close your eyes," she said to Broussard.

Finding all this rather entertaining, Broussard did as she asked. There was a rustle of taffeta and then a sharp pain on the top of his head.

"Ouch!" he said, rubbing the spot.

Grandma O showed him the hair she had plucked from his scalp. "It don' work if you cut it off with scissors."

She spread out on the table what she had gathered: a spool of thread, a piece of aluminum foil, a ball of yarn, a matchbox with some gray powder in it, a pair of scissors, and a small vinyl pouch with a drawstring. She filled a glass half-full of whiskey and sat down.

First, she tore off four long pieces of thread and doubled each strand four times, laying the folded strands parallel to each other a finger's breadth apart. Then she picked up the first strand and tied a knot near one end. She took a small sip of whiskey, spread the thread on the table, and spit a tiny amount of whiskey on the knot.

She did this three more times, producing a strand with four, more or less equally spaced knots on it. Then she picked up the second strand, saying, "Four times four times four is da luckiest number dere is."

She proceeded to tie four knots in that strand, anointing each with whiskey and saliva. This time she placed the second strand much nearer the first than before. When each strand had its full complement of knots, she spread out the foil and laid the four strands in its center. "Da foil represents light to drive away darkness," she said.

From the matchbox, she tapped some gray powder over the soggy strands of thread. "A little grave dust for strength." To this, she added the hair she had taken. After carefully folding the foil into a three-cornered packet with the threads, grave dust, and hair inside, she wrapped the packet round and round with yarn until she had a small ball. She tied the yarn and snipped it so as to leave a free end. Holding it by the free end, she dipped the ball in and out of her glass of whiskey, closed her eyes, and mumbled something Broussard couldn't make out.

"Now le's test it," she said. "Spirit of da ball. Are you dere?"

With a talent Broussard had never suspected she possessed, Grandma O threw her voice into the ball. "Yes, I am here," the ball said without an accent.

"Leave us now and go to da other side of da room."

From faraway, a voice said, "Is this far enough?"

"Yes. Now come back."

"I'm back," the ball said.

Grandma O looked at Broussard. "It's got an obedient spirit. Dat means it's gonna serve you well."

She put the ball into the vinyl pouch, pulled its drawstring shut, and gave it to Broussard. "It don' matter where you keep it. Long as it's under your roof it'll protec' you and those you care for. All you got to remember is to give it a drink of whiskey every two weeks."

Broussard searched the old woman's face trying to figure out if she was serious or just playing an elaborate joke on him. But there was no sign of humor in her and he accepted the gift with great seriousness.

Late the next day, a telephone call to Barry Hollins's sister, Daphne Parks, turned up the car Kit had been searching for. It was in the possession of Daphne and her husband, Ned. At first Daphne had been puzzled at Kit's request that she go to the car and determine the first five letters on the silver tag behind the engine but eventually agreed after being told that the information might help explain her brother's behavior the day of the fire. After learning that the Hollins car *was* assembled in New Orleans, Kit got Daphne to agree to discuss the matter face-to-face if Kit could get there before Ned came home.

She arrived at the Parks household at exactly three fifty-two and pulled in behind a red Escadrille. As she went up the walk, she wondered who the mastermind was that thought the lawn needed a birdbath and six plastic flamingos. Afraid to touch the doorbell, which was dangling with its wires exposed, she knocked sharply on the peeling front door. While waiting for Daphne to answer, she noticed that the Parkses had not yet taken down the Christmas lights under the eaves. The drapes over the tiny windows in the front door moved. An eye appeared in the lowest of the three, and then the door opened.

Daphne Parks was probably in her late twenties. Her thin brown hair, which she wore chopped off at her jawline, framed a face with finely drawn features and a smooth translucent skin. The lack of color in Daphne's cheeks and her dull lifeless eyes made Kit believe, as she had on the first visit to the Parks home in the days immediately following the fire, that Daphne was anemic.

She waved Kit to a chair covered in a brown check. Choosing the sofa for herself, Daphne sat on its edge, her back rigid, hands folded tightly on her knees. "I can only talk for a few minutes," she said.

"A few minutes is all I need. I know you're upset about what happened to your brother and his family and perhaps a little . . . ashamed?" Daphne nodded. "There's a possibility that your brother was not in control of himself that day but was the victim of a toxin that may have originated in the car outside. How did you get it here?"

"Ned took me over and I drove it back. We planned to use it as my car. You know, for grocery shopping and things. The lawyer said it would be all right."

"Do either of you know your blood type?" Daphne shook her

head. "Well, don't let Ned near the car or the results might be disastrous."

Daphne's forehead became as wrinkled as the skin on the elephant head in Bert Weston's office. "What exactly is wrong with the car?" she said.

Before Kit could reply, the front door opened and a bucktoothed little boy about ten years old came in and said, "Look what I found."

He was wearing the sunglasses Kit had left on the dash of her car.

"Why Eddy, where ever did you find those?" Daphne asked.

"That dopey looking car in our driveway. Can I keep them?" Daphne looked at Kit. "Can he?"

Kit was shocked by Daphne's audacity. Suppressing a desire to grab the brat by his ears, she smiled sweetly and said, "Of course he can," immediately hating herself for being so spineless.

As the boy headed out of the room, Daphne called to him, "Didn't you forget something?"

Kit prepared herself to say, "You're welcome," when the boy said, "Thank you."

Instead he shouted, "Dad says I don't have to shut the door," and fled from the room.

Without a hint of annoyance, Daphne got up and shut the door. "You were about to tell me what was wrong with the car."

"I don't know exactly. But you can help me find out by allowing me to take it away for testing."

Again the door opened and an angry voice filled the room. "Who the hell's that blockin' the driveway?"

Kit turned and saw Daphne's husband with a stormy scowl on his fleshy face.

"It's Dr. Franklyn," Daphne said pleasantly.

"Oh yeah. How ya doin'? You shoulda parked in the street. If I get a ticket out front for not havin' an inspection sticker, I'm gonna expect you to pay it."

Ned then disappeared into the back of the house, leaving the door open even wider than his son had.

"Don't take that personally," Daphne said, shutting the door. "Ned acts that way toward everybody. It's just his way."

"Well, will you allow me to run some tests on the car?"

There was a loud belch and Ned appeared in the doorway with an aluminum can in his hand. "This is the last beer," he said. "Finish up with what you're doin' there and take your brother's car down to the corner and get me another case."

"Ned, Dr. Franklyn wants to take the car away."

"Take it away? What for?"

"There's something wrong with it. It may have . . ." She hesitated, then seemed to find the word she wanted on Kit's face. ". . . a toxin in it. That's what made my brother . . . act funny."

"No way. No one is takin' that car anywhere!"

"But she said it's dangerous."

"The car stays here. End of discussion." Ned turned and stalked away.

By this time, Kit had written Daphne off as a doormat and had lost all hope of getting the car. But Daphne went to a small chest and withdrew a ring with two keys in it. She pressed the keys into Kit's palm. "You take the car and find out what really happened."

"Look, I don't want to cause any trouble between you and your husband."

"You won't. Ned's always had a weak spot when it comes to . . . You know." Finally a bit of color came to her cheeks. "If he doesn't get what he needs, he gets terrible headaches. Somewhere around ten o'clock tonight, he'll see that I did the right thing. How are you going to move it?"

"I'll send somebody by with a tow truck."

As she walked to her car, Kit mentally gave old Daphne a hearty pat on the back.

* * *

Kit had no trouble deciding what to wear for her date with Al Vogel. She simply chose her favorite outfit; a pale-yellow two-piece knit with a button-front cardigan and a lace collar. David had seen it so often she had been reluctant to wear it again. Now she could. Just another advantage of seeing a new man. Vogel arrived, equally resplendent, in a cool-looking linen suit, cream with a thin, gray stripe.

At K-Paul's the line was a block long. The couple in front of them, a cardiologist and his wife from Grand Forks, North Dakota, said that the way they had it figured, it would be thirty or forty minutes before they were seated. While waiting, Al questioned the physician about North Dakota and what it was like to be a cardiologist. When the man ran out of things to say, Al entertained them all with colorful descriptions of items on the K-Paul's menu, so that by the time they finally got inside, each of them knew exactly what to order.

Kit had seafood stuffed eggplant topped with a sauce that, according to Al, was made with eggplant pulp, cayenne pepper, peeled shrimp, and heavy cream. Whatever was in it, it was sinfully good. Al had oysters en brouchette, a sort of shish kebab of fried oysters, mushrooms, and bacon, topped with a hot browned garlic butter sauce served next to a bed of seafood dirty rice. Though totally happy with her own choice, Kit couldn't help but cast an occasional covetous eye toward Al's plate.

To finish, it was warm pecan pie and coffee, and finish them it did. For when the pie was gone, both felt the need to consume a little less in the future to make up for what they had just done. Al offered the opinion that he didn't have the willpower to live in a city with such food.

After dinner, Al and Kit strolled over to Bourbon Street, which they quickly found too congested and too noisy.

"Let's see if Jackson Square is any quieter," Al suggested.

A block further on, a crowd had gathered around three musicians in the street, two men and a girl in turn-of-the-century costumes. They strummed their guitars with such force, sang with such bravado, and were so lousy that Kit found herself mesmerized. Finally concluding that she was indulging in much the same behavior that had drawn the crowd to the scene where Freddie Watts had jumped the curb, she forced herself to move on.

"They're enthusiastic, I'll give them that," Al said.

In the next block there was a *real* musician; a bearded fellow in a denim shirt and worn jeans. They listened to him sing "Rocky Mountain High" for several minutes. At the completion of his song, Kit threw a half dollar into the Styrofoam cup at his feet, realizing only when it was too late that there was coffee in the cup and everyone else was throwing money into his open guitar case.

Thankful that she was not with Broussard, Kit took Al's arm and pulled him from the scene, her face a cheery pink and getting pinker.

"Well, that'll just be a nice surprise for him when he finishes his coffee," Al said, laughing.

Kit looked at him and smiled sheepishly. Then *she* started to laugh. Suddenly what she had done seemed hysterical and they both laughed until tears came to their eyes and people began to stare.

She hadn't laughed like this with David in a long time. This man whom she had known for such a short time had a rare ability to make people open up. First the cardiologist and now her. David had better watch out.

At night, Jackson Square was a ghost of itself in daylight. Where earlier there had been dozens of artists making pastel portraits of the tourists, there were now only the artists' heavy metal lockers sitting quietly, waiting for the sun. No kids on skateboards, no clowns squeaking as they made balloon animals, only couples walking quietly, admiring the great cathedral, looking at Andrew Jackson atop his green copper horse, or heading for Cafe Dumond for beignets and coffee.

Kit and Al went into the park and sat on a wrought-iron bench.

"So how long have you lived in New Orleans?" Al said.

"A little over five years."

"Then you've just gone from hating the city to loving it." Kit's eyes widened. "How did you know?"

He shrugged. "That's just how it works. This town is like an addictive drug. It hooks you gradually and then if you try to leave, you suffer withdrawal."

"Have *you* ever tried to leave?"

"I've lived either in the city or nearby all my life." He got a faraway look in his eye. "I could leave though, if I had to. But it wouldn't be easy. A part of me would always still be here."

"Because it's the only home you've ever known."

"More than that. It's the history, the feeling of permanence you get here." He gestured toward the Cabildo. "Not many places in the country where you can see buildings that old still standing. When I close my eyes, I can almost feel the presence of the people who built it. Try it. Go on."

Kit shut her eyes and did her best.

"Feel them?"

She opened her eyes. "Well . . . maybe a little."

He laughed. "More likely, I've just got an overactive imagination."

A young couple in jeans and Reeboks passed them sharing a bag of potato chips. The guy, a kid with a short face and orange-blond hair, scoured the inside of the bag with his fingers, licked the salt from them, and threw the bag on the sidewalk. Al went over, picked up the bag, and put it in the green waste can beside the bench.

"He probably parks in handicapped zones too," Kit said.

". . . at a sharp angle so he also takes up a legitimate space," Al added, sitting down again.

"And he laughs at the sad parts in movies," Kit countered, sensing that Al wanted to make a game of it.

"And . . . refuses to bus his tray at McDonalds."

"And . . ." Kit hesitated.

"Your turn," Al said.

"I'm out of gas," Kit admitted.

"And he has gas," Al said.

They both laughed and Al said, "I like it when you do that."

"Do what?"

"When you laugh." He touched the bridge of her nose. "Your nose gets all crinkly right here, like a happy little girl."

"I guess right now that's a pretty good description of me."

"Now?"

"Now that my job is going better."

"What was wrong before?"

"It's a long story and would probably bore you."

"Anything to do with that rash of suicide-murders we've been having?"

"How did you . . . ?"

"I ran into Charlie Franks the other day and he mentioned it. Doesn't sound boring at all. Just the opposite."

"Well, if you're sure . . ." Over on Decatur, reins smacked a horse's neck and the sound of hooves against pavement drifted over the square. "About three weeks ago . . ."

Kit talked for nearly half an hour, telling everything that had been happening to her, encouraged now by a nod of Al's head, later by a pertinent question, and always by those hypnotic blue eyes . . . alert and interested. Yes, David had better watch out.

Chapter 11

At eight-thirty Monday morning, Bubba backed into the Parkses' driveway in a police tow truck, his fingers tapping the seat in time to a Cajun two-step on his portable radio. Here in the city, with the sun shining and the radio playing, Bubba gave no thought to the swamp superstitions that so firmly guided his grandmother's life. In less than ten minutes, he had a towing dolly under the Escadrille's front wheels and had its rear dangling from his tow chain.

Broussard had designed the work bay in his garage for car restoration. Expecting that some of his acquisitions would have to be towed home, he had installed Dor-O-Matic overhead doors at both ends. When Bubba arrived, he pointed his remote control at the door and eagerly pushed the button. The device had been in place for three years and Bubba had used it so often that he didn't find it nearly as amusing as he once did. Now, he only made the door go up and down a few times before going in.

Together the truck and the car filled the work bay. To center the car, Bubba raised the far door and eased the truck partway through the opening. He jacked up the Escadrille's front end, removed the dolly, then lowered both ends to the pavement, unaware of the green eyes that watched him intently from the doorway to the adjacent room.

He hooked the dolly onto the tow chain, raised it until it

cleared the floor, and walked over to set the car's emergency brake, a habit acquired after a car he had once towed rolled down a tiny grade and struck another car.

When he opened the Escadrille's front door, Broussard's old tomcat slipped through it and jumped onto the platform behind the backseat. It was only then that Bubba remembered Broussard's warning about staying out of the car. But if it was dangerous for humans, it might also be bad for cats. What was he to do now?

He began to coax the cat as seductively as he could. "Here kitty. C'mon Chuck. Come on, big boy. Come to Bubba."

Sensing that Bubba was up to something, Chuck stayed put.

"Kitty, kitty. Come on fella, come and get dat old head scratched."

But Chuck was unmoved.

From the back of the tow truck, Bubba got a thick rope and tossed its frayed end into the back of the car. He skillfully twitched and jerked and pulled it slowly over the seat. But Chuck just yawned and lay down on his paws. Growing impatient, Bubba looked around and spied a broom. He prodded the old cat with the handle but might as well have been poking a bag of sand for all the effect it had.

Now Bubba was stumped. He couldn't get in the car and drag the cat out, and it certainly wasn't coming out on its own.

"Okay, have it your way. It gonna be nobody's fault but your own if you get sick."

Leaving the door open far enough for Chuck to get out if he wished, Bubba got in the truck and drove off. He felt a bit guilty but told himself Chuck would be all right.

As the garage door banged shut, Chuck dropped onto the backseat. After turning in circles for several seconds, he put his chin on his paws, curled his tail over his nose, and drifted off to sleep.

Before long his left ear flicked and he whimpered. A trickle of saliva ran from his mouth and formed a small puddle on the seat. Abruptly, his eyes popped open. Their pupils, which in the dim light should have been widely dilated, were mere slits in the center of his rheumy green irises. Tiny hemorrhages dotted the thin rim of his dingy sclera.

The soft rumble of contentment that earlier had filled the car's interior stopped and through quivering lips, he began to bark like a small dog. Oozing through the open car door, he went looking for the female Abyssinian with which he shared Broussard's home. Under the T-birds he went, moving slowly, the fur on his tail standing out like the bristles on a bottle brush. When he saw her with her head down, lapping at the water in the large plastic bowl that Broussard brought out when he would be gone for a day or two, the old cat dropped to his belly and began to slide over the floor, his feet barely showing. Whiskers quivering, he studied her for a few seconds, then moved slowly around the bowl.

When he was directly opposite her, he went down on his haunches, rocked from side to side a few times, then flung himself through the air. His weight drove her muzzle deep into the bowl. In her surprise, she inhaled a noseful of water. She struggled for her life, but Chuck was too big and his teeth and claws too sharp for her to escape.

The door to the kitchen opened. Broussard, back from his trip, gaped at the cats—then ran toward them, yelling and waving his arms. Chuck jumped aside, barely eluding a broadside from Broussard's hand. The female came up coughing and sneezing and ran for the kitty portal to the yard. Chuck crouched low, his hind feet drawn under him like tightly wound springs, his ears flat against his skull. Broussard stared in wonder. He had once seen the cat Cuisinart a Labrador's nose, but beyond that one incident, Chuck had always been gentle and good-natured.

Broussard leaned down, his hand extended. "What's the matter fella? Not feelin' well?"

Chuck's lips drew back at the corners and he spit his answer. Fearing that the animal might be hurting from an undetected abscess like the one that had nearly killed him a year earlier, Broussard reached for the cat to examine him.

Suddenly the old pathologist was covered with snarling muscle. Fangs went into the fleshy fold under his chin. He grabbed at the burrowing head and got a handful of loose skin and an ear. He pulled the creature loose and suffered three deep scratches to the side of his cheek from scrabbling claws. The animal's mad struggle made him impossible to hold and he squirmed loose and dropped to the floor. But not before Broussard had seen the hemorrhages at the corners of his hate-filled eyes and the matted fur on his muzzle.

Broussard ran his hand over his cheek and looked at the blood in his palm. Chuck crouched again. Fearing another attack, Broussard took an uncertain step backward. He touched the back of two fingers to the fire under his chin and came away with more blood. Suddenly the old tom's good ear stood straight up and he swiveled toward the work bay as though hearing a voice denied to human ears. In a single fluid movement, he was on his feet and headed toward the far end of the garage, Broussard following.

The cat slipped through the door to the work bay and jumped onto the Escadrille's fender and from there to a shelf affixed to the wall, where he sat staring at the stub of the car's vandalized antenna. From outside the work bay, Broussard tapped on the window, but the cat would look only at the jagged metal rod with the sharp point. Broussard was puzzled. What did the cat see that was so riveting?

Chuck shifted into a crouch and the muscles in his hind legs began to tremble. In an instant, it was done and Broussard put his hand over his eyes to blot it out. With his eyes covered, he saw Chuck as he had that first day on the porch, the tip of a steel-jacketed arrow pushing through the cat's white ruff. The scene he had just witnessed was not so different, except now Chuck had fallen victim to a car antenna.

Not looking was not acting, and he reached for the door, the memory of the cat's wet muzzle making him wonder whether Chuck had rabies, a prospect that held considerable consequences for himself as well. But then a different explanation hit him and he stepped back to the window. That was an

Escadrille in there . . . with one door open. Had Chuck been inside it? If so . . . No! He was unwilling to believe that a cat had the intelligence to commit suicide. Yet Chuck *had* learned to fear sharp objects from his experience with the arrow. And there were other points that fit; the unprovoked attack, the hemorrhages in his eyes. Kit had been right about that. Because of her, he had gone over the records and had found several murder-suicides where scleral hemorrhages were present despite being contraindicated by the cause of death. But it all seemed so unlikely. He had suggested some tests on the car because that seemed prudent and proper. But he had not really believed they would prove anything.

He glared at the car. Kit had said that people with blood type O were particularly susceptible. *He* had type O. And the door to the car was wide open. It might be dangerous in there. He could hold his breath, but what if the toxin could enter through a wound? He looked at Chuck's lifeless form impaled on the stump of the car's antenna and could tolerate the obscenity no longer.

Taking a deep breath, he burst into the work bay, lifted Chuck gently into his arms, and carried him to the house where he laid him on the kitchen floor and smoothed his ruffled coat. Had Chuck been in the Escadrille? The question would not go away. He dialed the number of the impoundment station, and he and Bubba exchanged stories. Bubba wanted all the blame for what happened, but Broussard pointed out that there was as yet no proof that the Escadrille was responsible and if it was, the blame should fall on his own shoulders for leaving the door to the work bay open.

After washing the blood from his face and beard, Broussard changed clothes and set out for the morgue, Chuck wrapped in a soft towel next to him. Bubba's account had made rabies a much less likely explanation, but for his own safety, he felt he should have Chuck's brain examined for Negri bodies, the accumulations of virus particles typically found in the nerve cells of rabid animals. From the parking lot, he went directly to the autopsy rooms where he left Chuck with Charlie Franks and then went to his office to wait for the results of the frozen sections.

While he waited, he tried not to think of how shiny Chuck's fur had looked lately and how he had such a small meow for such a big cat. He tried not to remember how Chuck liked to tunnel under the rugs when he was in a playful mood and how he would flatten out on the floor like a flounder when scolded. He tried to suppress the image of Chuck and Princess grooming each other.

Finally, the phone rang and Franks informed him that the sections were negative. That left the Escadrille. It was time for a hard look at that damn car.

There was a formidable amount to do before the testing could begin. But, before thinking about that, there was another more pressing matter at home. On the west side of his house was a stand of dwarf lantana. In the summer when it was in full flower, Chuck could often be found, head stretched forward, nose against the blooms. Here, next to this plant, Broussard dug a small deep grave. It was inconceivable that a man who had lived daily with human death for over thirty years would cry at the passing of a cat. But he did. . . . Not much, and wiped away quickly, but tears all the same.

By late that afternoon, the necessary equipment had been collected and the experiments on the Escadrille began. Because it had been designed to vent the fumes when spray-painting cars, the work bay had a ventilation system that turned the air over once every three minutes without creating a negative pressure. Not satisfied with this safeguard, Broussard had borrowed two respirators from the firefighting academy. Also on hand were three dozen mice from an inbred strain that, at Kit's insistence, had been tested by the hospital blood bank and shown to resemble human blood type O, the blood type of Barry Hollins and Freddie Watts. Another dozen were from a strain whose blood type resembled human type A, the type not present in any of the recent suicidal murderers. All the O-strain animals had been marked on each side with a yellow dot. Those from the A strain were marked in green.

"Still a shade out," Broussard shouted, peering at the fuzzy image of the Escadrille's front seat on the video monitor in front of him. In the work bay, a TV camera on a tripod was trained on the Escadrille's windshield. Kit slowly twirled the focus ring and the blurred image on the monitor sharpened.

"Stop!" Broussard yelled.

Kit emerged from the work bay and pulled off her mask. "Pttttghh. This thing smells like the inside of a volleyball."

Broussard plugged the monitor into the video recorder on the cart's lower shelf. "I'm goin' to start recordin' just before you put 'em in," he said. "I'll point when I'm ready. Be prepared to yank that cage out and separate 'em if things get rough. If what *might* happen, *does*, this tape will be seen by a lot of folks and I don't want the animal-rights people on my back sayin' we were stagin' cock fights with mice."

Kit strapped on her mask, pulled on a pair of rubber acid handler's gloves, and picked up a wire cage. In the cage were two mice, one from each strain. She carried the cage into the work bay, went around to the driver's side of the Escadrille, and pulled the door open. Through the window, she saw Broussard's signal. In the next room, he clicked his stopwatch.

Their universe became the experiment. Kit ceased to smell the rubber in her mask. Broussard temporarily forgot his remorse over Chuck. Only the mice mattered. One marked in yellow, one in green. And nothing was happening.

The mice stood on their hind legs and wiggled their noses. They rooted in the wood shavings on the cage floor. Occasionally one would sniff the south end of the other.

"One minute," Broussard sang out.

At one twenty-three, the mouse from the O strain seized the other animal by the throat. Broussard thumbed the stopwatch to a halt. Kit yanked the cage from the car and thrust her hand inside, the terrified squeals of the victim making her sweat even more beneath her mask.

Suspending the aggressor by his tail, she tried in vain to shake him loose from the other mouse. Something had to be done to stop that squealing!

With the joined animals dangling above the cage, Kit pulled the glove off her free hand with her knees and pinched the aggressor on one ear. His victim fell to the floor and scampered into a tail pipe that lay under a workbench. When Kit looked back at the animal she held, he was climbing his tail, presumably wanting a taste of her fingers. Despite Broussard's earlier assurance that a mouse could never bite through the gloves, she yelped into her mask and dropped him.

Broussard heard her muffled cry, but the car blocked his view. "What happened?" he shouted.

"He tried to bite me," Kit said, looking at her feet where the tiny ball of fur was tugging at her canvas shoe with his mouth. Again taking hold of his tail, she pulled him loose and carried him into the next room, using her loose glove to brush away further attempts on her fingers. Dropping him into the spare cage Broussard held out to her, she pulled off her mask. "He tried to bite me," she repeated, knowing he couldn't have understood her the first time. "That is one mean rodent. He went after my shoe just like he did his cage mate."

Broussard held the cage up and brought it close to his face. "He's salivatin' like crazy. I wonder if that's part of it? Let's try it again."

Kit reached into the cage holding the O-strain animals and was chasing another tail when there was a faint metallic clatter behind her.

"Look at this!" Broussard said.

She joined him at the cage holding their first subject. "Oh my . . ." Her hand went to her mouth as the little creature rammed headlong into the hardware-cloth enclosure with a *twang* that she could feel in her own nose. He backed up and charged again. Twang! His snout was driven nearly flat by the impact. Kit had seen enough. She reached into the cage and drew him out by the nape of the neck.

"Hold on, I'll get somethin' to stop that." Broussard came

back with a towel and used it to line the cage. Kit replaced the animal and together they watched him resume his bizarre behavior, but now without injuring himself.

"That remind you of anything?" Kit asked.

"Is there any precedent for believin' that animals are capable of suicide?"

"It's been argued for lemmings, and no one knows why whales beach themselves. But is precedent really all that important? Would its absence change the way Chuck died or alter the behavior of this mouse? We could be dealing here with a toxin that opens neural pathways ordinarily never used."

"Mice, cats, and men," Broussard mused. "Must be affectin' an aspect of vertebrate neurophysiology as fundamental as dirt. I wonder how many of those cars are still on the road?" His eyes took on that distant look she had seen before, and he stroked his nose with two fingers of his left hand. Presently, he said, "We've got to issue a warnin' about these cars. But before we do, we better have all the answers. If we get off on the wrong foot with this and the papers start to make a joke of it, it'll take forever to set things right and more people may die. On the other hand, we can't take forever to get our story together either or people may die. So let's get movin'."

He brought out more towels to protect other subjects that might try what the first one had, and the work went on.

They repeated the initial experiment with identical results except that Kit was able to intervene before any harm was done to the A-strain animal. As before, the O-strain mouse came out of the car drooling. "Looks like you were right about blood-group specificity," Broussard said. "Somethin' about havin' the A antigen confers protection from the toxin. What's *your* blood type?"

"If you had asked me yesterday, I couldn't have told you, but I had the blood bank type me this morning. I'm an A."

"Well, keep your mask on all the same when you're in there. We don't want to take any chances."

"How do you suppose having the A antigen protects against the toxin?"

Broussard shrugged. "Tough question. That'll be for somebody else to work out when all this is over."

"What's happening there?" Kit cried.

Together they went to the cage holding the first susceptible mouse tested and saw convulsions racking the animal's little body. Then he lay limp and still. Kit lifted him from the cage and felt for a heartbeat. There was none.

"Jesus," Kit said, looking up from the tiny form in her hand. "If the victims don't kill themselves, they die like this." A puzzled look spread over her face. "But what about Shindleman? *He* recovered."

"Maybe mice are different in that regard. Let's do some more and see if any recover."

Of ten more susceptible mice tested, nine developed seizures and died. The third one in the series, however, recovered completely.

"There's Shindleman," Broussard said, pointing at the recovered animal. "A small percentage of affected individuals don't progress to the last stage."

"I'd like to know what part of that car is toxic," Kit said.

"Will the owner allow us to take the necessary steps to find out?"

"I won't know that until I make a phone call."

"In the kitchen."

She returned with the news that Daphne had given them permission to do whatever they wished with the car. She then asked Broussard whether he had any single-edge razor blades and got, instead, a scalpel he used to make radish garnishes. As he handed the instrument over, he anticipated her next question.

"There are some five-gallon cans in the work bay that should make good incubation chambers," he said. "They're big enough so that with the lid on, there'll be plenty of air, and small enough so that any vapors from the pieces of fabric you're goin' to put in 'em should accumulate in sufficient concentration to be effective . . . *if* that's the origin of the problem."

Except for the lids, which fit so tightly that she broke a fingernail pulling them off, the shiny bronze cans were ideal. There seemed to be three possible fabrics to test: the roof liner, the carpeting, and the simulated-leather seat coverings. the door panels were covered in the same material as the seats, so they were not considered as a separate category.

With the scalpel, she removed a piece approximately six inches square from each of the three fabrics and dropped them separately into the three cans she had prepared. After spreading a towel on the Escadrille's hood and placing a cage containing a nonsusceptible animal on the towel, she adjusted the video camera and focused it. An animal from the susceptible strain was then placed in the can that held seat-cover material and the lid was pressed firmly in place. After the animal had been in the chamber for five minutes, Broussard started the VCR. Kit plucked the animal from the can and dropped him into the cage on the hood.

Six dull minutes later, Broussard suggested that they move on to the carpet sample. It, too, turned up nothing. The roof liner, however, was a different matter. No mouse could have been more crazed than the one that came out of the last can.

"What now?" Kit asked. "Make an announcement?"

"Not yet. I'd like for Al Vogel to examine that fabric first. He should be able to analyze it and characterize the toxic component." He looked at his watch and frowned. "We'll never get to the lab before five. Cut us a few more pieces of each sample. I'm goin' to see if he'll stay until we can get there."

Chapter 12

In the four outbound lanes on the Mississippi River bridge, much of the working population of the city sat baking in the late-afternoon sun. As Kit sped by going the other way, jealous eyes watched her pass. Up ahead, in his white T-bird, Broussard abruptly changed to the inside lane without signalling.

They reached the Justice Center at five-twenty. The figs in the lobby seemed, if anything, a little yellower than on Kit's previous visit, but the trash in the planters had been cleaned up and the slashed wallcovering had been replaced.

With their arrival, Vogel flicked the light off his microscope and jumped up to greet them. "You made good time," he said.

"Not much traffic comin' in," Broussard replied.

Vogel's eyes shifted to Kit. "Hello Kit, did you hear? Doctors say that fellow on Bourbon Street who swallowed the half dollar is going to be just fine."

"No Al, I didn't hear that," Kit said, unable to keep from smiling.

Broussard gave them an uncomprehending look.

Vogel gestured toward the manila envelope in Broussard's hand. "That what you want me to test?"

"These are the fabrics that weren't toxic. Dr. Franklyn has the toxic samples."

Kit gave Vogel the thermos they had used to safely

transport pieces of the Escadrille's roof liner. "If I were you, I'd label it so it doesn't get opened without proper precautions," she said.

Vogel pulled a piece of red tape from a spool on the counter, ran it around the seam where the cup met the body, and scrawled on the tape with a Magic Marker. "That should do it," he said, holding his handiwork up for Kit's appraisal.

"There's pretty good evidence that the toxin's effect is blood group specific," Broussard said.

"Type O is susceptible, type A is not," Kit added.

"Glad to hear that," Vogel said, "since I'm an A."

"Me too," Kit said, as though through their common blood type they shared other things as well. She gestured toward Broussard with her head. "He can't be in our club. He's an O."

"I don't think you want to trust your life to the kind of data we have so far on that point," Broussard said to Vogel. "Have you got a way to protect yourself while you work?"

"There's a fume hood in the other room with arm sleeves in it. I can do everything inside that. You say this toxin came from a car?"

Kit gave Vogel a condensed version of the day's experiments. When she finished, Vogel sucked his teeth and said, "Boy, you watch your diet, cross only at the corner, wear seat belts, and somebody sells you a dining-room table with radioactive legs, or something like this happens." He shrugged and turned his palms to the ceiling. "But what can we do . . . ?" He put his hands in his lab coat. "I can't possibly have anything for you in less than forty-eight hours."

"That long?" Broussard said.

"Even then, I'll have to work practically around the clock."

"Two days it'll have to be," Broussard said.

As they walked to the elevator, Broussard pushed a lemon drop into his cheek and offered Kit one, which she declined. On an illuminated wall panel, they followed the elevator's descent from the floors above. When the doors opened, the rich aroma of pipe tobacco spilled out.

"You and Vogel seem to know each other better than I thought," Broussard said, pushing the "L" button.

"We had dinner together Saturday night. He's a nice man. I just wish he could work faster. Two days is a long time."

"I've got another case back at the office you can work on, and I'd also like for you to get together with the photography people at LSU and work with them to edit our film down to a concise story of five minutes or so. That'll keep you busy until Vogel's through."

As Broussard pulled from the parking lot, his thoughts were on the strange new syndrome they had discovered. Excess salivation, scleral hemorrhages accompanied by a preoccupation with childhood songs, and a compulsion to kill. It was a bewildering array of symptoms for which he had no explanation. And that made him angry. He could spot cancer of the pancreas, myocardial infarction, peritonitis, tertiary syphilis, and a bookcase full of others in an instant because they all produced symptoms that could be explained by the physical findings at autopsy. So why should the effects of the Escadrille toxin be any different? He was sure they weren't different, and that in turn meant he had missed something when he had done the postmortems on the toxin victims. He had been fooled! Death from a severed spinal cord. It was such an obvious conclusion in the Huey P. Long case, he had dropped his guard and let something get past him. But what? What the devil could account for those apparently unrelated symptoms?

A growl from behind his belt announced the dinner hour, and he responded by popping another lemon ball. As current president of the Southern Gourmet Society, he had kicked off the year's annual dinner six weeks ago by raising his glass and saying, "To the enjoyment of good food, an activity better than sex, as it can be practiced three times a day for as long as you live and has virtually no possibility of producing unwanted children." It was a toast made only partly in jest. But while he rated food above sex, he did not rate it above work, especially when his ability was in question. Dinner tonight would be late. He had an urgent appointment in the tissue-holding room off the morgue.

In the vending area just inside the hospital's side entrance, his belly sang out again, much louder this time, and he had to slip two quarters into a snack machine and eat a packet of chocolate cookies to keep it quiet.

In all the years Broussard had been medical examiner, he had never thrown away a single slide made from autopsy material. They now nearly filled a room next to his office, where they stood on edge in dark green cabinets, the reference numbers on them allowing him to locate any case he wished in under two minutes. While useful, the slides only represented a minuscule sample of tissue, and he had often found himself wishing he had kept the organs from which they came. As that was physically impossible, he had done the best he could, keeping all viscera from each autopsy for one month before discarding them. Tonight he was glad he did. There was a brain he wanted very much to examine, and because of his reluctance to discard remains, he still had it.

The morgue lay behind a pair of windowless double doors off the vending area at the end of a dingy tunnel illuminated by bare bulbs in wire cages. To those unaccustomed to old hospitals, it would have seemed a cheerless place. But Broussard had breathed its air and trod its worn cement floor so long, it had become a part of him, an integral piece of all he was. And he was satisfied with the way it looked.

Near the corridor's end, he slid a key into the lock on a pale-green door with THR stenciled across it and went inside. The fixtures overhead flickered and caught, bathing the porcelain pots on the wooden shelves lining both sides of the room with a cold impersonal light. The Hollinses' fire had made Barry Hollins's brain difficult to study and Leon Washington's had been impossible. That left him only the brain of Freddie Watts.

He checked the logbook for the accession number of Watts's brain, then scanned the shelves for the correct pot. When he found it, he carried it to the stainless steel table at the far end of the room. From a shelf over the table, he pulled out a pair of disposable rubber gloves and slipped them on. Placing the pot lid on the table, he reached into the formalin and withdrew a gauze bundle. A few quick snips with a pair of surgical scissors and he was able to peel the gauze away from the brain inside, which earlier he had sliced crosswise like a loaf of bread to study its internal appearance. Since he now wished once again to examine its surface, he pushed the slices together and reached for the combination desk lamp and magnifying glass clamped to the back of the table. Through the magnifier, he scrutinized every furrow and every sulcus. With a gloved finger, he slowly traced each of the major blood vessels to their smallest ramifications . . . and found everything normal.

He then took up each slice and examined the patterns of gray and white that rippled and changed from region to region and section to section. His medical-student days were long behind him now and he had forgotten the names of most of the structures he saw, a situation that gave him no concern. The brain had more named structures in it than anyone could be expected to remember, but they could all be looked up in books. The important thing was to be able to tell the normal from the abnormal, and he was as good as anyone at that. . . . So why couldn't he find the answer? Everything looked so tormentingly healthy. The ventricles were clear and undilated, the white matter was smooth and flat, the gray zones were . . . Hello! There! . . . A gray mass the size of a small marble in the lower portion of a section through the frontal lobes seemed to be . . . Yes, it most certainly was. And the one on the other side, too. Both definitely had a reddish tint superimposed on the gray.

He brought one of the suspect areas closer to his eye, but the magnifier was too weak to provide the needed resolution. With the thrill of possibility racing through his veins, he dashed from the room, ignoring his own rules against carrying human material uncovered through the hospital halls.

The elevator had never moved so slowly and he was practically dancing with impatience by the time it arrived. It was empty, as he had hoped, and he made it all the way to his office on five without a stop.

He plopped into the chair in front of his ancient Nikon dissecting scope and slipped off his glasses, letting them dangle against his chest. Anxiously, he shifted the brain slice around until the suspicious area was centered in the field. He then zoomed up on the mag and clamped his tongue lightly between his teeth in glee. There was loose blood among the neurons. The owner of this brain had suffered a tiny stroke! There it was! A thread linking the symptoms. Scleral hemorrhage—brain hemorrhage. The toxin selectively damages the small blood vessels in both areas! But it was such a *small* area of the brain to produce such diverse effects.

He reached for his glasses and scanned his bookshelves. From a cross-section atlas of the human brain, he located the affected area and traced a label line to the words "amygdaloid nucleus." Seeing the word again after so many years sent a synaptic flutter through his own brain. But it quickly fizzled. In Willingham's *Medical Physiology*, he found a section titled "Function of the Amygdaloid Nuclei in Behavior Patterns." The first sentence leapt off the page at him. "Stimulation of different portions of the amygdaloid nuclei can cause almost any type of behavior pattern." He ripped through the remaining text, devouring it like a starving animal. "Stimulation of some regions produce fear, some produce aggression, and others, gastrointestinal activity such as vomiting, sniffing, salivation." . . . "Salivation! Aggression!" He spoke the words aloud as he closed the book.

He had been exposed to enough neurophysiology to know that partially compromised circulation can cause neurons to fire uncontrollably, much as if they were being stimulated electrically. It all fit! The Escadrille victims were being driven by hyperactivity of certain amygdaloid neurons! He lay back in his chair and sunned himself in the light of his intellect. But suddenly, he thought of a symptom as yet unaccounted for and the light dimmed.

What about the childhood songs that each victim heard? There was nothing about that in the section on the amygdala. He tapped the table impatiently with the fingers of one hand and probed the dark corners of his memory. Hiding there he found another fundamental of neurophysiology. The center of auditory sensation was the superior temporal gyrus and adjacent areas.

Off came his glasses. Sliding the brain section to the left, he examined the cortical material making up the auditory area. Carefully, he moved along the rippling gray line of neurons that lay just below the surface. Clear there . . . Clear there . . . He moved slowly, methodically. Clear there . . . *But not clear there!* He had found another affected area, much harder to see than the amygdaloid lesion and barely bigger than a lentil. It was also present on the opposite side.

One by one, he pulled down every book in his library that might contain information on the location of musical memory. Finally, he found the case of Mr. "M," a thirty-six-year-old construction worker who had been struck in the head by a falling hammer. Every time the surgeon's forceps touched a particular bone chip in the man's brain, the patient said he heard a song he hadn't heard since he was a child. So clear was the sound that he later maintained that the surgeon had been playing a recording while he operated. A diagram accompanying the case study put the bone chip right where Broussard had found the lentil-size lesion in Watts's brain.

When Charlie Franks solved a difficult problem, he had to tell someone about it. But with Broussard, it brought an inner peace that did not need to be shared with anyone. Now he could eat.

On the way home, Kit stopped at Gambini's, a small grocery with a high-priced deli that was worth the extra money. She started her shopping trip at a tall wicker basket full of long loaves of French bread in red-and-white paper sleeves. Feeling the bread give deliciously beneath her grip, and remembering that it was also good in the morning, hot with lots of butter, she decided on two loaves instead of one. A half-pound of imported Swiss and the same amount of pastrami, both sliced thin but not paper thin, and a big pickle that they allowed customers to fish out of a glass jar with a pair of wooden tongs rounded out her purchases. As Mr. Gambini, a thickly built man with deep lines etched in an olive complexion, wrapped her pickle in white butcher paper, he asked for perhaps the twentieth time whether she was engaged yet, and she responded as always, "Not yet. I'm waiting for your missus to let *you* go." As usual, he laughed convincingly.

Her mailbox was jammed absolutely full, an event that had become all too common since buying two magazine subscriptions from a little girl with bright brown eyes who was "this close" to winning a trip to Washington, D.C. She tossed the mail into the bag with the groceries, made sure the little dog was nowhere around, and took it all inside. After checking her answering machine for messages, she sorted everything on the kitchen counter.

Boyd-Jenkins was having a big sale and their "special" customers were invited to a one-day preview before the rabble would be allowed in. Congratulations KIT FRANKLYN, you are a winner. . . . All of it but one piece went back into the grocery bag for deposit later in the blue Dumpster in the rear of the building. The single item she saved carried the return address of her parents back in Speculator, New York.

Judging by the familiar hand that had printed the address all in caps, it was a letter from her father. In truth, any letter from her parents would be from her father, now retired from the bank of Speculator, where he had progressed to first vice-president. Like Kit, her mother was no letter writer.

The envelope had a bulge in it caused by a pen with BANK OF SPECULATOR printed in white down two sides. Puzzled, she put the pen on the kitchen counter and unfolded the letter.

"Dear Kitten,"

She dropped the letter to her side and sighed at the ceiling. Would he *never* understand how much she hated that name? She continued reading.

Everything was fine; her mother was as busy as ever with her charities and women's groups. They had to replace the hot-water heater and got Bob Drinnan to do it. "You remember Bob; Lester and Ida's boy (she didn't). And since we haven't heard from you in months, figured maybe you needed something to write with."

As she replaced the letter in its envelope, she wished her father would just forget his crazy vendetta against the phone company and have the thing put back in. He'd stand a lot better chance of getting a call from her than he would a letter. But as this was not likely, she would try to get off a few lines to them real soon. Maybe tomorrow.

Conscience salved, she made herself a sandwich, filled a tall glass with cold buttermilk, and carried them into the living room to catch what remained of the local news.

She had just sampled the buttermilk when a woman who would look great if it weren't for her nose said, ". . . and here's David with the weather." *David! Yikes!* She jumped to her feet. In all the excitement of testing the car, she had completely forgotten she was to have dinner with David at Commander's Palace.

When David arrived at seven, she was ready, and he had no idea how close he had come to finding her in her pajamas. The date was one of their better ones. They managed to get through the salad without a single disagreement. And the memories of all past arguments faded when the Reisling and prime rib arrived.

It was around nine-thirty when the phone rang in Kit's empty town house and the caller failed to leave a message. A few minutes later, a figure dressed in dark clothing slipped through the rear gate to the patio and, hidden by the stockade fence, examined the lock on her back door with a penlight.

Shortly after he had begun work on her door, the sound of voices and music drifted over the fence. Dropping to his knees, the figure switched off his light and waited motionless for the danger to pass.

"You really think Darryl is cute?" a young girl said.

"Don't you?" her companion replied.

"I asked you first."

"Well, yeah, I guess he is . . . unless you don't."

The voices and the music went by and began to fade. When they could be heard only as muffled sounds in the distance, the figure went back to work and soon had the door opened.

He was pleased to find himself in the kitchen; precisely where he wanted to be. After placing his small metal tray of tools on the kitchen counter, he took a flashlight with a flat base and a pivoting head out of the tray and set it up on the counter so that its beam played over the refrigerator. He spread out the tools he would need and set to work. When the job was finished, he scooped the counter clean and dumped everything in his tray. As he left, he paused and placed an object on the cement apron beside the back door, then stole back to his car, which was waiting in the shadows.

Chapter 13

Kit and David returned to her town house four hours after they had left. Both were slightly wine-giddy and Kit's defenses were down. So she agreed with David's suggestion that he come in for awhile, the first step in a sequence that usually led to the bedroom. While she sought the lock with her key, the dust mop of a dog that liked to visit came wagging out of the night, sniffed the back of her shoes, and began to paw the door.

"Yours?" David said, squatting to rub its head.

"No, but I think he'd like to be. Hold him will you? If you don't, he'll run inside."

"I've got him," David said. But when the door opened, the dog gave a quick squirm that left David looking at empty hands.

Kit felt the furry projectile brush her legs. "Oh David!" she moaned, flicking on the lights.

"Sorry."

"You let him in, so you've got to get him out."

The little dog couldn't have been happier, and he began to yap with joy and rush from one wall of the living room to the other. "Don't use up *all* your energy chasing him," Kit said slyly. Beaming, David went down on one knee and made coaxing noises to the little creature, who would go a few steps in his direction, drop to his belly, bark a few times, and run off.

While David and the dog were matching wits, Kit, feeling

just the tiniest bit drunk, remembered how to trick the dog
out of the house. She stepped into the kitchen and let out a
yelp of her own.

"What's wrong?" David asked, lunging for the dog and
missing.

"Water!" Kit moaned. "It's everywhere."

David got to his feet and went over to see what had
happened. "Jeez, Kit. I think you've got a plumbing problem,"
he said, looking at the sheen of water covering the floor. "Is
there a cutoff under the sink?"

She shrugged and David sloshed across the floor to look. As
he did, the dog dashed into the kitchen and ran to the back
door barking happily. He bounced off the door, then ricocheted
off David's back. The dog was in ecstasy and seemed to want to
touch *everything*. But when he pushed off the refrigerator, he
gave a sharp cry of pain and fell quivering to the wet floor.

"What the hell happened to him?" David said, no longer the
least bit tipsy.

Kit went to the dog and carried him into the living room
where, after a few minutes, he struggled to his feet and began
once again to explore, now with a slight limp.

"Poor thing," Kit said. "Maybe he'd like something to eat."

Before she could reach the refrigerator, David grabbed her
around the waist. "Stay away from there," he snapped,
suddenly knowing what had probably happened. "I think the
dog got a jolt from the fridge. Where's the fuse box?"

Again, a shrug.

"How about a flashlight?"

This time a shake of the head.

"Never mind. There's one in my car. Stand right here and
don't touch anything! I'll be right back." He went out the front
door and returned with a mammoth silver flashlight. "When I
find the fuse box, I'm going to cut the power, so when the
lights go off, don't panic."

Because of the circumstances, he got off scot-free with his
"panic" remark. He found the fuse box outside, next to the

back door, pulled the main, and went back inside, where he yanked the plug on the refrigerator.

With power restored and the fridge pulled away from the wall, the source of the water on the floor was now clear. "Here's your leak," David said. "A pinhole in the waterline to the ice-maker."

"Can you fix it?" Kit said from the kitchen doorway, the little dog cradled in her arms.

He held his answer until he had a look under the sink, where he saw a copper tube coming off the cold-water line above the cutoff. It ran in the direction of the fridge. "Can't fix the hole, but I can shut off the water." He turned his head to one side and reached deep under the sink. The water spouting from the breached line slowed to a trickle, then stopped. He lifted the refrigerator cord from the water and ran it through his fingers. "Ahhh, just as I thought. The damn cord is frayed clear through." He held it closer and studied the bare spot. "Have you got mice? This thing looks like something's been chewing on it."

"I haven't seen any other signs," Kit said, coming over to have a look.

"Better get some traps anyway," he said, handing her the damaged portion of the cord. He looked at the wet floor and sucked his teeth in thought.

"And?" Kit prompted.

"I was just wondering why the fridge itself didn't drain the current away. The chassis was grounded to the plumbing through the line to the ice-maker. The current should have gone from the exposed wire to the water, into the fridge, and out the waterline. There shouldn't have been enough extra current to do that dog any harm." He removed the kick plate. "Well, no wonder." He pointed to one corner of the chassis. "The leveling legs are sitting in rubber casters. Somebody must have put them under there to keep the legs from denting the linoleum. They did that all right, but they also insulated the fridge from the water and made this whole situation more dangerous than it had to be." He stood up and scratched the poodle under the chin. "You owe this little pooch your life . . . or maybe I owe him mine. If he hadn't dashed in here when he did, one of us could be dead. It's a good thing he was acting so crazy. If he'd been moving a little slower, *he* might have bought it. Here, when I rock the fridge up off its legs, kick the front casters out. That's it. Now, can you get to the back ones?"

When all four pieces of rubber had been dislodged, he gathered them up and fired them into the grocery bag from Gambini's. "So much for those little bastards," he said. "What are you going to do with the dog?"

"Put an ad in the paper and try to find the owner, I guess. Considering what the dog did for us, maybe *I* should offer the *owner* a reward."

"Be a sure way to get a response. Where's your mop?"

"That's okay. I'll do it. Would you mind awfully if we called it a night? I'm feeling a little weak in the knees."

"You sure you want to be alone?"

"I'm sure. Thanks for a lovely dinner . . . and for helping with the mess." She leaned over and kissed him lightly on the lips.

He leaned back and studied her face. "Kit . . ."

"Yes?"

"I know sometimes I'm an ass and I often say the wrong thing, but I do care for you and I think we could make a good life together . . . maybe each of us give a little . . . find a common ground. What do you say we give it a try? I don't mean marriage; I know you don't want that. Move in with me. Let's find out if we can cut it." He put his finger to her lips. "Don't say anything now. Give it some thought and we'll talk later. Okay?"

Kit nodded and he kissed her on the forehead. They parted with her feeling much less sure about their incompatibility. At the same time, her growing feelings for Al Vogel and her wish to remain self-sufficient and independent made things difficult to sort out.

She cleaned up as much of the water as she could, then made the dog a bed next to hers by taking some silk flowers from their woven basket and lining it with a flannel nightie. By this time, the dog appeared pretty much recovered but tired, and he settled into the basket and closed his eyes, opening them every few minutes when she passed.

After brushing her teeth, she put a small bowl of water next to the basket and gave him a last scratch on the head before getting into bed. It was against the rules for tenants in the complex to have pets, so she'd have to find the dog's owner quickly, and if she didn't, well . . . she'd tackle that problem when and if it was necessary.

As she lay staring at the ceiling, there was still a bad taste in her mouth from a couple of things associated with the evening's events. She had not followed David's reasoning at all when he was talking about "current flow" and the refrigerator being "grounded," and her ignorance might have cost her dearly had she been alone. Ignorance could be remedied and she decided to stop by the library in the morning and pick up a book to brush up on the fundamentals of electricity. Nor did she like standing there like a dimwit not owning a flashlight or knowing where the fuse box was. She could learn about fuse boxes from the book she was going to get, and by tomorrow night, there was going to be a flashlight in the house.

The refrigerator held its temperature through the night and in the morning the dog had ham and buttermilk for breakfast. Kit had a generous helping of hot buttered bread and coffee. After breakfast and a short walk outside, where he showed no trace of a limp and did what was expected of him, the dog went back to his basket and fell asleep. This made Kit much less apprehensive about leaving him alone than if he had been bouncing off the furniture.

She called the manager of Givenchy Village and he promised

to send someone around before noon to repair the refrigerator. When she complained about his practice of using rubber casters on refrigerators to protect the linoleum, he denied any knowledge of them, a response she mentally filed under "B.S." Now to place the ad to find Lucky's owner. *Lucky!* She hadn't planned on giving the dog a name, but there it was, unintentional and perfect. So he would be "Lucky" until his owner came for him.

The ad cost three dollars and fifty cents and they would mail the bill. As she hung up, she found herself smothering a half-hope that no one would answer the ad. She couldn't keep a dog, didn't *want* a dog.

Having lived in the village long enough to know the ways of its repairmen, she did not plan on waiting for them to show up but had given permission for them to enter with a passkey and work unsupervised by her, a decision with which she was not entirely at ease. Before leaving for the hospital, she took a last peek at Lucky, who was still sound asleep, and gently closed the bedroom door.

Chapter 14

As Broussard pulled into his driveway the night following Kit's adventure, he wondered whether there were enough eggs in the house for the crab quiche he had planned for dinner. If not, he'd simply have to make do. There wasn't time in his schedule tonight for a trip to the market. Beyond settling on the title, "Insect Larvae as Time-of-Death Indicators in Cases of Advanced Decomposition," he'd made very little progress on the paper he'd been meaning to write for the last three months. But he was determined that his head would not touch his pillow until the entire rough draft was completed. That would take the sting out of the job and it would not be so hard to pick up again.

There was a package on the porch that made him forget the quiche. It was wrapped in brown paper and was tied with hemp twine precisely as the previous thirty-six packages had been. It was his monthly delivery from Thomas Garroway Ltd. and his spirits soared. What would it be this time? French truffles? Handmade Normandy Camembert? Perhaps a blue-veined English Stilton?

He took the package inside, set it and his briefcase on the refectory table, and went immediately for a pair of scissors. The contents of the package were always a thrill, but he enjoyed nearly as much the knowledge that he was dealing with a firm over three hundred years old.

He snipped the twine and opened the package as he had opened the gauze bundle holding Freddie Watts's brain, using just the index finger and thumb of each hand, keeping both pinkies raised as though drinking tea from a small cup. With the tape removed, the wrapping fell away from a shiny green pasteboard box bearing the image of a narrow two-story Victorian store building. He lifted the top from the box and eagerly scanned the shipping manifest resting on the contents. He was now in possession of a five-hundred-gram broccio, a liter of Bolognese sauce, and a large package of tri-color fusilli. The manifest also listed a dozen maid-of-honor cakes, a dozen stuffed cabbage rolls, half a dozen smoked brill, two bottles of marinated eels, a package of black radishes, and a bag of dried shitake mushrooms.

Putting aside the manifest, he surveyed the bottles and tins, cellophane bags and plastic sleeves carefully packed in a bed of fake grass. In their wrappers of multicolored tin foil, the twelve cakes looked like chocolate eggs in an Easter basket.

With a light step, he carried the box into the kitchen and stacked its contents on the counter. Drawing on a few things already in his larder, dinner would be an event.

Before tending to his own needs, he went to the garage to feed the cats. It was only when he found the food bowl still half-full that he remembered. There was only Princess. Chuck was gone. He closed the bag of Feline Feast and went back inside, not feeling nearly as chipper as he had.

Dinner, which he ate as always in the dining room with the lights turned low and Placido Domingo on the stereo, restored his sagging spirits. During particularly brilliant passages, he imagined himself onstage, the source of those glorious sounds. It was his own complete lack of ability in this area that made him so admire those who had it. By dinner's end, he was in a writing frame of mind.

Since he could eat but not think with opera playing, he switched off the stereo when he retrieved his briefcase from the great room. Seated at his desk in the study, he spread the contents of the briefcase over the tooled red leather and set to work. In addition to the title, he had drawn up a list of seven points he wished to make in his paper. He began by rereading them.

From the moment he had entered the room, a vague sense of change had been nibbling away at his subconscious. There was something about the study that was different; different from the other rooms, different from the way it usually was. He lifted his eyes from the seven points and looked uneasily about without knowing why. Immersed again in his seven points, he soon found himself trying to name all the seven dwarfs. Doc, Dopey, Sneezy . . . He scribbled their names on the margin of his paper. Bashful . . . He began to hum "Whistle While You Work" and tried to remember the other names.

A drop of moisture fell on the paper and spread out in a fuzzy sunburst. He looked at the ceiling expecting to see a water stain and felt a trickle of saliva run down the corner of his mouth. Leaping to his feet, he knocked the chair behind him out of the way and charged across the room, arms crossed over his face. As he went through one of the tall windows, he took the draperies with him.

The ground came up with a blow that drove all the air from his lungs. Facedown in the newly manured east flowerbed, he fought for air and tried to divest himself of the tangled drapes that held him. In his struggle, he managed to roll onto his side and soon got hold of a good healthy breath. Heart hammering, chest heaving, he had no thoughts beyond his need for air, and he lay there for nearly two minutes, till the strobe lights behind his eyes quit flashing. Then he worked himself free of the drapes and got to his feet.

He patted the dirt from his clothes and combed the debris from his beard with his fingers. In the light from the study, he looked at the shards of glass on the ground around him without comprehension. How did the glass get there? For that matter, how did *he* get there? Dazed and confused, he ran a finger over the splintered remains of his study window. At that moment, the immediate past had never been.

But soon his mind, accustomed to years of sorting and cataloging, put itself in order and he remembered. He had realized what was happening to him and had crashed through the window to escape before the final symptoms appeared. Somehow, the Escadrille toxin had found its way into his home. . . . No, that wasn't exactly true . . . into his *study* was more correct. He had been all through the house earlier and had no symptoms until entering the study. He recalled now how uneasy he had felt just before the symptoms began. What was it that had made him feel that way?

Favoring his left leg, he went to the garage and let himself in through a side door. With all that had been on his mind lately, he had not returned any of the equipment he had gathered for testing the Escadrille. Consequently, his respirator was right where he had left it. Protected by it, he went into the house through the kitchen.

From the study doorway, he scanned the room. Only the shattered window to the right of his world globe on its gleaming oak stand seemed out of place. The hunting prints on the oak overmantle hung as straight as ever, the spines of the books behind the glass doors of his towering oak bookcase were still perfectly aligned, and the . . . He cocked his head to one side.

Inside the mask, each breath was transformed to an alien hiss that resounded in his ears; but between breaths, he heard something. He suspended his breathing and listened, then turned and listened again. When he could hold it no more, his breath escaped into the mask in a rush that blocked out all other sounds. But he had heard enough. Unlike the other rooms in the house where the central air conditioner produced a steady hiss much like his own exhalation into the mask, here in the study the sound was pitched higher, almost a whistle.

The vent, which delivered hot air in the winter and cool air in the summer, was above and to the left of the hunting prints, just under the crown mold at the ceiling. By standing on his movable library stairs, he could easily reach the vent but could not see into it.

He left the room briefly and returned with a long screwdriver with which he removed the screws holding the vent in place. Inside the mask, his face was flushed with exertion and he was breathing heavily. A fog was beginning to build up on the mask's faceplate.

Using the screwdriver as a lever, he pried first on one side of the vent and then the other. When it seemed loose enough, he pocketed the screwdriver and worked the vent with his hands. One side and then the other, back and forth, back and forth. A final impatient tug and it came off so easily that he nearly went over backward. With the screwdriver, he probed the ductwork and felt the tip hit something soft. Two quick rachetlike movements of his wrist brought the edge of a piece of blue terry cloth into view.

He put the screwdriver in his back pocket and got hold of the cloth with his fingers. It seemed oddly heavy when he pulled on it and as it slid out of the duct, something hard fell from its folds, bounced off his foot, and hit the carpet. Descending from the stairs, he bent down and retrieved the object—a black egg-shaped stone worn so smooth it felt like it had been honed and polished. A cross within a circle had been scratched on one side.

His thoughts turned to the blue towel in his other hand. He felt certain this was the cause of his symptoms. Since the mice obtained for the experiments on the Hollins car were also still in the garage, he was able to verify that feeling very quickly. Someone did not want the investigation of the toxic Escadrilles to continue. The realization that a prowler had entered his home and made an attempt on his life affected him in a curious way. He was, at once, angry and excited. How dare they walk across his carpets and touch his things without permission! It was contemptuous. At the same time, he found the danger stimulating. He sealed the toxic towel in one of the five-gallon cans in the garage and went into the kitchen.

But why the stone? He took it from his pocket and turned it over and over in his hand, then thought, What am I doin'? He put it down on the kitchen counter, knowing he had probably already ruined any prints that might have been on it.

Suddenly he recalled Grandma O's story about suicides and stones and finally the phrase she had used . . . how did it go? "Beware the songs you loved in youth," sank in. The story of the man hanged long ago in a public execution . . . what was his name . . . Albair Fauquel. Could there be some connection? Was someone trying to make it appear as though the Fauquel prophecy was coming to pass? But to what end? And how were they able to develop a toxin to fit the story?

Mentally sifting recent events and testing them for relevance, he thought of what Kit had told him that afternoon about nearly being electrocuted. He had thought at the time it was an unusual set of circumstances. Now he believed it was more than that and he dialed her number. She answered on the first ring. Five minutes later, without making any attempt to cover the damaged window, he was on his way to see for himself the appliance that had so conveniently sprung a leak and developed a frayed cord at the same time.

The T-bird slipped through the night air like a phantom and its gears meshed with liquid precision, sensations he ordinarily prized as highly as the pungent gumbo Grandma O occasionally sent his way. Tonight, they went unnoticed.

As she opened the door to him, Kit said, "I'm not clear on exactly what . . ." When she saw the tendrils of ruptured blood vessels in his eyes, her mouth gaped. "Gawd, are your eyes ever bloodshot. What have you been doing?"

He brushed past her. "Time for that later. Right now I want to see your refrigerator." In the kitchen, he dropped to his knees and squinted at the leveling legs on the fridge. "These were up on rubber supports of some sort the other night?"

She knelt beside him. "Yes, why?"

He didn't answer but instead began crawling around the room, looking along the baseboard and under the cabinets, accompanied by Lucky who kept trying to push his wet nose into the old pathologist's hand. Presently Broussard pressed his index finger against the floor where the kitchen door molding met the wall, then tried to get up using only one hand, an act requiring Kit's help. Breathing heavily, he placed his hand, palm up, on the kitchen counter and gave her his penlight. "Shine this on my finger," he panted. From his pants pocket, he produced a small magnifying glass and began to study the end of his finger through it. "More light," he said.

Kit moved the light closer. He turned his finger from side to side and his alarming respiratory sounds gave way to satisfied pathologist noises.

He offered her the glass. "Take a look."

They traded tools and she bent over his finger eager to see what he had found. "Looks like salt," she said, seeing the geometric crystals that littered the hills and valleys of his fingerprints.

"There's a ring of these crystals around the entire room. I don't suppose you recently dropped a box of salt in here?"

"No."

He nodded wisely. "You said the power cord on the refrigerator was damaged. Has it been repaired?"

"They replaced it today."

He peeked into the grocery bag she had been using as a wastebasket and with a grunt of satisfaction, pulled out the damaged cord. After examining the plug with his naked eye and the missing insulation with his pocket magnifier, he said, "Have you got a flashlight?"

Proudly, Kit produced her new flashlight and Broussard went out the back door with it, where he played the beam around the small cement stoop. Abruptly, he brought the beam to a halt and asked for a saucer. When she brought it, he had her hold the light while he teased a smooth stone into the saucer with the back of one finger. Inside, he didn't even have to turn it over to see the cross and the circle etched on one side.

"Just like mine," he said.

Bewildered, Kit replied, "What do you mean, 'just like yours'?"

He led her into the living room, sat her down, and explained what had actually taken place in her kitchen. ". . . your refrigerator up on insulating casters, the fact that someone added salt to the water on your kitchen floor to make it a better conductor, and razor cuts that exposed only the hot wire on the old power cord show that your adventure the other night was no accident." He then related his own experience earlier and told her Grandma O's tale.

"Jesus," she said when he finished. "Sounds like someone is trying to act out that story. You don't think Bubba or his grandmother . . ."

Broussard shook his head. "Absolutely not. He's the most guileless man I ever met and I've known him and Grandma O for years. I guarantee you they've got nothin' to do with this."

"That leaves Bert Weston, the guy at Crescent City Industries. He lied when I interviewed him and it's pretty clear that the toxic fabric in the Escadrille in your garage was manufactured by his company. Maybe he's trying to cloud the issue with this Fauquel thing so he won't get sued for the deaths those cars caused."

"I thought he assumed control of CCI *after* North American Motors quit makin' Escadrilles. I hardly think he could be held liable after the fact. And if he isn't liable, why would he want our investigation stopped?"

"Maybe he took over after the fact and maybe he didn't. For all I know, he lied about that, too."

"You think he's capable of murder?"

"You should have seen his face when he told me he'd do whatever was necessary to keep his company profitable."

"He said that? Those exact words?"

"Not verbatim. But it's close."

"I'm goin' to talk with Phillip and see if I can get a tail put on Weston. And I think I'll suggest that he let him know he's bein' watched. That should put a crimp in any future shenanigans he might feel like initiatin' when he discovers the first ones didn't work."

Kit frowned. "You sure you want to put this in Phillip's hands?"

"Maybe not. I'll talk to him and then decide. In the meantime, want to spend the night at my place? I've got plenty of room."

The thought of being left alone was not a pleasant prospect, but neither was playing the frightened female. With definite misgivings, she said, "No thanks. I'll be okay."

"You're sure? It'll be no trouble."

"I'm sure."

"I'll get the patrol car for this area to keep an eye on you tonight."

"Thanks."

"You got somethin' to put that stone in so I can take it to Phillip without smearin' any prints that might be on it?"

With the stone safely secured in a small snap-top freezer container in one hand and his other on the doorknob, Broussard paused. "By the way. I've got to be in Hammond all mornin' tomorrow. Vogel's forty-eight hours will be up at five-thirty and I think you ought to drop by his lab sometime before noon and let him know how anxious we are for his results and how disappointed we'll be if they're not ready on time."

After shutting the door behind him, Kit found herself wishing this was not the eighties and that women could admit they were afraid without concern for their image. With Lucky in her lap and her big overstuffed wing chair enveloping her in its protective embrace, she turned to page forty-two in

Understanding Electricity: A Primer for Every Homeowner and tried to get back into it. Finding that her mind would rather dwell on shadows in the night, she put the book down, placed Lucky on the carpet, and went to the telephone, thinking she might ask David to come over and spend the night. But when she thought about how helpless that would make her look and how David might use it to pressure her about moving in with him, she hesitated.

Relax, she told herself. The attempt on her life and on Broussard's had been indirect and sneaky. Nobody was going to attack her in her own home. That just wasn't Weston's style. Just the same, she was *not* going to let herself fall asleep.

Had she not had the TV on earlier and therefore knew it to be safe, she would not have turned it on now with her bare fingers. With Lucky in her lap, the late show came and went, followed by another of those endless Godzilla things that she watched with little interest until nodding off.

Phil Gatlin lived in Kenner on a winding street lined by modest little homes that tried unsuccessfully to disguise their kinship to each other by insignificant architectural variations. In their long friendship, Broussard had never been inside the Gatlin house and had spoken barely a dozen words to Mrs. Gatlin, a raw-boned woman with sharp disapproving eyes. And while Gatlin often spoke of his daughter Shelby, Mrs. Gatlin (Broussard wasn't even sure of her first name) might never have existed at all.

Phillip answered the door dressed in a robe. One side of his face looked like he had been lying on a tennis racket.

"C'mon in," he said. Then with his back turned, leading the way from the cramped foyer, said, "You look like hell."

The living room was lit by a single floor lamp, a spindly creation with its brass pole threaded through a circular wooden table. Within the feeble light the room was orderly, but on the dim fringes, newspapers and magazines littered the carpet. Phillip waved his guest to an early-American sofa that looked as limp as its owner. Fearing that the sofa wasn't up to the job, Broussard went to an armchair with a shallow firm seat.

Phillip dropped into the sofa, folded his arms, and looked at his slippered feet stretched out in front of him. "Andy, I'd like to offer you somethin' but I . . . that is we . . . you caught us with a bare cupboard. We been eating out a lot lately. . . . You know . . . hardly worth cooking for only two people."

"No apologies necessary, Phillip. This is more business than social. I need your help. A few hours ago, someone tried to kill me."

"Kill you? Come on, who'd want to do that?"

Disappointed in Phillip's reaction, Broussard pressed on, telling of the recent increase in murder-suicides, its relationship to Escadrilles, and the organic explanation for the symptoms. The more he talked, the less wilted Phillip looked. He described his own close call and Kit's experience with the shorted-out refrigerator, then related Grandma O's story and gave him Kit's stone. He finished by naming their number-one suspect. ". . . so what I need now is for someone to catch the responsible party and put him away before he scores. So far, he's battin' zero. I don't want to give him a chance to better that record. I want the best detective I ever knew workin' on this. I want the old Phillip. The one we've all seen lately might get me killed. It's up to you. Give me the best that's in you and I'll be satisfied. If you can't do that, I'll get it assigned to Ed Hilton." It was a lie of course. He would never have put his life in the hands of the police chief's incompetent nephew.

The suggestion that Ed Hilton was preferable to the current Phil Gatlin in a life-threatening situation had its desired effect and Phillip stiffened as though the sharp end of one of the sofa's springs had worked its way through his robe. His eyes, which earlier had all the luster of those on a manikin, were now active and bright. He sat up straight, smoothed the lapels on his robe, and ran a palm over his rumpled hair.

"You forget about anyone else," he said. "This is *my* case. I'll be out first thing tomorrow to take a look around. Unless you'd like me to come now and help you close up that window."

A warm feeling spread through Broussard's tired body. "Appreciate the thought, but I can manage. I've got to be in Hammond early, so I may not be there when you arrive. I'll put a key . . ."

"You got deadbolts on the doors?" Phillip interrupted.

"No."

Phillip shook his head. "Andy, you know better than that. Get some installed. If you'd had them, your visitor probably wouldn't have gotten in. Never mind the key. If I need to get inside, I'll do it the way he did. Where you spending the night?"

"Home." Then responding to Phillip's critical expression, he added, "Don't worry about that. He won't know for awhile that he failed. Oh, before I forget, would you arrange for a patrol car to keep an eye on Dr. Franklyn's place tonight. She wanted to stay there and its been long enough for *that* failure to be noticed."

After Broussard left, Phillip called the west precinct, then ironed a shirt and shined his shoes.

With his eyes fixed on the white center line flashing by, Broussard took pleasure in the knowledge that some good was going to come out of a bad situation. If what he had already endured was all it was going to cost to get Phillip straightened out, it was a bargain.

He was due in Hammond the following day at 9 A.M. to testify in a murder trial. The fifty-mile drive would require that he leave no later than eight. There would not be time in the morning to get the broken window covered.

When he got home, he went to the kitchen telephone and called Bubba. While waiting for him to arrive, he put on his respirator and opened all the study windows to air the place out. By the time Bubba's old Ford pickup came up the drive with a sheet of plywood and Bubba's tools in the back, the room was safe.

Broussard met him at the truck and took him around to the destroyed window.

"Whooee! What da devil you been doin'?" Bubba said, clapping both hands to the orange Pennzoil cap perched on his head. "Somethin' explode in dere?"

"You get that plywood nailed up and we'll talk. I'll put on some coffee."

With the damaged window secured, Broussard set a cup of chicory-laced coffee in front of Bubba and brought him up-to-date. Then he showed him the stone that had been on the table the whole time under an upside-down coffee cup. The sight brought Bubba out of his chair, a reaction that Broussard was sure was genuine.

"Don't worry my friend," Broussard said, "It's not Monsieur Fauquel come back to make good on his threat."

"Den what is it?"

"Right now I can only tell you what it *isn't*."

"Please don' take dis personally, but Ah'm gonna use some of ma vacation time and stay out on da bayou till you do know what it is. Why don' you come, too. Jus' for awhile till we see if somethin's about to happen."

"I can't do that. I've got responsibilities here."

"It'd be better if you come with me, but since you won't, at least you got Gramma O's luck ball to protec' you. Hadn' a been for that, you might not have figured out somethin' was wrong in time to save yourself."

Broussard nodded noncommittally and wished he could admit to Bubba that he had thrown the ball away days ago. It was not luck that had saved him, it was his own quick wits. But to say anything was to risk hurting Grandma O's feelings. Still, it would have been good for Bubba to see that the ball couldn't have anything to do with his escape.

In the garage, Princess lay on her belly trying to retrieve

her newest toy, a vinyl bag with a drawstring, from under the garden tiller where she had batted it. Catching the drawstring in her claws, she pulled the bag out in the open and picked it up with her teeth. Holding it firmly, she jumped to her feet and disappeared through her personal door to the outside.

Chapter 15

Phil Gatlin hitched up his pants and took a deep breath. Where Broussard's circular drive curved back toward the road, it was bordered for a short distance by a white brick wall covered with honeysuckle whose fragrance hung heavy and sweet in the morning air. The first breath was so good that he helped himself to another and marveled at how bright the flowers were in front of the house. The canopy of huge oaks that clothed most of the property served as a great natural air conditioner, and Phillip was happy to be there. Having shed the shackles of depression, he had found a new sense of optimism. He hadn't suddenly learned to live with the absence of his daughter but had become convinced she would be back unharmed, if not this week, the next.

He set off on a tour around the house, looking for footprints in the flower beds and handprints on the windows. When he came to the window that Broussard had gone through the previous night, he shook his head in wonder that his friend hadn't been badly injured by that alone. Turning to complete his circuit, something on the ground near the brick wall bordering the drive flashed the early morning sun into his eyes. The object lay under a small flowering tree whose upper branches he had admired earlier from the opposite side of the wall.

When he reached the spot, he dropped on his haunches and

saw that it was a piece of red plastic, smooth on one side, textured on the other. The tree nearby had many trunks growing from a common base. Some of them had been cut off and their ends sealed with black paint. On one stump, which jutted out almost horizontally, the paint was scuffed and raw wood showed through. Looking back the way he had come, Phillip saw faint evidence of tire tracks.

With a twig, he flipped the piece of plastic into a zip-top Baggie and placed it in his jacket pocket. As he stepped from behind the wall, the front door opened and Broussard emerged rump first, briefcase in one hand, suit coat pinched under his armpit while he locked the door.

"Halloo, Phillip," Broussard said, spotting his friend. "Never thought I'd see *you* this early."

Phillip pulled the Baggie from his pocket and they met at the foot of the front steps. "Found this next to the tree behind that wall." He held the bag up for Broussard to see.

"Looks like plastic from a taillight."

"Yeah, broken on a low branch on that watchamacallit tree back there."

"Crape Myrtle."

"What?"

"The tree. It's a Crape Myrtle."

"Oh, right. Guess these're not from any of your cars then?" Broussard shook his head. "No."

"How about a gardener's car or truck?"

Broussard thought for a moment about Bubba's truck, but that had been left in the driveway while Bubba fixed the window. "Couldn't have been the gardener. He drives an old Chevy pickup that's had broken-out taillights for years. Besides, he knows not to be drivin' over the property."

"Did it rain out here Monday?"

"Like to wash me away. That's a good point. No mud spatters on the fragment . . ."

"Means it's pretty recent."

"That's another reason it didn't come from the gardener. He hasn't been here since the rain."

Phillip jiggled the fragment up and down. "I think your would-be assassin left it."

"Kind of amateurish thing to do."

"Probably didn't even feel it happen. Guess I'll go on over to Crescent City Industries a little later and see if Bert Weston has a busted taillight. How long you gonna be gone?"

"Be back sometime this afternoon. Hard to say for sure when. You know how trials go."

"Don't I though. But then, that's why you make the big monoy."

Despite the gravity of the situation, Broussard grinned, not at the joke but at what it told him about Phillip. He fumbled in his pocket for a lemon ball. "I've got to hit the road," he said, slipping the candy between his cheek and gum. "Good huntin'."

Kit woke at seven-fifteen to a stiff neck and the sound of Willard Scott saying how hot it was going to be again today in the southeast. Her first clear thought was that perhaps it had been a hired killer and not Bert Weston himself who had rigged her refrigerator and Broussard's air conditioning. If so, that would mean the police could follow Weston till their tongues touched their shoes and it wouldn't have the slightest effect on a contract that had already been let. Suddenly she wanted the whole thing over. Once it was announced to the press and there was all that publicity, there would be no point in killing anybody.

There had been only one response to her ad for Lucky and that was from a woman who thought Kit wanted to *buy* a dog with Lucky's description. The little animal was now too rambunctious to be left alone indoors, so she took him to a nearby vet and arranged to board him there until she could figure out what to do with him. She should have just handed him to the girl and left without looking back instead of following her to see where he would be kept. The cage was terribly small for such an active dog and he looked *so* sad there behind the bars. As she walked to her car, she couldn't forget

172 / D. J. DONALDSON

the hurt in his liquid eyes. No! She couldn't *keep* a dog, didn't *want* a dog.

At the hospital, she went first to the Biomedical Photography division, viewed and accepted the film of the mouse experiments they had put together, and returned to her office with it. A few minutes later, Broussard called from Hammond to tell her not to worry about anything, that Phillip was not only already at work on their case but was certainly back in form. He reminded her to nudge Vogel, then hung up before she could convey her doubts about the usefulness of any detective's services. So that everything would be in order for an announcement of their findings, she spent the next hour drafting and polishing a press release, planning to add Vogel's data later. Then she set out for the Justice Center.

As Phil Gatlin put his hand on the doorknob of Gil Bertram's lab in forensics, he was pretty sure he knew what Bertram would say. After finding no damage on Bert Weston's car in the CCI parking lot, he had checked with motor vehicles to see whether they had any other car registered to Weston and found they didn't. In almost any other circumstances, he would not have confronted Weston this early in the investigation but would have watched from the fringes of the man's life, waiting for him to do something meaningful. But this was different. Two lives were being threatened and he had agreed with Broussard's suggestion that he show himself now to throw a little scare into the suspect. In fact, Weston had acted more angry than scared, demanding to know why his whereabouts for the last three days were being questioned. Having shown himself to Weston was going to make things more difficult than they already were. All he had to work with was a piece of taillight and the stone Broussard had given him. The faint hope he had held for the stone had been dashed when no prints were found on it. And he *never* had any illusions about the usefulness of the taillight fragment. Still, he had to give Bertram a shot.

The lights in the lab were out and Bertram was hovering over a sheet of plate glass set up on cement blocks. He was concentrating so much on aligning a headlamp fragment in the beam of the fiber-optic light source hanging from the ceiling that he didn't hear Phillip enter.

"Interesting case?" Phillip inquired.

Bertram stepped on a floor switch and the lights came on. "Hey, Phillip. You know me. I think they're all interesting." He slid his thumb and index finger down his mustache as though he was afraid it was coming off. "What brings you to these hallowed halls?"

Phillip produced the Baggie. "What can you tell me about this?"

Bertram's long veined fingers put a jeweler's loop in his eye, and he briefly examined both surfaces of the fragment in the bag. Shaking his head, he handed it back. "Plastic is a lot like glass, give me two pieces and I can tell you if they came from the same object, providing the original wasn't too big. But as far as telling you anything useful about the origin . . . What can I say . . . a taillight from any of a dozen different makes. There's just too many common suppliers of components these days to draw meaningful conclusions from something like this. Get me a piece of plastic from a suspect's car to go with it and I'll be able to do something."

While one elevator took Phillip to the squad room on the eighth floor, Kit stepped from its companion into the hallway in forensics. When she arrived at Vogel's lab, the place was empty. A beaker bubbling over a Bunsen-burner flame said he would soon return. The main lab was a long rectangle that ran parallel to the hall. Nearby, on a bench against the wall to her right, three lamps were trained on a Plexiglas chamber that held a small piece of unfamiliar fabric resting on a Plexiglas cylinder. The chamber was connected by a rubber hose to a pump that filled the room with a rhythmic asthmatic wheeze.

At the far end of the lab, there was an open doorway

between a double sink and a stand-up workbench. Thinking that Al might be in the adjoining room, she called his name but got no response. As she wandered in that direction, she saw the thermos she had given him the previous day sitting on the sink drainboard. It had to be Broussard's thermos because it was the same olive green and still bore the red tape Al had wrapped around it.

Since he had taken the trouble of resealing the thermos, she surmised that Al must have used only a portion of the contents in whatever tests he was running and that the remaining pieces were still inside. But when she got closer, she noticed something odd. When he had taken the thermos from her the previous day, he had sealed it *before* writing "Danger, Do Not Open," on it with a felt-tip marker. He had scrawled the warning hurriedly and the tail of the "g" in "danger" and the lower part of the "p" in "open" had run off the tape onto the thermos. Now, presumably after having been opened at least once, here was the tape positioned exactly as it had been originally, with the parts of the "g" and "p" on the thermos perfectly aligned with the parts on the tape.

This could mean only one thing. With only a few hours left before he was to make his report, Al had not yet opened the thermos.

Confused, Kit wandered about the lab, her senses sharpened. Against the back wall was a low bench that Al was using as a desk. On it was a technical journal lying on its back, its pages open. When she got closer, she saw something so startling, she could scarcely breathe.

Nestled in the groove between the open pages was a pen . . . a pen with BANK OF SPECULATOR written down the side in white letters. Vogel must have been in her home! *He* had been the one that rigged her refrigerator! But why?

The pump that had been wheezing away suddenly stopped and Kit froze, the pen still in her hand. She turned and her saliva suddenly tasted like brass. There, standing by the pump, was Vogel. He reached over and turned off the Bunsen burner.

She took the opportunity to reach behind her and put the pen back on the desk.

"Didn't expect to see you until later," Vogel said. "I've still got seven hours before my report is due and it'll take at least that long to finish."

"Of course," Kit said. "My morning was rather light and I was passing by anyway . . ." Christ, I'm rambling, she thought. She wanted desperately to run her tongue over her lips, which suddenly felt dry and cracked, but feared that it would look like a nervous gesture. The taste in her mouth seemed to be getting worse and her hands fluttered about, looking for a natural position. She pulled at her dress and stopped talking, not at all sure she had expressed anything coherent.

Vogel moved toward her. "Go back to your office. I'll call you when the tests are complete."

Liar! Kit thought. "I wasn't trying to hurry you, just got curious is all." She made a big show of looking at her watch. Jesus, what a bush move. "God, look at the time, I'm late for an appointment." Even as she said it, she remembered telling him a few seconds earlier that she had a light morning. "Talk to you later."

When she had gone, Vogel leaned into the hall and his eyes followed her to the elevators. As she stepped inside and turned around, he pulled his head back and softly shut the door. Why had she been so nervous? He went to his desk, then moved through the lab looking and checking, touching everything. His eyes came to rest on the thermos. Instinctively, he studied it until he realized what Kit had seen. He began to pace. He thought, Why now, just when things were coming to a head, did this have to happen? It shouldn't have worked out this way. So many things gone wrong. And none of them my fault. Up and down the aisle he went, thoughts whirling through his head. Broussard and Franklyn should be dead. But no, that'd be too easy.

As he steamed past his desk chair, he caught it with the toe of his right shoe and kicked it into his path, where he struck it hard with his knees. He let loose an animal cry, more of frustration than pain, and sent the chair spinning against the far wall with his foot. Rubbing his knees, he tried to imagine himself in Kit's place. What would she do now? . . . Tell Broussard, of course. He flipped through his Rolodex. To the woman who answered the phone, he said, "Is Broussard there?"

"I'm sorry," she replied in a coldly official way that made it clear she wasn't at all sorry. "He's in Hammond this morning. May I give him a message?"

His lips curled in a feral grin. "When will he be back?"

"Probably not until late this afternoon. May I tell him who called?"

He hung up without answering, his mind already at work on a solution.

While Kit walked briskly from the Justice Center to the hospital, she reflected on what had just happened. The fact that Vogel had not even *begun* any tests on the fabric samples was a shock, but not nearly as big as the jolt she'd received when she saw her pen on his desk.

"Yes, he *did* leave a Hammond number in case of an emergency," Broussard's secretary said. "Would you like for me to try it?"

"Please." But before the other woman had completed the call, Kit said, "Never mind." There was nothing Broussard could do from Hammond. Phil Gatlin was the one she should be calling. "I'll just wait until he gets back," she explained.

In her office, she pulled out the phone book and looked up the number of the VC squad.

Chapter 16

Phil Gatlin was at his desk. Avis had just told him that no one named Weston had rented a car in the last week, nor had any recently been returned with a broken taillight. He ran his finger under the number for Budget Rent-a-Car, fixed the number in his memory, and was reaching for the phone when it rang.

Even though he had spent the greater part of his life uncovering hidden vices in outwardly respectable people, Gatlin was shocked at what Kit told him. Vogel? It seemed unlikely. Why would he want to harm Andy and Kit? But apparently he *had* been in her house uninvited. It was something that had to be looked into.

Berta in the parking office always talked into the receiver as though she was shouting out a window, a fact he remembered only after she had nearly broken his eardrum identifying herself. He asked her for the number of Vogel's parking space, then held the phone a foot from his ear while she answered.

The parking lot was a black asphalt inferno radiating heat waves that made the rows of cars look like the picture on a failing TV. By the time he reached space sixty-four, the moles on his back could be seen through his wet shirt. There was a white Cutlass with undamaged taillights in the space. A receipt in the glove compartment for a lube and oil change was made out to Vogel.

Back in his office, he learned from motor vehicles that in addition to the Cutlass, Vogel also owned a black Ford Galaxie. Next to Vogel's name in the phone book was a Chartres Street address not five minutes away.

The vinyl seats on his own car seared the backs of his legs, and he had to wait for the air conditioner to cool the steering wheel before he could touch it. Thank God it was not his turn for night duty. After such a scorcher, the blood would flow in the city's bars as freely as the beer.

At the Chartres Street address, he paused, pulled to a stop, and studied the structure on the opposite side of the street. Not much to look at, he thought. Or rather, not much to see. In typical New Orleans tradition, the exterior of the three-story house with its gray cypress board-and-batten siding and shuttered windows wouldn't give a passerby cause for even a glance . . . the kind of house you could pass every day and never miss if someone moved it one night.

Behind him, he heard the steady blare of a car horn. In the rearview mirror, an old lady with an immense wattle was pointing at the driveway he was blocking. Since he'd seen enough from this angle, he eased around the corner and kept his eye out for the alley. At its mouth, he pulled carefully past a garbage can that had been tipped over by a dog or a can-picker and began to count garages and yards. When he got to eight, he stopped.

The garage was much like the house—cypress board and batten, but showing signs of deterioration: battens missing, rotted places where the wood had turned black, green things growing in moist crevices. The matching fence was in even worse shape, leaning inward and outward like an abstract artwork. Legally he could not enter the yard without a search warrant. But then, he really didn't need to. His quarry would be in the garage.

Forsaking the air-conditioned comfort of his car, he went to the garage and, with his cheek against the rough wood, set one eye to exploring the interior through a battenless joint between boards. At first, he could see nothing, but as his eye dark-adapted, the dim bulk of a car took shape. The interior of the garage was illuminated only by a single dusty window in the front, and because the hole through which he was looking was small, he could only see a little of the car at a time. That was enough, though, to discover that the left taillight was disgustingly intact. To see more, he shifted to his left eye and waited the requisite time for it to grow accustomed to the gloom. Suddenly, he stood up and threw a short punch at the air. The right taillight was smashed.

He fingered the brass padlock on the hinged garage doors, looking for the manufacturer's logo. The initials R. O. G. pressed into the lock's base brought his lips up at the corners. It had been a long time since he had smiled and he was surprised at how good it felt. A Rock-of-Gibraltar lock. Christ, the guy might as well have secured the doors with a stick, he thought happily, slipping behind the wheel.

An hour and ten minutes later, he was back, a search warrant in one pocket, a petty-cash slip for $2.32 from Gravois's hardware in another. On the seat next to him was a brand new Rock-of-Gibraltar lock, still sealed in plastic. Snatching up the lock, he peeled the cardboard backing away and threw the lock into the glove compartment. It was not the lock he wanted but the key. The good old Rock-of-Gibraltar Company made very strong inexpensive locks that were impossible to pick, but they all opened with the same key.

He was soon on his knees beside the taillight. From his pocket, he produced the Baggie with the plastic fragment and tried to fit it into the part of the puzzle still attached to the car. It matched perfectly.

A mile away, Broussard's secretary relayed a call to Kit's office.

"This is Lieutenant Reynolds, state highway patrol," a voice said. "We've got a body out here at the end of the dirt road near the abandoned church on Highway 8 and Dr. Broussard would like for you to get out here as soon as possible."

She made a quick call to David, told him that she would not be able to meet him at three o'clock as they planned, explained when he asked why not, and practically ran from the office. Broussard surely would not have anything more interesting for her than she had for him.

She shifted impatiently back and forth from one foot to the other, waiting for the hospital's old elevator. When it finally arrived and the doors clattered open, an unhappy voice from within said, "Dr. Franklyn. I'd like a word with you."

It was Bert Weston, wearing a look that matched his angry tone. She stepped back, afraid to get on with him. Vogel had become her prime suspect, but that didn't mean Weston wasn't also involved. They could be working together.

He stepped off the elevator and its doors banged shut behind him.

"I'm already late for an appointment," she said.

"You'll be a little later then. This morning I spent over an hour describing my movements for the last four days to a particularly unpleasant member of the police department. From the questions he asked, it was pretty obvious his visit had something to do with you. What's going on? I saw you pumping my secretary the other day. What did you tell him?"

"That someone tried to kill me."

"And you think . . . Hey, lady. If it'd been me, you wouldn't be here now." When he realized what a stupid thing he had said, his face reddened. ". . . I didn't mean that. What I meant was, why pick me?"

"Maybe because you lied to me."

His face relaxed a bit. "Okay, I lied. But you shouldn't have taken it personally. Ever since the Health Department had me cough up twenty thousand for an emission-control system for our chimney, I lie to everybody that comes snooping around. Those questions you were asking just sounded like another kind of trouble—one that was going to end up costing us money. Sure, I lied, but I didn't try to hurt you. Believe me, I didn't. To prove it, I'll tell you whatever you want to know, right now if you like."

"Maybe later. As I said, I'm on my way somewhere and I need to get going."

He pushed the Down button. "You just call me whenever you're ready."

Weston's frontal attack had her confused. It didn't seem like the action of a guilty man, but that might have been exactly why he did it. She certainly wasn't going to get on the elevator with him. So when it arrived, she rolled her eyes toward the ceiling, snapped her fingers, and said, "Nuts, I've forgotten something. I'll catch it later." She strode purposefully to her office, where she waited until he had gone before heading for the stairs.

As Kit left the hospital parking lot and turned south, Broussard was just entering the city from the north. Because of a drawbridge that wouldn't go down after letting a Chriscraft full of sunburned men with big bellies pass, she was still ten miles from the old church when Broussard rolled into his office and found Phil Gatlin waiting.

Chapter 17

Prickling with excitement, Phillip sat across from Broussard's desk and told him how quickly things had developed since they had last spoken. Abruptly, Broussard reached for the phone.

"What's up?" Phillip said.

For a reply, he got Broussard's fat fingers waving him to silence. Not finding Kit in her office, Broussard tried her home and got only the answering machine. His secretary brought in some letters to sign. "Do you have any idea where Dr. Franklyn is?" he asked.

The woman looked over his head and sorted through her day. "She was here about ten o'clock, so anxious to talk to you that we nearly tried to reach you in Hammond," she said. "That's the last time I saw her." She turned to go, then pivoted on one heel. "Just remembered. I transferred a call to her about thirty minutes ago, so you didn't miss her by much." Her face clouded over. "She usually keeps me pretty well posted on her whereabouts. Maybe, she's at lunch." Looking at her watch, she added, "Kind of late, though, for that, wouldn't you think?"

A chill started at the nape of Broussard's neck and ran down his spine. On impulse, he dialed Vogel's lab in the Justice Center. Each unanswered ring was a Highlighter drawn through his fears. He banged the phone down.

Gatlin saw the worry in his eyes. "Who'd you call?"

"Vogel. He's not around, either."

"I don't like *that*."

Broussard lugged out the phone book and flipped to the blue pages where state offices were listed. A few seconds later, at the other end of the line, a pleasant female voice said, "David Andropoulas? One moment, please."

The half-dozen bars of canned harp music that followed seemed in poor taste considering the possibilities. He didn't wait for David to say anything but started talking as soon as he heard him pick up. "David, this is Andy Broussard. Do you know where we could find Kit?"

"I thought she was with you."

The chill came back. "What made you think so?"

"She was going to help me pick out some new carpeting for my condo, but a half hour ago, she called and said she couldn't make it. Said she had to meet *you* somewhere."

"She say where?"

There was a pause and Broussard winced in anticipation of a useless answer. "Highway . . . Eight," David said. ". . . near the old church, I think. What's the . . ."

The receiver bounced off the cradle and fell onto the desk, but Broussard was in too big a hurry to worry about it. "Come on, Phillip. I know where she is."

They didn't wait for the elevator but took the stairs instead, Broussard in the lead. "Vogel has lured her to a deserted spot near the old church on Highway Eight," he said, his flushed cheeks bouncing in time with his belly.

"We'll take my car and radio the state police," Gatlin said. "They may already have men in the area."

Phillip left a dollar's worth of taxpayer rubber on the street in front of the hospital and made a U-turn in front of an old man whose glasses flew off and fell in his lap when he hit the brakes to avoid being hit. Producing a red light from under the seat, Phillip set it turning and put it up on the dash, next to his plastic statue of Saint Christopher. Broussard greatly admired the way Phillip maneuvered the car in and out of traffic with one hand while working the shortwave with the other, but that didn't stop him from hooking up his seat belt.

The drawbridge that had delayed Kit for so long had finally come down. Now, ten miles beyond the bridge, the road was flanked on the left by a swamp twelve miles long and four miles wide. Looking at the gaunt cypress trees that stood as sentinels in its shallow water, Kit found it a place of ominous beauty, something nice to look at from a distance but nothing she wanted to see any closer. Over the tops of the willows on the opposite side of the road, a church steeple appeared, and Kit turned her attention from the swamp to the search for an unpaved road. The church was a red-brick building with all its windows shattered and too little of the gold lettering left on the portico for her to identify the denomination. She passed it and went on for nearly two miles before pulling to a stop. Where was that road?

Slowly, she returned the way she had come, this time alert for a break in the tall grass and cattails on the swamp side. Two hundred yards beyond the church, she found one and turned in, going only far enough to get fully off the road. Ahead of her, little more than a path barely wide enough for a car twisted and turned away into the grass, which obscured any view of what lay ahead. On each side of the path, she could see patches of duckweed and black water showing through the grass. Once committed, it would be impossible to turn around.

She rolled her window down to listen for voices that would tell her this was the place. Hot air rich with pungent odors of decaying vegetation rolled thickly into the car. She listened and heard the snapping sounds of grasshoppers springing from one grass stalk to another. Something unseen buzzed close to her ear. She heard the liquid warble of a bird and off in the distance, a muffled splash. But no voices. She was hoping for the crackle of a car radio, a shout, or maybe snatches of conversation. Then, she could proceed without concern. But there were only animal sounds: grasshoppers and birds, buzzing insects and an occasional fish cracking an open patch of water with his tail.

It was the absence of frog noises more than anything that was making her uneasy. She thought about climbing up on the car to try and see over the grass but decided against it after picturing what that might do to the roof. Figuring that even a wrong decision was better than no decision, she traded the brake for the gas and proceeded slowly into the swamp.

The path was so full of turns, she could see ahead for only a few feet at a time. Then it straightened and she saw that it went up into a stand of cypress a city block away. Well before she got that far, she came upon a wide ditch full of black water and duckweed. Damn! This wasn't the right place after all. Now she would have to *back* out, and she was terrible at it.

She put the car in reverse and gave it a little gas. As she did, there was a sharp crack and the car slumped to one side. Even without looking, she knew a tire was gone. Not recognizing the sound she'd heard as a gunshot, she got out to deal with the problem. The tire was as flat as she feared and she damned and kicked it. Having never used it, she began to wonder how the jack worked. It was only a skipped heartbeat from there to wondering whether there even *was* a jack.

Perched on a knot of roots behind a big cypress, Vogel had her shapely neck in his sights. His heart was still thumping from the effort of poling his old pirogue through the grassy swamp. Sweat matted his hair and ran in erratic paths down his cheeks and onto his neck. It dripped off his nose and was inhaled as his chest heaved against his wet shirt in a fight for the heavy swamp air that seemed devoid of oxygen. Anyone else would have also had to contend with the vicious mosquitoes that protected the glory holes in the area from the local fishermen, but for some reason, he was not to their liking. He drew his index finger slowly toward his face and tried to relax.

The bullet shattered the Nissan's left-rear window and for a moment, Kit stood rooted in confusion. Then she dropped to her belly and crawled to the other side of the car. Now it was clear to her: the bogus phone call, the freshly dug ditch. And she was pretty sure who was behind it. "Vogel, don't do this," she called out.

Hearing his name ring openly through the swamp, Vogel felt like a snake whose rock had been turned over. He licked his lips and looked nervously about him.

"Vogel. Can you hear me?"

His name again. But what did it matter? There was no one to hear her and she was trapped. If he just followed through, this would end as he had planned.

Kit searched for her next words, wondering how to reason with someone who is trying to kill you when you don't even know why. She looked behind her, thinking she might escape into the grass, but saw the head of a turtle or a snake staring at her from the water. A turtle she could deal with, but not a snake.

Vogel realized that if he didn't move in, she could just stay put and they would be here forever. He stepped into the water.

She could see him now. "Why are you doing this? If you're going to kill me, surely I have the right to know why," Kit shouted.

"The only rights anyone has are the ones he can force people to grant him," Vogel shouted back.

"It has to do with the fabric we brought you, doesn't it?"

"It might."

"Having worked in forensics, you must realize you'll be caught."

"That's exactly why I *won't* be caught. It takes a body to prove murder and yours is going into a bottomless muckhole a short way from here. So what if your car is found with a few bullets in it? Rifling marks can be matched to a gun only if they find the gun and this one is going into the muck along with you."

She had no real hopes of talking him into throwing his rifle down, but she was simply buying time until she could think of a way out. And it was working . . . at least for now. Since she had called his name, he had not moved. She glanced back the way she had come. Sure, when you need the path to twist and turn, it was open and straight. He could drop her before she got ten steps. Behind her, the dark water swirled as something came near the surface and returned to the bottom.

She had waited too long to reply and there was splashing from Vogel's direction. Through the grass that grew between the faint tire tracks on the path, she saw him fighting his way through the thigh-deep water and she prayed for a hole that would suck him under. But instead of falling away, the bottom rose up and the water went to his calves. She was certainly not going to just wait for him. Compared to the odds at Vogel's hands, the swamp was a far better risk.

With her first steps, the mud and rotting matter on the bottom covered her deck shoes and oozed into them. Ripples spreading across the stagnant water announced her arrival and a cloud of gnats came to pay their respects.

On the edge, the water was only as deep as her knees, but a step more and it went to her thighs and then played around the V where her legs joined. There was a dense stand of wire grass a few yards away. If she could get to it, she would at least have a chance. Surely, it could not be but a few seconds more before he was upon her.

She fanned the air with both hands to clear the gnats from her eyes. The warm water now became as much of a nemesis as the man stalking her. It held her legs in a leaden grip, holding her back. It was a nightmare as the water rose to her waist.

"Dr. Franklyn!"

Vogel's voice so close at hand caused her stomach to roll. She snatched a look over her shoulder and saw him on the bank, his cheek resting against the stock of an ugly rifle. The malevolent black mouth of the barrel seemed enormous.

"This *is* going to happen," he said. "But it's for you to decide how. Stand quietly and it'll be over quickly. Move, and it could be much more unpleasant for both of us."

She froze, not because of his words but because she simply found herself unable to move. She closed her eyes to wait for the end.

"If it's any consolation, you were just in the wrong place at the wrong time," Vogel said.

Kit was only half-aware of what he was saying. She was wondering how it felt to be shot. Would she just black out or would there be pain first? Did your brain know you were dead before you fell? Would her body ever be found? The thought of an eternity that would go on without her seemed unbelievable. There were things left undone, people she needed to see again. This couldn't be happening.

There was a sharp crack of gunfire and she felt as though the muck had suddenly fallen away from beneath her. The contents of her stomach rose hot and foul into her mouth.

Chapter 18

Either they allowed shouting in heaven, or Kit was not dead. She opened her eyes and saw Vogel racing down the road. There was another shot and he lurched to the right. The rifle slipped from his fingers, but he kept running. As Phil Gatlin sprinted past her, Vogel leaped into a hundred acres of tall grass. Kit jumped in surprise as strong fingers closed on her shoulders.

"You all right?" Broussard asked, holding her at arm's length and looking her over.

She shook her head and together they sloshed back to shore. Phillip returned, his pants soaked halfway to his knees. He held Vogel's rifle cradled in his arms.

"Sonofabitch just disappeared," he said. "But there's blood on the grass, so he's hurt."

A blue state police car pulled in behind Phillip's Pontiac, and the driver, a lean fellow with one temple of his sunglasses stuck down the neck of his sharply creased shirt, got out and walked toward them. Phillip met him halfway, badge in hand. "Gatlin, New Orleans PD," he said, pocketing his ID. "I've got a killer hiding down there in the weeds and I could use some help flushing him out."

"Just how do you plan to do that?"

"I figured we could spread out and sweep the area where he went in."

"Sweep the area, as in get in the swamp and sweep the area?"

"Can't be done from the road," Phillip said, his temper beginning to rise.

"We got no snake boots with us and there's no way we're goin' in there without boots."

Before Phillip could respond, his radio crackled, "Unit Thirty-eight, please respond. Unit Thirty-eight."

He went over to his car and put Vogel's gun in the trunk. Dropping into the front seat, he thumbed his mike. "Unit Thirty-eight, go ahead."

"Your wife asked us to relay the following message; Shelby is home. Do you copy?"

For a moment, the words he had been longing to hear didn't sink in. He sat without moving. "Do you copy, Unit Thirty-eight?"

He put the mike slowly to his lips. "I copy, Thirty-eight out." He hung the mike under the dash, moving as in a dream. But then the words took hold. Shelby was home! His baby was safe! The desire to see his daughter dwarfed all other concerns and the parent side of him saw why it was reasonable to leave.

Those knuckleheads from the state police were going to be no help, and they had a point. It *was* foolish to go crashing around in a swamp without the proper gear. He looked at his watch and blindly convinced himself that by the time he could get a properly outfitted crew in to comb the area, it would be too dark to search properly. Then too, with each minute that passed, Vogel was probably working his way deeper and deeper into the swamp. There was nothing to be accomplished by staying here. At the same time, the detective in him could not ignore one possibility.

He walked over to where the lean patrolman had gotten back into the air conditioning. At his approach, the driver lowered the car window a few inches. No sense letting all that heat in just to conduct a little police business, Phillip thought, fixing the number on the side of the car firmly in mind in case these guys refused or screwed up the favor he was about to ask.

"Boys, I need your help . . . and you won't even have to get wet." He dropped his voice so that should Vogel still be within earshot, he wouldn't hear. "This guy we're after must have a car somewhere in the area. It's a white Cutlass with Louisiana plates, 1BC388L." He rattled off Vogel's plate number after having seen it only the one time in the Justice Center parking lot. It was one of the talents that had helped him earn his nickname.

"He may head for his car and somebody should stake it out just in case. I've got urgent business in town and can't do it myself. Will you fellas cruise the area and if you find the car, keep an eye on it for awhile? He's a big fish and the collar would be something nice for your jackets."

The driver looked at his partner, who nodded and pushed his sunglasses back against the bridge of his nose with his middle finger. "Sure we'll take a look," the driver said.

"I'll get out a description in case you miss him. If you boys ever need a city favor, call me." The driver gave him a slow two-fingered salute and backed out.

As he went to where Kit and Broussard waited, Phillip was so excited and pleased that even the mud in his shoes felt pleasant. "Andy, my daughter's home. I've got to go."

Broussard clapped both hands to Gatlin's shoulders. "I'm glad, Phillip. I really am."

"Thanks, Andy, but I've got to leave." He leaned closer and whispered, "Don't worry about Vogel. We'll get him when he comes onto dry land." Then in a more normal voice, said, "Could you ride back with Dr. Franklyn, that way I . . ."

"Sure, you go on."

While Phillip was talking to the state police, Kit had begun to tremble uncontrollably. Try as she might, she couldn't stop. Now, in a quivering voice that she could not believe was her own, she said, "I'm afraid I have a flat . . . and I'm not sure I have a jack."

Despite his desire to be quit of the place, Phillip took her keys and opened her trunk. He made a point of showing her each piece of her jack as he assembled it. When he and Broussard finished changing the tire, Phillip jumped into his car and backed up the road at a furious pace. With Broussard at the wheel, the Nissan followed at a more cautious speed. Kit was still shaking and Broussard was concerned that she might be about to go into shock. As they turned onto the highway and headed for town, Kit fought the trembling and said, "How did you know where I was and that I might need help?"

"Phillip followed up on what you told him and found some evidence in Vogel's garage that proved he was at my house the night my air conditioner was rigged."

"What kind of evidence?"

"Whoever tried to do me in left part of a taillight in my garden. Phillip found the car it came from in Vogel's garage. When I couldn't find you or Vogel, I called David. He told us where you'd gone and why."

"What's the rest of the story? What does it all mean?"

Broussard shook his head. "Beats the stuffin' out of me. But I'm gettin' a real strong urge to snoop around Vogel's house myself. I'm gonna call Phillip a little later and see if he's willin' to take me over there tonight. But right now, I'm gonna get you home."

As they drove, Kit had time to reflect on what had taken place. Not only had she walked willingly into Vogel's trap but she was standing there like a chump, with her eyes closed, when help arrived. And now, here she was, shaking so badly Broussard was afraid to let her drive her own car. Some example of independence and self-sufficiency *she* was.

"If you think you're going to Vogel's without me, you're mistaken," she said abruptly.

Broussard took a quick look at her and said, "We'll talk about it later, after we get cleaned up and you have a chance to relax."

* * *

The two patrolmen quickly located Vogel's car at a boat dock two miles from where he had set his trap for Kit. They backed in behind a row of boats that were sitting upside down on sawhorses and waited for him to appear. Two hours later, as their shifts drew to a close, they drove off, believing that he did not intend to return.

After Phillip had seen for himself that his daughter was unharmed and had spent a little time with her, he was willing to leave her for awhile to comply with Broussard's request. Thus, nine o'clock found Kit, Broussard, and Phillip on Vogel's back porch.

"Not gettin' much from this flashlight," Broussard said as Phillip fiddled with the lock on Vogel's back door. As he said the words, the pale beam died completely and Phillip was left to work by touch alone. Broussard put the useless flashlight on the porch rail and waited quietly for Phillip to get them inside.

Being here was not something Kit particularly wanted to do but felt that it was something she *had* to do. By placing herself in the most intimate surroundings of the man who had come so close to taking her life, she hoped to rid herself of the fear that even now was blowing its cold breath on the back of her neck and making her legs feel like they had run a marathon.

Phillip pushed the back door open. "The department better hope I never turn burglar," he joked over his shoulder. "Wait here until I find the lights."

Phillip found the cool air inside a welcome respite from the soggy New Orleans night, but the musty smell, like old newspapers, was something he could do without. In the gloom, he saw the dim outline of a light switch and reached for it. He beckoned for the others to join him, then took a good look around.

Even now, after years of seeing that it doesn't work that way, he wanted all lawbreakers to be dirty, shiftless, and of low intelligence—people who spit on sidewalks and put a little extra in it when they fart. He was therefore disappointed to find that except for a bowl and a spoon in the sink, and a box of cereal on the counter next to the sink, there was nothing out of place. He noted with irritation that Vogel ate the same kind of high-fiber cereal he did.

There were two doors off the kitchen, both almost featureless from untold layers of paint that had built up over the years on their decorative beading. Philip felt smug in the knowledge that had *he* owned the house, those doors would have been stripped and painted properly. He wrapped his fingers around one of the painted doorknobs and gave a pull.

The door groaned open and he thumbed another light switch. "Look here," he said. He felt Broussard's soft stomach against his elbow and heard Kit's rapid breathing behind him. Here was the clutter he expected.

"A laboratory!" Kit exclaimed.

The two men went inside, where Phillip picked a beaker up off a bench that ran the length of the room and sniffed the oily contents.

"You keep that up and we might be *carryin'* you out of here," Broussard warned.

Clearly unnerved, Phillip quickly put the beaker down.

Kit waited in the doorway, her arms folded to still their quaking. On the way to Vogel's house, she had felt reasonably calm and in control. Now, in the very bosom of his existence, the shaking had returned. The image of Vogel's cold blue eyes swam before her and she could again feel swamp muck in her shoes.

Phillip went over to a fume hood and pressed all the buttons. The sound of an exhaust fan was heard and he felt the hairs on the back of his hand tingle as air was sucked from the lab into the hood. Annoyed by the sound, he turned it off.

Broussard reached into the wastebasket and pulled out a sheaf of dried foliage.

"Something meaningful?" Kit asked.

"Could be," Broussard replied. "Seems like he was only interested in the roots."

Phillip idly felt the tip of a soldering iron hanging on a clipboard with a lot of other tools and junk. Broussard's eyes locked on a calendar a few feet away on the wall over an antiquated black double sink and Kit wondered with amusement whether he was looking at the girl of the month; a big-breasted bimbo with the nozzle of a gas pump in one hand and wearing a shirt open to the waist.

He walked over and tapped the calendar where a date was circled with a red grease pencil. "Somethin' important comin' up next week," he said. "Let's have a look at the rest of this place."

Where Phillip had been their leader at first, now Broussard took over and it was he that led the small party through the other door off the kitchen.

They were now in a part of the house that appeared much older than the kitchen. Here, the ceiling loomed high over a floor laid with large wide boards, ancient with dark scars. The walls were soft, old brick with crudely mortared joints, and were dotted with second-rate landscapes in simple gilded frames. There were no carpets and the only furniture was a primitive pine dining table and a sideboard. Beside the far doorway, two coarsely carved brackets held up a rough plank on which stood a row of plain pewter cups.

"Remind me never to use his decorator," Kit said.

"Look at this," Phillip said. He was peering into the opening in a circular wall of bricks about four feet high. Joining him, Kit and Broussard saw that it was a well that went right through the floor. Light from floodlamps halfway down reflected off the red-and-white patches on a half-dozen fat Japanese Koi suspended in the crystal clear water.

"Big goldfish," Phillip muttered.

The two men moved off toward the front of the house and Kit followed. The next room was a parlor, not unlike the dining room—same high ceilings, brick walls, and planked floors. The furnishings were again sparse and simple. A pair of spindle-backed settees with thin cushions faced each other in front of a fireplace with no mantel. Over the fireplace was another rough plank, like the one in the dining room. On this one, there were two hurricane lamps and a small bronze casting of a sleeping dog. Between the settees was a low pine table. On the floor beside the fireplace, a fake Boston fern had been jammed into a black iron kettle.

"That's what I'm lookin' for," Broussard said, heading for a two-tiered pine secretary against one wall. He lowered himself into the ladder-backed chair in front of the secretary and began to open drawers.

While Phillip disappeared up the stairs that led to the next floor, Kit sat on the edge of a settee and watched Broussard paw through an accordion file. Finding nothing of interest in the file, he put it back and began to ransack the little drawers and compartments above the writing surface. After thoroughly searching them, he sat back in his chair and slapped the tops of both legs. "Nuts."

With a hand still on each leg, he saw something of interest on the floor near Kit's feet and he bent forward for a better look. He came over and kicked the rug up.

"What is it?" Kit asked.

"That floorboard's been screwed down, not nailed."

He disappeared back toward the kitchen and reappeared with a screwdriver and a broom.

Phillip came down the stairs. "Look's like Vogel's getting ready to take a long trip. There're a couple of big trunks . . ." He saw Broussard on his knees. "What are *you* doing?"

"Ruinin' my back," Broussard said, pulling on the loosened screw with his fingers. "Kit, move that table over a little, will you?"

With the table out of the way, Broussard rolled the rug back a little more and went to work on the other screw. When it was out, he forced the screwdriver under one end of the suspect board and pried it up. Phillip grabbed the raised end and pulled the board free, opening a black hole in the floor about eight inches wide and two feet long. Kit leaned over and peered into the darkness.

"Step back!' Broussard said sharply.

Puzzled, she watched Broussard put the handle of the broom in the hole and move it around. It clanked against something metallic.

Satisfied that it was safe to do so, he thrust his hand in the hole. While he was feeling around, a glistening cockroach ran up his arm and perched on his neck, its antennae probing the air. Shuddering, Kit knocked it off him and watched it disappear through a crack in the floor a few feet away. Broussard pulled his hand out. In it, Kit caught a glimpse of a metal box just before everything went black.

"Great," Phillip muttered. "And no flashlight."

With the windows tightly shuttered, they were clothed in a void where eyes were a useless luxury. In the dark, Kit's anxiety at being in Vogel's home mushroomed to outright terror. They had left Vogel in the swamp hours ago, more than enough time for him to have found his way here before they did. He might even be in the room with them now.

A floorboard creaked and fingers went around her arm. She screamed.

"It's only me," Phillip said.

Before she could scold him for frightening her, they heard a distant sound, like a marble rolling across the floor, at first faint and faraway, then louder. Disoriented by the total absence of light and confounded by the slight echo in the sparsely furnished room, Kit could not tell from which direction the sound emanated.

Relentlessly it came, slowly and steadily, closer and closer, mixed with the sound of her own ragged breathing and that of her two colleagues. Together, they waited expectantly.

Abruptly, on the floor a few feet from where she stood,

twinkling lights appeared like a sparkling jewel in the dark-ness—a small exquisitely detailed carousel. Slowly, it began to turn and a tinny calliope played its first brave notes.

Fascinated, they watched the tiny toy gain speed, its brightly colored horses moving up and down to the music. Faster and faster it went, the music speeding up as well. The detailing on the canopy became a blur and the music ran together.

Broussard heard a rustling and someone brushed past him. His nostrils filled with a heady aroma.

Something hit the floor hard and the carousel vanished, leaving behind only its music, now muffled and faraway. A heartbeat later another sound, like rice being thrown into a metal bowl, drowned out the muted carousel. Then the room became as quiet as the inside of a coffin.

By now, Broussard had realized that the metal box in his hand had probably been holding down a button that regulated the lights. He lowered himself to his knees, felt around for the hole, and put the box back where he had found it. The lights returned.

The room was just as it had been before the lights went out except that the fake fern lay in the fireplace and the kettle that held it was now upside down on the floor where the carousel had stood.

Phillip picked up the kettle. There was the carousel, surrounded by a glittering carpet of tiny objects. He reached down.

"No!" Broussard shouted, struggling to his feet. "Don't touch them."

With his American Express card, Broussard coaxed a few of the objects onto his driver's license and took them to the secretary. There, he examined them with his pocket lens. Satisfied, he handed the lens to Kit. "Look, but don't touch," he warned.

"Little metal spheres," she said. "With tiny points on them."

"A trap, set off by picking up that box," Broussard said. Kit handed Phillip the lens. "Doesn't look very dangerous," she said, ". . . unless of course the points have been poisoned."

"Not much doubt about that," Broussard replied.

"Damn quick thinking to use that pot like you did," Phillip said, returning the lens to its owner.

"I'll say," Kit added.

Calmly, Broussard folded the lens and said nothing, giving no indication of how his head was spinning. He had been about to congratulate one of *them* for quick thinking. Who the devil had brushed past him in the dark? He remembered the rustling sound as they passed and the aroma they left behind; the smell of . . . gardenias.

He put the lens in his pants pocket, then unbuttoned the pocket on his shirt and fished for a lemon ball to help him think. Instead of candy, his fingers found something else.

"What's that?" Kit said as he drew a vinyl drawstring bag from his pocket.

"Nothin' important," he said, stuffing the bag into the pocket with his magnifying lens. He didn't have to look in the bag to know that inside was the luck ball Grandma O had given him. In his mind, he saw her as he had on his last visit, the wooden dock at her home shaking with her step, her black taffeta dress rustling as she walked, the scent of gardenias heavy around her.

He forced his thoughts from things he couldn't understand to those he could. Picking up the bronze of the sleeping dog, he carried it to the hole in the floor. "Phillip, you get the box that's down there and I'll put this where it was. That ought to keep the lights on."

The exchange was made so swiftly that the lights didn't even flicker. Phillip took the box to the secretary, where Broussard brushed the carousel shrapnel to one side with Vogel's utility bill.

Eyes burning with curiosity, Kit and Broussard watched Phillip work on the lid with the screwdriver. Finally, the lock gave way and the lid popped open.

Inside, on a stack of papers, was a TWA ticket folder. Phillip flipped the folder open and read the destination. "Rome . . . one way."

"When's it leave?" Broussard asked, reaching into the box.

"Week from today."

"Same day as that circle on the calendar." He took a sheet of paper from the box, examined it, and gave it to Phillip. "Two weeks ago, Vogel leased a building on Rampart Street," he said, reaching back into the box.

The rest of the papers in the box were held together with a black spring clip. Broussard thumbed through them and handed them to Phillip. "Guess who Weston's boss is."

Phillip glanced at the papers and offered them to Kit. Among the documents he gave her were profit-loss statements for CCI and ownership papers for the plant itself made out in Vogel's name and dated long before Shindleman had had his trouble out there.

"What does he do with all his money?" Kit said.

"Guess you haven't priced real estate in this part of town lately," Phillip said.

"And this is all authentic period furniture," Broussard added, unzipping a flat leather bag he had found in the bottom of the metal box.

In the bag was a book bound in worn and cracked red leather, its two covers held together by a tattered spine. Broussard put the empty metal box on the floor and gently placed the book on the secretary. He probed his shirt pocket and popped two lemon balls into his mouth. Carefully, he lifted the book's cover and laid it flat.

Kit could see that the first page was yellow with age and water-spotted. But with Broussard hunched over it, that was all she could see.

"I'm going to find the can," Phillip said, wandering off.

Kit went back to her settee and waited for Broussard to share the contents of the book. After an eternity in which the only sounds were the clacking of lemon balls against Broussard's teeth, the old pathologist stood up and began to pace, his fingers stroking his nose.

Kit went to the secretary, sat down, and eagerly opened the book, noticing now its sour smell. On the first page, written in a beautiful flowing hand in ink that had faded to the color of a tea stain, was the name *Albair Fauquel*.

She turned the page and the brittle paper cracked under her touch. The second and third pages were filled with writing in the same elegant hand. But it was all in French, a language she couldn't read.

Turning the page, she came upon a roughly drawn map with street names she knew: Bienville, Chartres, Dauphine—all streets in the French quarter. But many downtown streets were missing; a map drawn before they existed. A large section of land on the side of Canal Street opposite the quarter from what was now Magazine Street to Rampart Street was lightly crosshatched.

Between the next two pages, she found a loose piece of yellowing parchment folded in half. Holding it as lightly as she would the wings of a butterfly, she unfolded it and found a detailed sketch of a plant with long slender shoots growing from what looked like a tulip bulb. The roots of the plant had clusters of nodular growths on them.

Under the sketch was another crudely drawn map, this time of the bayous south of the city, with Xs clustered in certain areas. At the bottom of the parchment, there was a long paragraph written in the same hand as before.

"So what's in the book?" Phillip said.

Lost in its contents, Kit jumped at the sound of his voice.

Phillip put a hand on her shoulder. "Sorry, kiddo, I don't mean to keep doing that."

"It's Albair Fauquel's journal," Broussard said.

"Who?" Phillip said. Then he remembered. ". . . Oh yeah, so the guy really existed, huh?"

"Most of it is Fauquel's account of the story Gramma O told me, how some land was taken from him and sold to satisfy a debt he owed." Broussard took the parchment out of the book and set it aside. He turned back to the city map Kit had seen. "This is the land in question—today, twenty square blocks of the financial district."

Phillip whistled under his breath.

"To get even with the judge who ordered the land sold, Fauquel cast a spell on him, one that drove him mad to the point of killing his wife, his daughter, and, then, himself. We already knew that from Gramma O, but Fauquel tells us how he did it." Broussard tapped the parchment. ". . . With this plant."

Phillip leaned over for a better look. "Same as the one you found in the lab wastebasket," he said.

Broussard pointed to the bayou map with Xs on it. "These are spots where the plant grows. And down here are instructions for its use. A powder made from the dried roots was usually sprinkled on a victim's firewood. Fauquel put it in the judge's tobacco. It's all here. He tells how the victims will think they hear songs their mother used to sing to them when the spell takes effect. They even knew that it didn't always work." He looked at Kit. "A stone like the one we found on your porch was supposed to be good luck for the one who left it."

"So that's what Vogel put in the fabric he shipped to the Escadrille plant," Kit said.

"For some reason, he wants the old curse to come true," Broussard said.

"I thought the powder had to be put in a fire," Phillip said.

Broussard tapped the parchment again. "There's a warnin' in here about keepin' it in a cool place after it's made. Apparently it's unstable and doesn't need a whole lot of heat to set it off. Puttin' it in fire not only activates it but makes sure it gets spread around."

"So when he shipped the toxin-impregnated fabrics, they weren't dangerous," Kit said.

Broussard nodded. "Not until the cars containin' 'em sat in the hot sun for a few days. I suspect Shindleman was an accident. Knowin' that heat could set it off, Vogel wouldn't have knowingly allowed the adulterated material to be exposed to those sunlamps. Probably some kind of foul-up at the plant."

"And when Shindleman shot the plant manager, Vogel got scared and shut the plant down for awhile," Kit said.

"Makes sense," Broussard replied. "Takin' the job in forensics put him in a position to know if anybody had caught on to what he'd done."

"How come no one figured out that those cars were dangerous before this?" Phillip said.

Some people are not susceptible," Kit replied. "And some that *were* affected killed themselves after they left the car, like Barry Hollins did. The common features in the related cases were hidden by so many extraneous facts, it took a computer to sort it out. And even then, we had to find the Escadrille tie-in ourselves."

"Which is why New Orleans Escadrilles that were driven to other cities never caught anyone's attention," Phillip said.

"Wouldn't have caused a ripple," Kit replied.

"All fine as far as it goes," Broussard said. "But it doesn't go far enough. We know why we might have found those plants in Vogel's wastebasket three years ago, but why were they there tonight?"

"Jesus," Kit moaned. "He's still at it."

"There're a couple of *other* things that are makin' my feet sweat. For one, there's the last page in that journal."

He flipped to the last entry, one clearly written by someone other than Fauquel, and read the passage aloud: "The hand that wrote these words was stilled July seventh in the year of our Lord seventeen hundred and thirty-eight." He looked up. "The date circled on the calendar in the lab off the kitchen is also July seventh; the two hundred and fiftieth anniversary of Fauquel's death. I want to see the building on Rampart that our friend just leased."

The building on Rampart was a run-down one-story with its plate-glass windows whitewashed on the inside. Phillip had no trouble with the lock.

Except for a five-gallon can of whitewash and a crusted paint roller, the place was empty.

"What do you think?" Phillip said.

"He obviously didn't want anyone to see what was going on in here," Broussard said.

Kit looked around at the peeling walls. "What's to see?"

"Nothin' yet," Broussard replied. "But I wonder what we'd have found on July seventh?" He shook his head and shifted the lemon drop in his cheek to the other side. "I wish we had Vogel where we knew he couldn't do any harm."

Self-consciously Phillip looked at his feet, fully aware that had he not put his personal life ahead of police business there in the swamp and run off to see his daughter, it was likely that Vogel would now be in custody.

"I have a feelin' there's more to be learned at CCI," Broussard said. "Let's pay 'em a visit first thing in the mornin'."

On the way home, all Broussard could think about was black taffeta and gardenias.

Chapter 19

Shortly after he had ducked into the swamp grass, the pain in Vogel's shoulder became so intense that he slipped into unconsciousness and slumped onto a fallen cypress, his hands dangling in the water. He woke with mosquito fish picking at the wrinkled skin on his fingers. When he tried to move, he found his joints stiff and unresponsive. Attempts to change position of his left arm brought breath-sucking pain to his shoulder, and he cursed Phil Gatlin's marksmanship.

The swamp was totally black and he could see nothing. The frogs that had been so quiet earlier were now singing madly. In the distance, there was a bellow from a bull 'gator and he cringed when he thought of how he had lain vulnerable for what must have been hours.

He got to his feet and a tom-tom began to beat on the back of his head. The bullet became a hot poker that buckled his knees. He braced himself on the fallen tree and waited for the moment to pass.

When he felt better, he looked slowly about, trying to guess where his pirogue might be, then realized that in the dark, a boat would be useless. The path was what he needed. He was sure that he had gone no more than fifteen yards into the grass to hide. Figuring three steps to a yard, that would be . . . The dust in his brain lay in drifts over the answer to this simple calculation. Forty-five . . . yes, that was it. No more than forty-five steps to the path.

He set off slowly, feeling the way in front of him, each foot testing the muck for stability. With each step, his shoulder throbbed and waves of pain lapped at his skull. When the required number of steps failed to produce solid ground, he stopped to think. But that made the pain in his head worse and, like a trapped animal, he felt the urge to flee in any direction. He quelled the panic and forced himself to concentrate.

If he had set off in the opposite direction from the path, it would now take twice as long to reach it if he went back the way he had come, providing he could even find his way back. But if he had set off parallel to it, he could still reach it in about forty-five steps. Since the odds of having gone parallel instead of perpendicular to the road were . . . two to one, he should now turn . . . left or right? That was the choice. Well shit! The chances of choosing the wrong way were even.

Screw the odds, he thought, slogging off to the left. After a dozen steps he fell sprawling into his boat. Now he knew the way, for the nose of the pirogue had been pointed toward the path. A few minutes more and he was on dry land, heading for the highway. As he trudged up the grassy trail, the hopelessness of his situation became clear. His plan was not going to work. How could Broussard and Franklyn be so goddam lucky? Three times between them, they'd managed to slip a trap he'd set. They probably knew it all by now and his years of preparation for that one glorious finale were going to be utterly wasted. The Escadrilles weren't enough. They weren't nearly enough. And it was all that *bitch* Franklyn's fault.

His boot caught in a vine. Growling, he ripped his foot loose and with his head thrown back like a howling wolf, he screamed in frustration. The resulting pain in his head and shoulder dropped him to his knees and he began to whimper. As his pain and the white heat of anger receded, he knew what to do.

He reached the highway and set out for the boat dock where he kept his pirogue, hoping that no one had realized that it was his car on the grass next to the minnow tanks. The road was a thin ribbon through a croaking bedlam and the dim white line along the shoulder was not enough to keep him from frequently wandering off course.

A pair of headlights appeared in the distance. Fearing that it might be the police, he dropped to his belly in the roadside weeds and waited for the car to pass.

It took a long time to cover the two miles to the bait shop, and near the end of his trek, the wound in his shoulder began to bleed again, causing him to fear that loss of blood might send him into shock before he could accomplish what he had in mind. Despite his wretched condition, he felt a flutter of pleasure when, in the floodlight at the boat dock, he saw his car right where he had left it.

His fatigues had deep pockets on the front of each leg. Button-down flaps insured that items placed in those pockets stayed there. Even so, he experienced a stab of fear that having lain in the swamp and fallen in the boat, he might have lost his keys. His spirits rose when he plunged his fingers deep into his right pocket and found the keys among a crushed pack of cigarettes, his lighter, and some extra bullets for the rifle.

The three tanks the boat dock used to hold bait minnows had been fashioned from fifty-five-gallon drums cut in half lengthwise so that the filling port could serve as a drain. Hanging on a nail near the door of the small air-conditioned shed that housed the tanks was an enormous crescent wrench that they used to work the screw-top caps when the water needed changing. He removed the wrench from its nail and carried it to the car.

The clock in the dash said 4 A.M. He was shocked at how long he had lain unconscious in the swamp. Without the exertion of walking, the bleeding stopped and as long as he didn't move the arm, there was minimal pain. His head didn't hurt quite as much, either. He pointed the car toward the city. At the intersection of Highway 8 and Gentilly, he wheeled left and held the course until it crossed Waring, where he also turned left—in the direction of Crescent City Industries.

At the entrance to the CCI parking lot, he switched off his lights. The lot was empty except for a blue Nova with gray primer around the lip of the front fender, probably the night watchman's car. He cut the engine, put the car in neutral, and glided silently to the far corner of the lot, where a cluster of bushes in a bed carved out of the blacktop concealed his presence. He picked up the wrench and got out, being careful not to slam the door.

At the loading dock of the detached warehouse, he found the metal overhead door secured with a padlock. Having not expected to need it, he had left the warehouse key at home. The sound of whistling came from the direction of the main building.

He froze. It was getting closer. The night watchman on his rounds. The night watchman who would have a key to the big padlock.

The dock was illuminated by a single floodlight aimed so that on one side the recess for the overhead door was in deep shadow. The darkened space was large enough to conceal him for a few seconds, and if he could think of a diversion to keep the watchman occupied . . . He patted his back pocket and remembered placing his wallet in the trunk of the car before setting out in the pirogue. And that's where it still was. What then could he use for bait? The whistling was getting closer.

The watchman stepped onto the dock, still whistling. In the light from the floodlamp he saw Vogel's cigarette lighter lying on the cement. No longer whistling, he went over to see what lady luck had brought his way. When he bent over, Vogel struck, bringing the wrench down with all the power he could muster. There was a dull crack as the wrench shattered the watchman's skull. He couldn't risk having the man wake up, and he was too weak to drag even a small man to the car, where he might have locked him in the trunk. This was the only way.

He slipped the watchman's pistol from its leather holster and put it in the pocket of his fatigues. Of the dozen keys on the watchman's ring, he tested nine before finding the one that opened the padlock. The overhead door made a horrible din as it lurched from his hand and disappeared up into the darkness. He waited, cringing, to see whether the noise would bring trouble but heard only the distant sound of a dog barking. Cool air poured from the warehouse, enveloping him in a refreshing embrace.

Since the loading dock faced onto an open field and the warehouse had no windows, he felt secure in turning on the lights. They produced a sight so stunning it momentarily made him forget Catlin's bullet: hundreds of drums, stacked three tiers high, each marked cryptically with the number 7–7; the date of their intended use. He reflected briefly on what might have been and cursed Kit again. With the big wrench, he set to work on the threaded caps atop a row of drums against the wall beside the entrance.

The caps were so firmly screwed on that he was able to remove only two of the eight, and then only by ignoring the hot flash that ripped through his shoulder each time he strained against the wrench. The red stain spread further into his shirt.

With two drums open, he discovered what he should have realized earlier. They were too heavy to tip over.

There was a yellow forklift in the wide aisle between the rows of stacked drums and he struggled into its seat. The On/Off switch was labeled, but its black-knobbed levers and shiny pedals were not. Never having driven the thing, he could only guess at their functions. His first guess sent the machine gliding backward. He found the brake a scant second before crashing into a wall of drums behind him. A minute more of careful trial and error and he drove flawlessly over to one of the open drums and nudged it off by itself. Then he rammed it!

Instead of tipping over, it slid across the floor, sloshing only a small amount of the contents down one side. A second attempt to topple it also failed. In anger, he spun the forklift around and charged a three-tiered stack on the aisle. The fork struck the lowest drum a glancing blow and slid it sideways, leaving the upper ones only partially supported. Another blow and the stack collapsed. As one of the drums hit the concrete, its seal ruptured and an oily fluid gushed onto the floor and ran under the fallen drums. The air became filled with the heady scent of the volatile liquid that he had chosen to carry Fauquel's toxin.

He straddled a drum that lay on its side and brought the big wrench into play. With a madman's single-mindedness he ignored his pulsating shoulder and pitted himself against the threads. Beads of sweat popped from his brow and his shoulder begged him to stop. The cap moved a fraction of a turn and then it was loose. Discarding the wrench, he spun the cap with fingers slippery from the fluid dribbling around the threads. Finally, the cap slid from his grip and bounced to the floor. With the forklift, he rolled the newly opened drum down the aisle to help spread its contents.

Feverish with success, he became more creative. Jamming the drum against the far wall, he got it fully onto the forklift and deposited it near the entrance, where it was now light enough that he could stand it upright. From a first-aid kit fixed on the dash of the forklift, he took a roll of gauze and held it under the waning stream of liquid still issuing from the drum that had ruptured. He unrolled the gauze, doubled it, and twisted it all along its length. One end of the makeshift fuse went down into the drum he had partially emptied. The other he carried to the entrance.

He wanted to do more, but the gray sky was changing to pink and he was afraid to linger. This would have to do. He searched his pockets for his lighter, then remembered where it was. Unwilling to touch the watchman's body with his hands, he turned it with his foot, careful not to look at the face.

Held to the edge of the dark stain that by now had spread over nearly three-quarters of the floor, the lighter's flame spread rapidly in a widening arc, producing almost from the first instant a thick black smoke. He applied the lighter to the free end of the gauze and paused only long enough to see the flame begin its race toward the drum. Then he ran.

He was barely thirty feet from the building when the homemade bomb blew, toppling the other drums like tenpins. The explosion took off half the metal roof, knocked dozens of cement blocks out of the wall, and threw Vogel onto his injured shoulder. A piece of sheet metal clanked to the ground a yard away and the contents of the blown drum rained on him in a fiery downpour. Groaning from the pain in his shoulder, he slapped at the sparks that threatened to ignite his clothing and dragged himself farther from the boiling hell behind him.

There were more explosions. From where he sat, fifty yards away, Vogel was awed at what he had created. Flames licked the air like tongues from perdition and a steady plume of black smoke fouled the new day. There was another explosion and a piece of cement block thrown from the conflagration like a missile struck Vogel in the chest, breaking his sternum and rupturing his liver. Through the pain and the sure knowledge that he was a dead man, Vogel prayed that the smoke with its heat-activated toxic vapors would find its way into the city.

Once again Kit felt swamp water lapping at her legs and gnats dancing in her face. Frigid blue eyes stared at her over a rifle barrel. This time her eyes were open to see the rifle buck against Vogel's shoulder as he fired. In the distance a muffled bell was ringing. Nothing could save her now. She was going to die.

She woke screaming, her nightclothes clammy with sweat. Hands to her face, she rocked herself gently, her hair swinging in soggy profusion against her ears. Gradually she became aware of the ringing telephone. She leaned over and picked up the receiver. At the other end, she heard Broussard say,

"There's a huge fire burning at CCI. If my suspicions are right, we could have big trouble."

She checked the voice against her memory and found it genuine. It was truly him and not Vogel.

"I'm headin' over there now with Phillip," he said. "You'd better come, too."

Chapter 20

Hearing the turnout bell, Tracy Gannon stopped beating her pancake batter and listened for the call.

"Pumpers eleven and twelve, to Crescent City Industries," the watchman's voice said over the fire-station loudspeaker. "Repeat. Pumpers eleven and twelve, to Crescent City Industries."

For Tracy, this call was special—the first one after learning that she had passed the lieutenant's exam. Today, she would automatically be the number-one nozzle man, the one responsible for working the big line. And to Tracy, that's what fire fighting was all about. The rest of it was really only support for the nozzle man. And today she was it. Hidden in that pleasure was hope that the battalion chief or pumper twelve from the other station responding would beat her to the scene. If she got there first, she would be ranking scene officer and would be in charge, a prospect that would have caused her no concern if this were a house fire. But a two alarm at a chemical plant? Not a comforting thought.

She was in her seat in the pumper a good ten seconds before Kent Davis, the driver, slid behind the wheel. "Shit, Trace, you musta been wearing your gear to cook breakfast."

"Don't you mean, 'Shit, Lt. Trace'?"

Davis grinned. He tried her title himself. "Lt. Gannon. Has a nice ring, don't it?"

Ben Eaves, the hookup man, swung into the jump seat behind Davis and they all waited for the rookie, Al Germain, to appear. With their heavy insulated parkas, boots, and helmets, the three firemen filled the spaces allotted to them. There was no air conditioning in the part of the station housing the rolling stock and the thermometer on the wall by the watchman's booth was holding steady at ninety-two degrees. Outside, it was not much less. Sweat was already beginning to soak into their underwear.

By Tracy's count it was fifteen seconds before she heard the flap of Al Germain's boots and felt him step onto the running board on her side. Even before he got seated, the pumper was rolling.

When Germain was settled in the jump seat behind her, Tracy slid open the window that separated them, looked stiffly over her shoulder, and said to the back of Germain's head, "Nice of you to join us." The siren began its slide to a shriek and she added in a shout, "You gotta cut fifteen seconds off your turnout time."

Germain nodded and said nothing, his eyes fixed on the back of the pumper. As soon as he could manage it, he was transferring to a different station house. He wasn't taking orders from a woman.

"What did you think of the suggestion Owen Everett made at the city-council meeting yesterday?" Kent Davis said, wheeling the big Pirsch around a corner.

"Didn't hear about it," Tracy replied. "What'd he say?"

"He thought we should just use the *old* equipment for the false alarms."

"Jesus, he really said that?"

"Kind of gives you the willies, don't it? Picture this. You pull up in front of a house that's in flames, the owner runs up to the truck, and you say, 'Oh, this is a *real* fire? We'll be right back with the *good* equipment.'"

Glancing over to see if Tracy was smiling, Davis saw she wasn't. He had been around long enough to know what she was probably thinking. "Don't worry. If we make the scene first, you'll do fine. They wouldn't have given you your stripes if they didn't think you could cut it."

He wheeled the pumper onto Parkland, a street that would bring them out right at the location of CCI. By using Parkland, he would avoid the commuter nightmare that, because of the construction over there, had recently become a daily occurrence on Waring. "Check our setup position, will you?" he asked. "I can't picture the place."

Tracy pulled a small notebook from under the seat, ruffled through it, and studied the CCI layout on page thirty-four. "Set up to best advantage," she said. "We get the south plug; number twelve gets the north."

Then they saw it, dead ahead. Black smoke boiling a hundred feet into the air . . . and something else.

"I hope that's not what I think it is," Davis said grimly, referring to the series of dull thumps they heard over the siren. Tracy said nothing but had the same misgivings. She remembered a training film that showed how fifty-five-gallon drums could become projectiles that made fighting a chemical fire a game of Russian roulette.

Her heart thundered in her ears when she saw that they were the first piece of equipment on the scene. Davis went down the drive and stopped a safe distance away. There was a dull whump that shook the truck and a drum hurtled obliquely into the air. It struck the chimney of the main plant, cutting a large gash in the brickwork near the base. The chimney leaned in slow motion and toppled in a heap onto the asphalt drive that ran behind the plant.

The black smoke from the fire rose high into the air, some of it dissipating in the atmosphere. Much of it settled back onto the meadow, producing a gray haze that covered many acres.

The flying drums were problem enough, but Tracy Gannon was just as worried about the proximity of the plant's two storage tanks for ammonium nitrate, a substance she knew to be extremely explosive. From the size of the fire, she guessed that those tanks were already dangerously hot. They had to get the flames under control. But that could be hazardous, too. Water made some chemical fires worse. She looked at the two cars in the parking lot and turned to Al Germain. "Scout the main building and see if you can turn up somebody that knows what's stored in that warehouse." While the rookie tried the plant's doors, she reached for the radio mike. "Pumper eleven to haz mat team. Pumper eleven to haz mat team."

A voice mushy with electronic clutter responded. "Haz mat team. Go ahead."

"We're at Crescent City Industries where there's a grade four in progress in a detached structure north of the main building. Nearby ammonium-nitrate tanks are at risk. Please advise."

On the highway, passing motorists were wondering why the pumper was doing nothing to put out the fire. While waiting for the hazardous-materials team to get in touch with a responsible plant official, Tracy realized that plant employees would soon be arriving for work. She leaned across Kent Davis and called through the window to Ben Eaves who was standing nearby.

"Ben, go out to the highway and keep the drive clear."

There was a crackle from the radio. "Haz mat team to pumper eleven. Pumper eleven, please respond."

"Eleven here, go ahead."

"Contents of warehouse water compatible. Repeat, contents . . ."

Al Germain stuck his head in the window. "Can't find anybody," he said.

"That's okay, we got what we needed," Tracy replied. "Let's go with the big line on this one."

In the periphery of her field of vision, something moved, something she earlier thought was a piece of sheet metal. She jumped from the truck and pulled one of the respirators off its rack. Slinging it onto her back as if it didn't weigh thirty pounds, she told Germain, "Get your unit on and come with me."

Another drum shot into the air, spinning end for end, and they both pressed themselves against the pumper. Vogel lay well clear of the smoke but was close enough to the fire for the firemen to feel its heat on their faces as they carried him to safety and laid him on the grass. He moaned and Tracy pulled off her mask. Directing her orders to Kent Davis, she said, "Put in a call for an ambulance. Then, let's get this thing knocked down before that ammonium nitrate goes."

When Davis got the pumper in position, Tracy attached the straight-tip nozzle to the three-and-a-half-inch line and, with Al Germain helping, began to drag hose toward the fire. Davis eased the pumper from the parking lot, laying hose as he went. At the end of the driveway, he picked up Ben Eaves. The inbound lanes were filled with traffic and it was fortunate that the plug was on the opposite side of the highway; otherwise, they would have had difficulty getting to it.

At the plug, Eaves connected the suction hose to the plug while Davis put the wooden suction blocks under it. Davis then disconnected the deployed part of the line at the five-hundred-foot connector and hooked into the discharge panel. He checked the pressure chart under the seat and set the gauge for 175 psi.

While Gannon and Germain waited for water, pumper number twelve and the chief pulled into the parking lot. With a chief at the scene, responsibility shifted to him, much to Tracy's relief. Al Germain straddled the hose and grasped it in both hands, steeling himself for the surge to come. The first water came at hydrant pressure and the hose was limp. But as the pumper took over, the trickle became a torrent and the hose tried to rip itself from his grip. Even though they were well clear of any smoke, the two firemen on the hose were wearing their masks and yellow compressed-air bottles. There was a muffled "whump" from the fire and a piece of shrapnel ricocheted harmlessly off Gannon's helmet. But another piece, no bigger than a fly, silently nicked the line that ran from her mask to the regulator at her waist. Soon, she was getting no air and she stripped her mask off to breathe. She did this without concern since the prevailing wind was carrying the smoke almost directly away from them.

A rogue breeze, spawned by pockets in the fire that were hotter than others, emerged from the fire as a tiny whirlwind, churning with black smoke as it advanced toward the two firemen. They were engulfed so quickly, evasion was impossible. With his mask in place, Germain was safe, but Tracy Gannon's lungs were filled with it. The whirling cone moved away and disintegrated. Tracy coughed.

Swiftly, the toxin made its way from her lungs into her bloodstream. In her scleras and parts of her brain, the cells comprising vessels no larger than spider silk contracted violently at the toxin's touch, ripping holes in the vessel walls through which blood quickly flowed. Like frightened children, neurons in the affected areas panicked, irresponsibly consuming the dwindling oxygen supply through wild activity. From far away, Tracy heard a sound she had not heard for ages: the sweet notes of the music box her father had given her for her tenth birthday.

As Ben Eaves approached to help maneuver the line, Tracy turned it on him. The powerful stream of water knocked him backward onto his left arm and it snapped with a sickening pop. Al Germain let loose of the hose and it began to swing over the landscape in an erratic arc. Though she now had minimal control, Tracy was able to rake the downed man every few seconds. Each time she did, he rolled over the ground like a puppet.

While Germain stood stupidly by doing nothing, the chief ran toward Tracy, his shoulder lowered. He hit her hard, waist-high, knocking her off her feet. Eyes glazed, she scrabbled at his face with her gloved hands. Her hands were everywhere. Suddenly, she was slashing at him with a ragged piece of metal. In desperation, the chief clipped her on the chin with his fist, knocking her unconscious.

"What the hell's wrong with this woman?" the chief said.

Germain shrugged and shook his head.

The chief went over to Eaves, who was writhing on the ground and holding his broken arm.

The two inbound lanes on the highway that passed in front of CCI were now packed with commuters from Cypress Springs, the mammoth housing development eight miles south of the plant. Where the new cement ended about a mile north of CCI, there was an abrupt ten-inch drop into a bed of sand that ran beside the old road for several miles. A hundred yards back, there was a flashing arrow pointing left and a string of orange barrels arranged in a curving arc. Here, the opportunists who had used the new stretch of road to get the jump on their more conservative neighbors were trying to buy their way back into the other lane with grins and waving arms. Except no one was going anywhere for awhile. Ten cars beyond the bottleneck, an eighteen-wheeler with a flatbed full of reinforcing bars had its hood up. Perched on one fender, the driver was scratching his head and staring into the engine. Under the cab, a large puddle stained the cement. Kit made a mental note to go home a different way.

Through the windshield Kit saw a bank of ominous black clouds creeping across the once promising sky, changing it to one that appeared fully capable of delivering the rain and gale force winds predicted by the weatherman. About a half mile north of CCI, on the other side of the cement median, a gray haze hung low over the landscape. On its fringe, she saw the bodies of dozens of cows.

At the entrance to CCI, a fireman was sending inbound traffic on Waring back the way it had come. Another was diverting outbound traffic onto Parkland. After identifying herself, Kit was allowed onto the plant grounds, where two teams of firemen were playing huge streams of water high into the air over the warehouse. Angry orange flames could still be seen leaping skyward from gaping holes in its roof.

Near a small fir tree to the far right of the fire, she saw what appeared to be the body of a man in civilian clothes. Not far away, she saw Phil Gatlin, Bert Weston, and a fireman in full gear standing around Broussard who was kneeling on the ground over a prostrate form in blue pants and a blue T-shirt. On the ground to the left of the group, there was another body dressed in blue, and beside it, two piles of fire gear.

As she joined the small group, Phillip looked at her in despair. "Quite a mess, huh?" He rubbed the back of his neck and shook his head. "If I was a better shot, none of this would have happened."

"What do you mean?" Kit asked.

"Vogel. He set the fire."

At the mention of Vogel's name, Kit stiffened. "How do you know that?" she croaked.

"He told us himself. That's him over there."

She followed his finger to the body by the fir tree.

"Some flying debris caught him in the chest. Could be he isn't going to make it if that ambulance doesn't get here soon."

Despite his inability to do her any harm now, Vogel's mere presence brought Kit's shakes back and she realized that if she didn't do something now to conquer this unreasonable fear, she might never be rid of it, might relive nightly for the rest of her life that horrible moment in the swamp. She felt she had to look into those frigid eyes one more time.

She detached herself from the group and cautiously went over to where Vogel lay motionless, his eyes rolled back in his skull. She must see those eyes! Softly, she spoke his name. But there was no response. She called it again and his eyes rolled into view. She made herself look deeply into them. "There's an ambulance on the way," she said.

His lips quivered and he pulled his right hand from where it lay under his thigh. In it was the watchman's pistol. It wavered in his grip, the barrel making tiny circles as he tried to hold it steady.

Kit's mouth opened to cry out, but the sound lodged in her throat.

Vogel struggled up on one elbow. "You," he hissed in a weak whisper. "You're to blame for everything." His finger tightened on the trigger and his hand grew white. Now she *would* die. And this was no dream.

Kit's fear turned to anger and her foot lashed out. The toe of her shoe struck Vogel in the wrist and his fingers splayed open. The gun flew from his hand and fell harmlessly in the grass several feet away.

Unable to hold himself up any longer, Vogel collapsed onto his back. His chest heaved. A frightful rattle issued from his dry lips and his frosty eyes grew colder still. She could see his life ebbing away, receding like a tide flowing back to its source. His mouth opened as if to protest and then it was over. There was no need to feel for a pulse. He was dead.

Slowly she walked over and picked up the gun. As much as she had reason to despise him, she could not rejoice at the death of anyone. Yet a part of her felt reborn. In kicking the gun from his hand, she had redeemed herself for her behavior in the swamp and she was sure her dream would not return.

Rejoining the others, she heard the fireman in the group, a heavyset black man with a gray mustache and the designation CHIEF on his helmet, ask Broussard, "How bad is it?"

The medical examiner struggled to his feet. "Fractured humerus, a broken nose, possibly a fractured rib."

The chief looked up and down the highway. "Where's that damn ambulance?"

"The one over there won't be needing it," Kit said, pointing to Vogel.

"Dead?" Gatlin asked.

"Yes. You better take this," she said, handing Phillip the gun.

"*He* had that?" Phillip said, shocked.

She nodded.

"Damn, but I hate it when my people go down," the chief said. "And it's even worse when it's freaky. This one was coming over to help with the hose when that one," he motioned to the other figure on the ground close by, "spun around and whap." He slapped his gloves into his open palm. ". . . she let him have it right in the chest. It was no accident either. It was deliberate because she had to turn all the way around to do it and then she kept it up even after he was down. When her helper on the hose saw what was happening, he let go, figuring that without him, she wouldn't be able to control it. But she's a strong one, stronger than some of the men, and she got along pretty good without him. I had to knock her down to get her to stop. Then she went after me with a piece of metal. Crazy she was. As sorry as it sounds, I hit her on the chin to quiet her down."

"Look there," Phillip cried.

The figure on the grass had begun to twitch. First it was her legs and then her arms. Soon her whole body was shaking.

"She's havin' a seizure," Broussard yelled, grabbing one of the chief's heavy gloves. He dropped to his knees and tried to force the woman's mouth open, but it was clamped tight. Helplessly, they watched convulsions rack her body until her eyes popped open and she stiffened in a last paroxysm. Saliva bubbled from between her lips and she stopped moving.

Broussard put two fingers against her neck. "She's dead."

The chief's mouth was hanging open.

"You said you hit her. Was her mask off when all this happened?" Broussard asked, getting to his feet.

"It shouldn't have been, but it was. Musta been something wrong with it."

"Was she in any smoke when it started?"

The fireman thought a moment. "Now that you mention it, a small eddy did blow over them, but it only lasted a few seconds, then it broke up and disappeared.

Broussard looked at Kit. "Unless I'm gettin' senile, this warehouse was full of toxin that would have ended up in the building on Rampart Street if Vogel hadn't been spooked."

"That explains the dead cows I saw in the meadow as I drove in," she replied.

"You saying that little bit of smoke killed this woman?" the chief said.

Broussard nodded and the fireman turned and surveyed the hazy specter that clogged the meadow. The wind had changed slightly and the cloud now lay in a long narrow band about half a football field from the highway. The fire was nearly out and a breeze that was causing the flag near the entrance to flap and snap sharply had opened up a small clear zone between the cloud and the remains of the warehouse as it pushed the sluggish cloud slowly toward the city. "If what you say is true," the fireman said, "we've got a helluva problem on our hands. That cloud looks like it's not going to disperse anytime soon and we've got people at risk in whatever direction it moves. East, and there's Oak Glen, five, maybe six thousand people; north, there's the city; south, Cypress Springs, another five thousand people; and then there's that crowd out on the highway. We've got to get that traffic moving before the wind changes."

"There's a big truck with a heavy load of steel broken down in the only passable lane about a mile down the road," Kit volunteered.

"Not the best time for the road to be under construction," Phil Gatlin observed, shaking his head. "The median has them trapped on one side and the shoulder is so soft, it'd never hold a car."

"Look, you folks shouldn't be hanging around here," the chief said. "If that wind shifts this way . . ."

At the warning, Bert Weston backed away, but Phil Gatlin grabbed him by the arm. "You stick around awhile. We may need your help. And even if we don't, I'd like a few words with you."

"I don't know anything about what's in that warehouse," Weston whined. "I was just following orders. Let the professionals handle this. They're experienced in these things."

"Thanks for the vote of confidence," the chief said. "Wish I had an idea to back it up."

"Maybe we could get the road crew to cut an openin' in the median so those cars out there could turn around," Broussard said.

Phillip shook his head. "You haven't got that much time. It'd take two hours to get through the cement and another hour for the rebars."

The flag, which had been flapping steadily in a northerly breeze, grew quiet. Everyone looked at it in apprehension.

"Any other ideas?" the chief asked, looking from face to face.

"How about sending your men down the road, explaining things, and have everyone back up here to where they can turn around," Broussard suggested.

"It'll be slow going, but I can't see a better answer," the chief said.

"We'll help," Phillip said.

"You, maybe, but not the others. If anything happened to them, I'd never be able to explain why I put them at risk."

They heard the yodel of a siren, and an ambulance hurried down the drive.

The chief checked the remaining pressure on Ben Eaves's respirator, then strapped Phillip into it and screwed the ribbed hose from the face mask into the regulator. He took Phillip's hand and pulled it around to the compressed-air bottle. "That's the valve where you turn it on," he said. "If you hear a bell go off, it means you've only got about five minutes of air left and should move to safety."

The flag ropes began to bang against the pole and the flag briefly fluttered feebly in a westerly direction, then fell motionless.

"We'd better move our tails," the chief said. "That wind looks like its getting ready to change."

He whistled through his fingers and waved his crew around him. After explaining the plan and the danger, he had them shed their heavy parkas, and sent them on the run toward the highway. Unnoticed, Bert Weston slinked to his car.

Chapter 21

The chief watched his men carefully until he was satisfied that they were spreading themselves out properly among the threatened commuters. Behind him, ambulance attendants gathered up the dead and injured. He went to the pumper and pulled a spare respirator from the rack. "If you two are gonna stick around, you better be in one of these," he said, holding it out to Kit with the harness open. "Doc, there's one over there for you, too."

The wind freshened and the sound of the flagpole being whipped by ropes and pulleys drifted over the grounds. Using a small tree as a point of reference, Kit watched the toxic cloud advance toward the road. Within a few seconds, the tree was completely enveloped. The cloud now lay barely thirty yards from the highway. "They're not going to make it," she said into her mask.

But then the wind ceased and the cloud stalled. It lay still now, quiet death biding its time . . . waiting.

As he watched the grim scene unfold before him, Broussard realized that clearing the traffic jam would do nothing to solve the primary problem. The cloud would still exist and would simply continue to move until it threatened others. The ropes on the flagpole signaled that the wind was starting up again, and he looked fearfully at the flag. It was pointing toward the road.

The first tendrils of silent death wrapped themselves around the wooden posts of the wire fence that lined the road ten yards from the new lane. In another few minutes, the haze would reach the cars themselves.

As the wind continued its steady push to the west, the ugly clouds that had been spreading across the sky blotted out the sun. The landscape took on a somber pallor and it became impossible to see into the creeping haze.

Out on the highway, Phil Gatlin knocked on the window of a car driven by an old lady whose eyes barely cleared the top of the steering wheel. The cars behind her had all backed up to the cut in the median and it was her turn.

Phillip made a sign for her to roll her window down. Instead of doing so, she locked the door and sat in stony resolve with her eyes on the back of the car ahead. Phillip leaned over the fender and tapped on the windshield. He pointed at his mask, then at the approaching haze. He jabbed the air in the direction he wanted her to go, but she acted as though he didn't exist.

Through the windshield, he saw that the door on the passenger side was unlocked. He made a dash for it, intending to pull the old girl from the car and move it himself. Before he got there, she had locked that door, too. The result of all this was that the right lane was completely blocked. Progress had also been slow on the left lane and there was still an achingly long line of cars to be evacuated.

The first ghostly fingers made contact with the old lady's car and with many others in her lane. Immediately in front of where Phil Gatlin stood, Broussard could see a station wagon full of children, going off to school probably, their faces pressed against the windows on the side of the approaching cloud. He was too far away to see their expressions but could picture innocent eyes, mouths agape with excitement. Here it comes. Hooray, we'll soon be in it.

Broussard's heart grew heavy with the same despair that

led him to put his fist through the bathroom door at the Hollins fire and weep when he buried his old cat. Overhead, the black clouds merged and separated, collided and boiled.

The image of bodies stacked like firewood floated in Broussard's brain. Vogel was going to have the last word. He turned away.

Two snowy egrets, approaching from the north, heard the sound begin and changed course to avoid the area. Initially as soft as a woman's sigh, the sound grew in intensity. The tip of a black funnel emerged from the angry clouds and telescoped downward, the sigh now a shriek. Broussard turned and saw the tip of the swirling funnel enter the haze over the meadow. He covered his ears to shut out the sound of the screaming wind. His hair flew into his eyes and pieces of flying grit stung the back of his neck as he struggled to stay on his feet. Kit and the chief sought refuge behind the pumper.

When it touched the ground, the whirling mass howled down the meadow, sucking up everything within reach. Small trees were pulled out by the roots. Large ones were stripped of every leaf. Held rigid by the wind's fury, bits of dried grass were driven like nails deep into the trunks of trees still standing.

On the highway, windshield wipers stood straight up and cars rocked on their tires. Phillip and the firemen pressed themselves against the lee side of whatever vehicle they were near to keep from being pulled from the road. Sheets of newspaper and Styrofoam cups flew by. In the meadow, the bodies of dead cows were lifted as if they were stuffed animals and they, too, disappeared into the gluttonous vortex.

Then as abruptly as it had appeared, the funnel receded into the cloud that had spawned it, leaving behind no trace of the toxic smoke.

Broussard pulled off his mask and took a deep breath. The air now held something disturbingly familiar. In the pocket of the pants he had hastily pulled on before bolting from the house, he felt Grandma Oustellette's drawstring bag against his leg. What had she said when she gave it to him? ". . . It will protect you and all you care for." He took another deep breath to verify the first and again detected in the air the unmistakable scent of gardenias.

EPILOGUE

The press conference to warn Escadrille owners of the danger took place at noon that day in the hospital auditorium, and no one doubted a word of their story. Afterward, under a now cloudless sky, Broussard took Kit and Phillip to the Court of Two Sisters for lunch.

"You're convinced, then, that Weston was not involved?" Kit said, spearing a tender crawfish tail with her fork.

Phillip generously buttered his bran muffin. "He was pretty much a toady when it came to those drums. Vogel was the boss and who was Weston to stick his nose in the boss's business. Sure, he thought it was odd that Vogel kept him in the dark, but he was willing to play along to keep his job."

The couple at the next table got up to leave and a flock of sparrows dropped from one of the courtyard's giant wisterias and began to peck at the bread crumbs on the white tablecloth.

"Still can't get over that funnel cloud," Kit said, attacking the mound of rice in the middle of her plate. ". . . came out of nowhere, sucked up the smoke from the fire, and left, like it had been sent just for that purpose."

Broussard cleaned the sweet meat from the last oyster on his plate and said nothing. In the last few days, he had come to see that there were forces and principles in the world that are not described in any textbooks but have to be learned through experience. Kit and Phillip would have to discover this on their own.

"You're awfully quiet," Kit said.

"There's at least one piece of the puzzle still missin'," Broussard replied.

"Motive," Phillip interjected. "Yeah, I don't get that, either. Where's the gain in what he did?"

Broussard patted his mouth with his starched napkin. "Could be, we'll never know."

After lunch, Kit set out to complete some unfinished business. Kicking the gun out of Vogel's hand had renewed her self-confidence and with that confidence came the answer to Minnie Mrocheck's situation—a solution that would resolve another dilemma as well. Minnie's primary problem was that she was alone. There was no one to share her life, no one who *needed* her. Then there was Lucky, still waiting at the vet for someone to claim him, *needing* someone to love him, *needing* Minnie. It was perfect. Each could fill a void in the other's life. Lucky could be a mascot for the home. Everyone could help take care of him, and Minnie could delegate the duties and take primary responsibility. It would give them all something to think about besides themselves.

It took five minutes of her most eloquent oratory to convince Ida Swenson to go along with the idea. When she finally agreed, Kit set out for the hospital. Outside Minnie's room, she knocked lightly.

"Come in."

It was a strong voice that spoke, probably a nurse, Kit thought, pushing on the heavy green door. But it was Minnie herself and she was not flat on her back with tubes in her nose as Kit had expected, but was sitting up, with color in her cheeks.

"Aren't *you* looking fit," Kit said.

"Dr. Franklyn, how nice of you to come and see me." Minnie's eyes shone as they never had at the home.

232 / D. J. DONALDSON

"Minnie, I have a problem that I think you could help me with. I found the cutest little dog, about this big, with huge brown eyes and the sweetest personality you could imagine. I can't find the owner and my landlord doesn't allow pets, so I was wondering . . ."

Minnie made a sour face. "I *hate* dogs," she said. "Always trying to lick you and stick their nose between your legs. Brrrrr." She shivered in disgust.

"But I thought . . ."

The door opened and a voice said, "I'm back, Min."

It was Shindleman with a copy of *Time* in one hand. "Dr. Franklyn," he said. "Shame on you for canceling your last visit to the home." He put the magazine on Minnie's lap and gave her a peck on the cheek. "Actually, I didn't mind. I've got Minnie to talk to now."

"We're leaving the home," Minnie said. "We found a nice little apartment that together we can afford."

"And it's on the first floor, so Min won't have to climb the stairs," Shindleman added.

"Then you're eating again?"

Shindleman chuckled. "Never seen such a woman for pancakes. How many did you have this morning, Hon?" Minnie shyly held up four fingers. "And they weren't those dinky kind either," Shindleman said.

"Does this mean I can stop worrying about you trying to . . ."

"Yes, dear," Minnie said. "It was loneliness, that's all. And Abraham has taken care of that."

Walking back to her car, Kit reflected on what an unlikely pair they were. But it was undeniably going to be good for both of them. As she drove back to her office, events of the past three weeks whirled through Kit's head.

Shindleman and Minnie, Lucky, David, Vogel; she thought of them all. Gradually she began to see how independence could be overdone. Reaching the office, she went directly to the telephone. When David answered, she said, "You've been wanting the patter of little feet around the house, how about I bring Lucky with me when I move in?"

David cheered.

In the morgue, Broussard put a fresh autopsy form on his clipboard. Across the room, Vogel's body, covered with a green cloth, lay on a stainless-steel table, a porcelain pot holding the head up so Broussard could get at the skull with a bone saw.

Before he could put his rubber gloves on, the phone rang. It was Phillip.

"I want to read you something," he said.

"What is it?"

"A little history lesson."

"A *very* little one, I hope."

"You'll want to be sitting down for this. Ready?" He started to read. "'Among the early settlers that came to New Orleans was a small group of Germans sick of the constant strife in their own country. As they disembarked from the ship that brought them, they were registered by French officials who spoke no German. The result was that most German names were changed to French equivalents. For example: Kamper became Cambre, Schoen became Chaigne, and *Vogel* became *Fauquel!*' There's your motive. Vogel was a descendant of the guy who was hanged. I guess when he saw what he would have inherited had his ancestor not lost that land, he snapped."

Albair Fauquel . . . Al Vogel! Of course, Broussard thought, mentally kicking himself. It was so damned obvious now.

"I'm sure with some more checking I could lay my hands on the records showing when he changed his name back to the original, but it's probably not worth the effort."

A little jealous of Phillip's coup, Broussard said, "What put you on to this?"

"Does Woolworth tell K Mart?"

Phillip was still laughing when Broussard hung up on him.

Turning back to the autopsy, Broussard slipped on a pair of rubber gloves and pulled the sheet down to the body's knees. Returning to the head, his shaggy brows arched in surprise and his mind took him back, back to 1738 and the hanging of Albair Fauquel. He saw the crowd jeer when Fauquel threatened to reach from the grave for revenge, and he saw the trapdoor drop. He saw Fauquel's eyes bulge and his tongue force his lips apart. He saw the slightly swinging body come to a stop. And clearest of all, he saw under the rope that broke Fauquel's neck, how it had cruelly bruised and raked his flesh, leaving a mark not unlike the angry red ring encircling the neck of the corpse in front of him.

For a moment, Broussard stood without moving, remembering the page in Fauquel's journal where he had named the judge whose death he caused, a name that Broussard had earlier thought a curious coincidence but which now seemed like much more . . . the name François Oustellette.

Not even fresh zucchini cake could make him more eager for his next visit to see Grandma O.